Acclaim for Ann Packer's

SWIM BACK TO ME

"Ann Packer's *Swim Back to Me* reminded me of why I fell in love with literature in the first place. Upon closing the book, I thought, 'I'll read this again.' . . . Packer's stories stick with you."
—Susan Baleé, *The Philadelphia Inquirer*

"Packer . . . is a master at getting to the heart of characters struggling on in the face of loss. . . . *Swim Back to Me* is best enjoyed for Packer's sharply focused snapshots of people at pivotal points in their lives, a focus so intense that we can feel as if we're spying on them."
—*St. Louis Post-Dispatch*

"[Beginning] Packer's stories feels as nonchalant as stepping into a puddle but results in a sudden plunge into deep water. . . . Potent and deftly written."
—*The Dallas Morning News*

"An author who speaks with her full voice. . . . The people in Packer's stories are so possible and so familiar, reading about them is like flipping through a photo album with someone you've always known."
—*San Francisco* magazine

"Anyone intrigued by the ways we both fail and save one another will find ample food for thought here."
—*People*

"Deeply engrossing. . . . Illuminates the instant, in the darkest hour of grief, when the heart opens wider than ever before—and shows us a new way of being."
—*More*

"Gripping. . . . A stunning look into how we learn and sometimes fail to live with each other."
—*The Daily Beast*

"Touching, tender and true."
—*Austin American-Statesman*

"Utterly readable. . . . Ann Packer has a talent for creating authentic, absorbing characters."
—*Ladies Home Journal*

"A keen observer of family dynamics. . . . Packer the novelist is equally adept at the short form."
—*The Oakland Tribune*

"Packer's descriptions of what crisis looks like from the inside out are almost always word-perfect."
—*Toledo Blade*

"Subtle, deeply personal. . . . [An] excellent collection."
—*Bookreporter*

"Powerful . . . satisfying. . . . Packer's characters are fully developed with emotions that feel authentic."
—*BookPage*

ANN PACKER

SWIM BACK TO ME

Ann Packer is the author of two bestselling novels, *Songs Without Words* and *The Dive from Clausen's Pier*, the latter of which received a Great Lakes Book Award, an American Library Association Award, and the Kate Chopin Literary Award. Her short fiction and essays have appeared in *The New Yorker*, *The Washington Post*, *Vogue*, and *Real Simple*. Also the author of *Mendocino and Other Stories*, she lives in northern California with her family.

·

Ann Packer is available for select readings and lectures. To inquire about a possible appearance, please contact the Random House Speakers Bureau at rhspeakers@randomhouse.com.

·

www.annpacker.com

SWIM BACK TO ME

· · · · · ·

ANN PACKER

· VINTAGE CONTEMPORARIES ·

Vintage Books
A Division of Random House, Inc.
New York

FIRST VINTAGE CONTEMPORARIES EDITION, APRIL 2012

Portions of this work were originally published in the following: "Walk for Mankind"
and "Molten" in *Narrative Magazine*; "Jump" in *Open City*; "Dwell Time" in *Avery*;
"Her Firstborn" in *Before: Short Stories about Pregnancy from Our Top Writers,* edited by Emily Franklin
and Heather Swain (New York: Overlook Press, 2006); and "Things Said or Done"
in *Zoetrope: All-Story*.

Grateful acknowledgment is made to the following for permission to reprint
previously published material:
Alfred Publishing Co., Inc.: Lyrics from "Without a Trace," words and music by David Pirner,
copyright © 1992 by WB Music Corp. (ASCAP) and LFR Music (ASCAP). All rights
administered by WB Music Corp. (Publishing) and Alfred Publishing Co., Inc. (Print).
All rights reserved. Reprinted by permission of Alfred Publishing Co., Inc.

Chris Bauermeister, Adam Pfahler, and Blake Schwarzenbach: Lyrics from "Save Your
Generation" and "Fireman," lyrics by Blake Schwarzenbach, music by Chris Bauermeister, Adam
Pfahler, and Blake Schwarzenbach. Reprinted by permission of the authors. *Gorno Music:* Lyrics
from "Add It Up," written by Gordon Gano, copyright © 1980 by Gorno Music (ASCAP).
Reprinted by permission of Gorno Music (administered by Alan N. Skiena, Esq.).

Hal Leonard Corporation: Lyrics from "Swim Back to Me," words and music by Carla Bozulich and
Kevin Fitzgerald, copyright © 1997 by EMI Virgin Songs, Inc. and Milk Pal Music. All rights for
EMI Virgin Songs, Inc. and Milk Pal Music controlled and administered by EMI Virgin Songs, Inc.
All rights reserved. International copyright secured. Lyrics from "Tame," words and music by
Charles Thompson, copyright © 1989 by Rice and Beans Music.
All rights controlled and administered by Songs of Universal, Inc. All rights reserved.
Reprinted by permission of Hal Leonard Corporation.

Hal Leonard Corporation and Jessy Greene Publishing: Lyrics from "Trashman in Furs," words and music
by Carla Bozulich, Bill Tutton, and Jessy Greene, copyright © 1997 by EMI Virgin Songs, Inc.,
Milk Pal Music, and Jessy Greene Publishing. All rights controlled and administered by EMI Virgin
Songs, Inc. All rights reserved. International copyright secured. Reprinted by permission of Hal
Leonard Corporation and Jessy Greene Publishing.

The Library of Congress has cataloged the Knopf edition as follows:
Packer, Ann, [date]
Swim back to me / Ann Packer. —1st ed.
p. cm.
I. Title.
PS3616.A33S95 2011
813'.6—dc22 2010051792

Vintage ISBN: 978-1-4000-7973-5

www.vintagebooks.com

Printed in the United States of America
10 9 8 7 6 5 4 3 2 1

To George

Contents

Swim Back to Me

Walk for Mankind

.

September 1972. It was the first week of eighth grade, and I sat alone near the back of the school bus: a short, scrawny honor-roll boy with small hands and big ears. The route home meandered through Los Altos Hills, with its large houses sitting in the shadows of old oak trees and dense groves of eucalyptus. Finally we came down out of the hills and arrived in Stanford, where the last twenty or so of us lived, in houses built close together on land the University leased to its faculty. A couple of stops before mine, a clump of kids rose and moved up the aisle, and that's when I saw her, a new girl sitting up near the front.

To my surprise, she shouldered her backpack at my stop. I waited until she was off the bus and then made my way up the aisle, keeping my eyes away from Bruce Cavanaugh and Tony Halpern, who'd been my friends back in elementary school. Down on the bright sidewalk, she was headed in the direction I had to go, and I followed after her, walking slowly so I wouldn't overtake her. She was small-boned like me, with thick red hair spilling halfway down her back and covering part of her back-pack, which was decorated with at least a dozen McGovern buttons, rather than the usual one or two. There was even a Nixon button with a giant red X drawn over his ugly face.

She stopped suddenly and turned, and I got my first glimpse of her face: pale and peppered with freckles. "Who are you?" she said.

"Sorry." I was afraid she thought I was following her when I was just heading home.

She came forward and offered me her hand. "Hi, Sorry—I'm Sasha. Or maybe I should say 'I'm New.' We can call each other Sorry and New, and then when we get to know each other better we can switch to something else. Shy and Weird, maybe."

I had never met anyone who talked like this, and it took me a moment to respond. "My name's Richard."

She rolled her eyes. "I know that. I didn't mean who are you what's your name—I meant who are you who are you. Your name is Richard Appleby and you live around the corner from me, in the house with all the ice plant."

Now I got it: she was part of the family renting the Levines' house. Teddy Levine was spending the year at the American Academy in Rome, and the Levine kids were going to go to some Italian school and come back fluent and probably strange. The Jacksons had spent a year in London, and afterward Helen Jackson had been such an oddball her parents had taken her out of public school.

The girl's hand was still out, and though I'd never shaken hands with another kid before, I held mine out for her, and she pumped it up and down. She had blue-gray eyes with very light lashes, and a long, pointy noise.

"Sasha Horowitz," she said. "Happy to know you. I was waiting for you to come over, but it's just as well we met like this—if you'd come over I'd've probably been a freak. Plus my parents would've co-opted the whole thing. Do your parents do that? Co-opt everything? When I was really little my dad would always try to *play* with me and my friends—he'd give us rides on his back like a horse, and he'd kind of buck sometimes, and one time a friend of mine fell off and broke her wrist. Her parents were really overprotective—she was never allowed to come over again." Still looking at me, Sasha shrugged off her backpack and ran her fingers through her heavy, carrot-colored hair. She gathered it into a thick ponytail and secured it with a rubber band from her wrist. She said, "There, that's better. So do you love San Francisco? We had a picnic in Golden Gate Park on Saturday, and we saw a guy on an acid trip—my little brother thought he was in a play. The only thing is, I'm expecting to be miserable about missing winter."

"Are you from somewhere cold?" I said. "Did you have snow?"

"New Haven. And God, yes—we had mountains of it. It was a huge pain in the ass. Do you want to come over? You should, because my mother'll ask me to tell her about school otherwise and I really don't feel like talking to her."

She stood there looking at me, waiting for me to answer, and I thought of my mother, in her shabby apartment across the bay in Oakland, where she had lived alone for the last seven months, an exile of her own making. I looked at my watch. In two and a half hours my father would bike home from his office on campus, and after he'd had a drink we would sit down to a dinner that Gladys, our new housekeeper, had left us in the oven. Telling him about school was my job, just as asking about it was his.

"Sure," I said. "I'll come over. For a little while."

Within two weeks I had eaten dinner at Sasha's house three times, had gone with her and her father to buy tiki lamps for the back-yard, had driven to San Francisco with all four Horowitzes to have Sunday morning dim sum. On election night, the five of us squeezed onto the living room couch and yelled at the television set together. In December I ate my first ever potato latkes at their house, and on New Year's weekend my father allowed me to skip a visit to my mother in favor of an expedition with the Horowitzes to Big Sur.

But I'm getting ahead of myself. That first day, once I was home again and my father and I were in the kitchen just before dinner, I found out what had brought Sasha's family to Stanford. According to my father, her father had been denied tenure by the English Department at Yale and had accepted a one-year renewable appointment at Stanford—which, my father said, was "quite interesting."

"Usually you'd stay on for a year or two, try to publish some work, get your CV in order, then go on the job market for a tenure track position somewhere else." He paused and drew his lips into his mouth, as he often did in thoughtful moments. He was a straight-backed man with neat gray hair and hazel eyes: handsome enough. But when he did this thing with his mouth his chin took over, and he looked like a ventriloquist's dummy.

He let his lips go. "Maybe there was some bad blood. There often is in a case like this."

I said, "Maybe he just wanted to leave." I had met him— Dan—on my way out, and he'd seemed far too friendly for whatever my father might have in mind. "Richard Appleby!" he'd said. "Excellent to meet you! Tell me, are the natives amicable? May we count on you for guidance? You must tell us what the customs are. The customs of the country. You'll help us, won't you? Correct our clothing, teach us the vernacular?" And all the while Sasha stood there rolling her eyes but unable to keep from smiling.

"I could ask Hugh Canfield," my father said. Hugh Canfield was my father's closest—really, his only—friend outside the History Department. They'd been at Princeton together. Hugh was chair of the English Department and therefore someone who'd have information about Dan.

"You don't have to ask," I said. "I don't care."

"No, of course not," my father said. "Though it's curious. To have been at Yale, he must be very promising."

He was far more than promising to me. He was promise ful-filled, one of those people who makes the most ordinary occasion brilliant. Build a blanket fort in the living room, which Peter, Sasha's little brother, loved to do? With Dan's help we built Peter a blanket civilization, with a theater and a civic center and a mau-soleum for Peter's stuffed hippopotamus, whom we named Hip-pocritz, the Czar-King of Egypt-Arabia.

He was tall and skinny, Dan, with Sasha's frizzy red hair and a great beak of a nose. He played endless games of Risk with us, lit-erally yelling when he lost hold of a continent; and he was fond of showing up at our school at dismissal time with the car packed full of quilts and announcing that he was taking us to the beach to watch the sunset. Joanie, Sasha's mother, possessed quieter charms, but she had a knack for making things special, too: on Halloween night, a little too old for trick-or-treating ourselves, we shepherded Peter around the neighborhood wearing caps she'd made for us, with badges that said "Official Halloween Escort—Will Say Yes to Candy." At home, she did quick charcoal sketches of anyone who happened to be nearby, and when she thought they were good she wrote a caption on them and taped them to the kitchen walls. There were a lot of Sasha and Peter, of course, but within a few months there were a couple of me, too, one in which I was holding a deck of cards in my hand, labeled "The Schemer," and another, in which I was looking off to the side, that said "Richard waiting." "He looks like a retard in that one," Sasha said. "Take it down." But Joanie didn't, and though I didn't say so to Sasha, I was glad.

Sasha. She had a little of each parent in her, Dan's gaiety, Joanie's warmth, plus something essential and not altogether pleasant that was entirely hers, like a back note of pepper in a rich chocolate dessert. It was a quality that made her—that gave her permission to—insist on what she wanted. We played Truth or Dare a lot, and her dares invariably had me taking risks that just happened to have as their end points some small reward for her: a stolen candy bar, the details of an overheard—an eavesdropped-upon—conversation.

"Someone has a sweetheart," Gladys said, but it wasn't that. For one thing, we hardly spoke at school, Sasha having found a niche among some other Stanford kids while I stuck with two guys I'd met during seventh grade, Malcolm and Bob, precisely because they weren't Stanford kids and hadn't known me when my mother was around. Occasionally Sasha would track down the three of us at lunchtime and plop down next to me with her brown bag (which contained, unvaryingly, an egg salad sandwich on pumpernickel, a handful of dried apricots, and a small can of pineapple juice). More often, we'd join up once we'd gotten off the school bus, or one of us would appear at the other's front door at about four o'clock and say, with heavy irony, "Do you want to play?"

"I've always had boys as friends," she said. "What's the big deal?"

I hadn't had a girl as a friend since kindergarten, and for me it was strange and exciting. But I wanted to seem as blasé as she was. "Yeah," I said. "People are so idiotic."

Gladys may have given me knowing smiles when Sasha came over, but my father hardly noticed I had a new friend. Right after my mother left, he reduced his time at the University, spending Saturdays in his study at home rather than going to campus. He was hard at work on a book about the New Deal, though, and by the time the Horowitzes arrived he was back to his old habits, and he clung to them through that fall and winter, working, working. Sunday was his only day of rest, and we always did something together: went to a concert or played a board game or even tried to navigate our way through some complicated baking project, in service to his ferocious sweet tooth.

He was fifty that year, the age I am now, but he wore fifty in the old way, with lace-up leather dress shoes and starched shirts. Sometimes when I'm out for a run, or just kicking a soccer ball with my kids, I think my father, if he were still alive, would not recognize me. He would see that I was his son, he would see that I was Richard—but he wouldn't be able to make any kind of sense of me as a middle-aged man.

In early March, posters began to appear at our school advertising the second annual Walk for Mankind, a twenty-mile walk around Palo Alto to raise money for the world's poor and infirm. Right away Sasha decided we should do it. "We'll be heroes," she said. "We'll make more money than any other kids our age."

And so we spent several weeks' worth of afternoons going from house to house collecting pledges: first around Stanford; then farther away, in College Terrace and some of the other nearby parts of Palo Alto; and finally, when we could get Dan to drive us, in the next town up the Peninsula, Menlo Park. We filled page after page with names and addresses.

One Thursday afternoon, waiting for Dan to get home so we could make another sweep, we lay on her parents' water bed, pigging out on Fig Newtons and half watching *The Edge of Night* on the small black-and-white they kept on their dresser.

"I don't think we should drink their water," Sasha said.

I was confused for a minute, thinking she meant the characters on the TV screen. But she meant the Walk—the cups of water that would be available at the check-in stations.

"Why not?"

"Or eat their food. Because it'll be a bigger sacrifice for mankind that way, duh. We'll carry our own water and bring gorp and maybe some beef jerky. Oranges would be good, but they'd get too heavy." She reached for a cookie and then looked into my face. "Were you looking at my boob?"

"No!" I said. "Sasha, God."

"You don't have to spaz out—that's what teenage boys do."

"Thank you, Dr. Kinsey."

"I'm just saying it's normal."

I hadn't been looking at her boob, but I'd been aware that her blouse was cut so that I could: it had a slit down the front, and when she moved in a certain way the slit opened. I took the Fig Newtons box out of her hand. "Did you eat the last one?"

"Go ask my mom if we have any more."

"You go."

"Am I the one who wants a cookie?"

I scooted sideways, riding the waves to the edge of the bed. Out in the dining room, Joanie sat at her sewing machine, working on a giant floor pillow. She was much younger than my mother—thirty-six to my mother's forty-two—but she already had some gray, shorter silver threads that kinked away from her near-black hair. It was a joke between her and Dan that she would soon be mistaken for his mother.

"I can't believe you two," she said, looking up at me. "Watching TV on this beautiful day."

"Are there any more Fig Newtons?"

"Poor Richard—Sasha isn't the most gracious hostess, is she?" She left her work and went into the kitchen, which was really part of the dining room, which was part of the living room: the Levines' house was an Eichler, with an open floor plan and floor-to-ceiling windows everywhere. It was the time of day now when the sun angled through the glass and laid a band of

light on the floor. Sometimes Dan stretched out in the light and announced he would never leave California.

"Sorry, honey," Joanie said, standing at the cookie cabinet. "No more Fig Newtons. I've got some of those chocolate mint cookies, though—heretic that I am." This was a reference to a little tantrum Sasha had thrown a week or so ago, prompted by the sight of chocolate mint cookies when she preferred plain chocolate.

"Well . . ." I said.

"Stand up to her." Joanie had high cheekbones and a long, straight nose, and when she stood like this, slightly affronted, her dark hair falling down her back, she looked a little like an Indian noblewoman. "It would do her some good," she added. "Shake her up."

I was about to take the cookies when the front door opened, and Dan stormed in, shouting, "Motherfuckers!" Then he saw me and stopped. "Richard Appleby. A pleasure as always. Please forgive the inexcusable language."

I shrugged. I'd heard him swear before, in a jokey, Dan-like way, but the look on his face now—mouth down-turned, cheeks flushed—suggested he was seriously angry.

"What?" Joanie said, rounding the end of the counter that divided the kitchen from the dining area. "What happened?"

"Nothing." He smiled a false smile. "I had a hard day at the office, dear."

This was his way of being funny, but I thought I should get out of there. I left them and made my way down the dark hallway. Sasha was where I'd left her, a Fig Newton an inch away from her mouth.

"What the hell?"

"I just found it," she said. "It was on the floor, I swear."

"Your dad's home. But I'm not sure he's going to want to drive us anywhere."

She shoved the cookie into her mouth and got off the bed. I followed her back to the front hall. Dan and Joanie were still standing where I'd left them, and now Joanie had her hand on Dan's upper arm. I wondered what had happened. My father sometimes came home from History Department meetings in a bad mood, though for him this meant only that he was particularly quiet and distracted. My mother, when she was still with us, had been unsympathetic to the occasional stories he told.

"Give us a minute," Joanie said when she saw us, but Sasha ignored her.

"Daddy, will you drive us?"

"Ah, the Walk," Dan said. "Noblest of causes." He ran his hand through his bushy red hair. "Do you kids know what a cretin is?"

Sasha put a finger to her chin. "Someone who has a different opinion from you?"

Dan barked out a single, loud laugh. His briefcase was standing on the floor next to him, and he lifted one foot and knocked it over, then kicked it several feet along the floor. He didn't look at Joanie as he faced us again and said, "I'm ready when you are."

"We'll get our shoes," Sasha said, but when we were out of her parents' sight, she stopped and held a finger to her lips.

"What?" I whispered, but she shook her head and then cocked an ear in the direction of the main room. I tried to listen, but I couldn't hear much—Dan's voice going up and down with occasional moments of sudden emphasis; Joanie's low, slow, soothing.

"Oh, never mind," Sasha muttered, and she continued down the hall. In her parents' room she perched on the padded leather frame of the water bed and wiggled her bare feet into her tennis shoes. "Now you're really a Horowitz," she said. "You've seen Daddy have a fit."

"What was the matter?"

"He gets into arguments with people."

"About . . ."

"Henry James! T. S. Eliot! He's an English professor, remember?" She grabbed the empty Fig Newtons box and headed out of the room. "Come on—before he gets even more wound up."

But when we got back out there, Dan seemed to have calmed down: he was standing in the kitchen with his hand in the cookie box. He saw us and grinned. "Caught in the act," he said. "Caught red-handed. Richard, may I offer you a chocolate mint creme sandwich cookie? I love how they spell it c-r-e-m-e instead of c-r-e-a-m. But I think we should pronounce it correctly from now on. It's a chocolate mint krem sandwich cookie, isn't it? Krem. *Merveilleux!*"

The last weekend before the Walk, I had to go visit my mother in Oakland. This happened every month or so, my father driving me across the bay on a Friday evening. When we arrived he'd pull to the curb in front of her building and we'd sit silently in the car for a minute or two, until at last one of us said, "See you Sunday," and the other said, "See you Sunday," and I'd get out of the car and go into the narrow vestibule of my mother's apartment building, where I'd have to wait for her to buzz me into the lobby.

That night she was working on dinner when I arrived, and once she'd hugged me she returned to the stove. I parked my backpack near the couch and sat at the table, thinking that the weekend was really just three units—Friday evening, Saturday, and Sunday—and reminding myself that in a few hours I'd go to bed, and already the first unit would be finished.

The apartment was tiny and so was everything in it, including the table: so tiny that my glass of milk nearly touched her glass of wine as we ate. "Tell me," she said, chewing quickly and smiling at me. "How are you? How was your week?"

"Fine," I said, and because it was best when I told a long

story, I described the Walk for Mankind, how this friend and I were raising money like crazy, how we had it all planned, down to the refreshments we were going to bring.

"Which friend?" she said. "Tony?" And I said no, not Tony, someone new. I'd finished my meal by then—a hamburger patty and carrot coins, little-kid food—and I stood to clear my plate.

There was a TV in the living room, and we settled in front of it once she was finished eating. She seemed antsy. She got up for a glass of water and then, just a few minutes later, a cup of coffee. She had slender arms, and when she came back with the coffee, the cuff of her blue work shirt had unrolled, making it look as if the cup were being held not by a hand but by an empty blue sleeve. I watched her sit down, watched her tuck her longish hair behind her ear. The way she wore her hair, hanging to her shoulders, made her look like a teenager from the back. She had wrinkles, though, framing her mouth and in deep grooves across her forehead.

At last it was time for bed. We unfolded the couch, and I waited for her to close her bedroom door and then undressed quickly, climbing between the sheets before she could crack the door again: "Just in case you need me in the middle of the night," she always said, which annoyed me even more than the silly dinner. I understand it now, of course, her babying me: parental tenderness is a night-blooming emotion, perhaps most robust when it's been kept under wraps.

I had a hard time falling asleep that night. I could hear the clock ticking on the stove and, in a little while, my mother's faint snores from the bedroom. Unit 1 of the weekend was over, or would be once I was sleeping. I pictured a map of the Bay Area, and I imagined a line drawn from our house in Stanford to my mother's apartment in Oakland, cutting right through the bay. That line was hundreds of times longer than the line from our house to the Horowitzes', but it was the second line—the shorter one—that mattered.

Saturday morning, my mother woke me early, saying she had something she wanted to show me. "Get up," she said. "We'll go as soon as you've had breakfast."

She drove a different car now, having left behind the family station wagon and bought an old white VW Bug. She kept it in an empty lot around the corner from her apartment building, and as we got into the car I saw on the opposite side of the lot a tall black woman in a low-cut dress and shiny gold high heels. She leaned against the hood of a rusty sedan, drawing every now and then on a cigarette.

"She's mankind, too," my mother muttered, and I began to feel nervous, wondering what she had in store for me.

And in fact our destination was the Oakland ghetto, a place I had heard about but never seen. We drove up and down the streets, past stores crammed close together and wrecked cars parked with their windows open. I'd never seen so many black people—walking up and down the sidewalks, sitting on the hoods of cars, crossing the street in clusters or alone. I was scared, but I knew I shouldn't say so.

"It's time you saw this," my mother said. "I realized last night."

Out my window, an old man hobbled along the sidewalk, shaking his finger as if he were scolding someone.

I said, "OK, but can we go soon?"

My mother frowned. "Yes, but don't you see? *We* can go. Do you think the people who live here can go? That's what poverty is, a place you can't leave. Honey, I'm thrilled you're doing the Walk for Mankind, but if you want to help, there's plenty to do right here." She held her palm up, extended toward the wind-shield. "In your own backyard."

I watched as a woman crossed the street in front of us, a large blue suitcase forcing her to walk lopsided, one shoulder lower than the other. I leaned against the door and rested my head on the closed window.

"Richard," my mother said gently, "I needed to do something useful with my life. Do you understand?"

These were the words she'd used when she decided to leave. She wanted to help the poor, to correct the wrongs our country seemed so content to live with. She'd come to Oakland to work in a social services agency that helped underprivileged and undereducated women learn the skills they needed to get decent jobs. That there were underprivileged and undereducated women over on our side of the bay, too, was something we never mentioned.

"I know seeing this might be . . . strange," she said. "Upsetting. But I needed to bring you. I needed you to understand."

"I already did," I said. And I looked at the clock on the dashboard, figuring I was at least 10 percent through Unit 2.

The Walk was on a Saturday. On the Friday evening beforehand, Sasha and I sat on the curb in front of her house and totaled up our pledges. Weekends with my mother often left me feeling weird, and I'd been distracted all week, unable to concentrate in class, burdened by a feeling that time had changed, slowed down: that it was getting slower each day and soon I'd find myself in Social Studies or somewhere staring at a clock with hands that didn't move. Sitting on the curb next to Sasha, I added a column of numbers, whispered the total to myself, and then forgot it halfway through the next column.

Sasha's lips moved as she flipped through the pages on her clipboard. She looked up. "I'm going to have more than you."

"What do you mean? We went to the exact same houses." We'd gone so far as to ask people to split their pledges between the two of us, to make sure we stayed even.

"I did some other ones," she said, eyes still on her pledge sheet.

"When?"

"When you were with your mom last weekend. My dad drove me to Redwood City and I did some there. You don't have to freak out, Richard—it's good, it's more money for mankind." She turned to her last page, and I saw her eyes fly down the length of it. "Twenty-eight dollars and seventy cents a mile," she said. "That's, let's see, five hundred and seventy-four dollars I'll earn tomorrow. How much do you have?"

I was still reeling from the news she'd just delivered. Why hadn't she said something earlier? I missed *everything* when I was with my mother.

"Well?" she said.

"I don't know. I lost count."

She reached for my clipboard and within a minute she was on the final page, her head nodding a little with the increasing sum. "Twenty-one even," she said. "That's good, that's four hundred and twenty dollars you'll earn." She handed me the clipboard. Then she pounded her thigh. "Shit, put that with mine and it's just six dollars less than a thousand dollars! We need thirty more cents a mile. We've got to get thirty more cents a mile."

It was the evening before the Walk, and there wasn't a house we hadn't hit in all of Stanford. I said, "Maybe we should just put it in ourselves."

"No way. We're walking, we're not going to pay, too."

"Well, what are we going to do?" Her parents were out— they'd gone to dinner in the city, taking Peter with them—and I knew my father wouldn't drive us. He was a creature of habit, and it was his habit to spend Friday evenings preparing his lectures for the following week, so he'd have the weekend clear for writing.

"I know," she said. "SCRA. Some old person'll be swimming laps and we'll hit 'em up and be done with it."

SCRA was the Stanford Campus Recreation Association, a little swim and tennis club a few blocks away. When I was younger I'd lived there in the summertime, going from pool to Ping-Pong to tennis for hours at a stretch. At the end of the afternoon I'd ride home with the latest layer of sunburn tightening my face and a damp towel hanging from my shoulders.

Sasha and I walked down the hill together, the scent of jasmine faint in the evening air. Through the falling light I looked at her, at her unruly hair and long nose. She wore a Mexican blouse, gauzy and decorated at the neckline with tiny blue birds. Look at me, I thought, but she didn't.

The SCRA parking lot came into view, and there were a couple of cars in it, an old blue Mercedes and a black Volvo. I recognized the Mercedes and my heart sank a little: it belonged to Harvey Bergman, my father's closest friend. I didn't feel like running into him.

Beyond the parking lot, right up against the back fence, some older teenage boys were gathered at an abandoned bike rack, some of them on the ground, others leaning against the rack or straddling it, their hair long and lank. "Great," I said, because they were a group I mostly recognized, sixteen- and seventeen-year-olds who attended the high school we'd go to year after next. They were known in the neighborhood to smoke pot, and I had a feeling they were smoking it now.

"What do you mean, 'great'?" Sasha said. "It is great, we can ask them."

"Ask them?"

"To sponsor us."

I stared at her. "We can't ask them."

"Why not?"

"Because . . . Because . . ." They'll laugh at me, I wanted to say, but didn't. "They're kids," I finally managed.

"We're talking about six dollars," she said. "Anyway, SCRA's probably locked, what choice do we have?"

"Let's at least try," I said, and I veered away from her toward the entrance, a set of double doors flanked by open railwork that allowed you to peer in or call to someone, but not to reach your hand in to unlock the door.

Which, it turned out, was locked. From inside, I heard the sound of water lapping against the sides of the pool, rhythmically, as from the motions of a swimmer. "Hello?" I called half-heartedly through the rails, but no one replied, and I figured Harvey and the Volvo driver were both in the water, one in each of the two lanes set aside for lap swimmers, both moving with the monumental slowness of the aged.

"Richard," Sasha said, and I turned and found her standing where I'd left her with a high-wattage smile on her face that told me the guys at the fence were watching. "Come on," she said loudly. "I want to ask these guys something."

"What?" I said, but after a moment I joined her and we continued through the parking lot and entered the dead field where the bike rack was. On the other side of the fence was the back playground of my old elementary school. The tether balls had been taken down for the weekend, and the poles stood like leafless trees in an even line.

I knew who two of the guys were: Eric Rumsen, the younger brother of a neighborhood girl who'd babysat me years earlier; and Kevin Cottrell, whose father was a colleague of my father's in the History Department. Two of the others looked familiar: Stanford kids, too, but college age now or from the older residential neighborhood, or the offspring of faculty in far-flung departments like Physics or Art. The only one I'd never seen before was a tall, lanky guy leaning against the bike rack, his hands stuffed into the pockets of his jeans. In place of a shirt he wore a vest of patched-together velvet, the pieces green and burgundy and navy blue, and his arms were muscled and tan.

"How's it going?" Sasha said, and a couple of the guys laughed.

"We're cool," Eric Rumsen said. "How about you? A little warm? Kind of hot?"

Dismayed, I turned to Sasha, but she was smiling. I thought of Eric's sister: she'd been nice to me, had brought me a book about fishing once, with glossy color pictures of all the fish you could catch in the western United States. She'd taken me by their house one day, to get something she needed, and I remembered her room, the walls covered with billowy cloths from India. I'd walked by Eric's room, too, could call up the B.O. smell, the unmade bed.

"Have you guys heard of the Walk for Mankind?" Sasha said. "It's this fund-raiser, and we're doing it tomorrow, and we need one more pledge to get to this higher level of earning."

Kevin Cottrell was looking everywhere but at me. I remembered a swimming party when I was about six and he was about ten—it was at the house of the then chair of the department, and while the grown-ups stood around on the patio and talked, the five or six kids all played in the pool, except Kevin. He had a book, and he sat reading by himself on a lounge chair the whole time. Now he nudged one of the other guys and turned to Sasha. "How much do you need?"

"Not much," she said eagerly. "Thirty cents a mile—just six dollars altogether."

"And what do we get?" said the guy Kevin had nudged. He had a pink face and a snub nose, and pale blond hair that reached halfway down his back.

Sasha glanced at me. "What do you mean?"

"You get six bucks, what do we get?"

"Yeah," Eric said. "We need something too, here. You want to keep us company, maybe smoke a joint with us?"

"Just you," pink-face said. "I think your little friend is too young."

I felt my face grow warm. I turned to Sasha and said, "We've got the Walk tomorrow."

Eric laughed. "Whoa, don't want to be too tired for that."

"Cut it out." The guy with the vest had pushed away from the bike rack, and suddenly there was something different going on. The other guys all looked at him, and I saw that he was not a teenager after all but in his mid-twenties, maybe older: his hairline receding, the inlets of scalp it had abandoned shinier than his forehead. His mustache drooped over his mouth, and his eyes were hooded and dull, but he was clearly in charge. He sauntered over, his walk somehow telling me he was from somewhere else: he leaned back as he walked, hooked his thumbs in his belt loops.

He stopped in front of Sasha and held out his hand. "Hi, I'm Cal. What's your name?"

She took his hand. "Sasha."

"That's really beautiful. Beautiful name for a beautiful girl."

She smiled. She seemed about to speak but didn't, which surprised me; she was not usually quiet or shy.

"I'll sponsor you," he said. "What do I have to do?"

She gave him her clipboard and showed him where to write his name and address, then the amount he was pledging. She said nothing about splitting the pledge between us, and I figured that with her trip to Redwood City it was too late, anyway.

"Thirty cents, that it?" Cal finished writing and handed the clipboard back to her. He asked my name, and when I told him he said, "Well, Sasha and Richard, you're welcome to join us for a smoke."

I'd been around pot before, had smelled it, had even seen a joint in an ashtray at a party my father had taken me to. But I'd never smoked it. Sasha hadn't either, but she was on record with me as ready to try.

"Want to?" she asked me, that same bright smile on her face.

I thought of my father, his lecture notes spread out on the dining room table. After dinner he'd produced a small box of See's Candies and told me we'd crack it open when I got home from the Walk tomorrow night. "Hand packed," he'd said. "Heavy on the chocolate butters."

"I should go," I told Sasha. She didn't reply, and I said it again. "Well, I'll see you tomorrow," I said at last, and she flicked a glance at me before turning back to Cal.

"OK," she said, and I didn't know if she was talking to me or him.

The next morning, Dan drove us to the starting point of the Walk, the playground of a Palo Alto elementary school. In the car I cast glances at Sasha, raised my eyebrows to show I was curious about the rest of her night, but she was slumped in her seat, her knees up in front of her, preoccupied. In the front, Dan talked idly to Peter, who'd come along for the ride.

"Isn't that funny, Richard Appleby?" Dan said over his shoulder to me.

I'd been staring out the window, thinking I'd been chicken to leave SCRA. "What?"

Dan maneuvered the rearview mirror until he caught my eye in it. "I said, isn't it funny how Sasha, the queen of the Walk for Mankind, had to be reminded this morning why she needed to get up?"

I looked at Sasha.

"You'll like this," he went on. "I said to her, 'It's the Walk,' and she said, 'What walk?'" Dan laughed a short, mystified laugh, then turned around and looked right at me. "Funny, you have to admit."

I shrugged.

He faced forward but caught my eye in the rearview again, and I saw that he was genuinely puzzled.

"I was tired was all," Sasha said. "I reread *To the Lighthouse* last night."

Dan chuckled. " 'And he would ask one, did one like his tie? God knows, said Rose, one did not.' Well, you missed a great dinner—right, Peter? The Cohens served cracked crab and asparagus and this incredible ice cream laced with Kahlúa. We all kept saying, 'Too bad Sasha and Richard Appleby didn't come,' but we knew you were busy working for mankind."

Sasha slumped lower, and I looked out the window again, relieved when Dan let it drop.

We had to wait in line to register, and then Dan and Peter stood at the starting point and saw us off as if we were embarking on an ocean liner, Dan waving a white handkerchief back and forth over his head, Peter humming on a kazoo, a tune I recognized after a moment as "So Long, Farewell" from *The Sound of Music*.

Sasha muttered something under her breath as we headed away from them.

"What?"

"I said, I wish Daddy would do something in a normal way for a change. And Peter's shirt was really nerdy."

I tried to remember Peter's shirt: striped, like most of mine. I turned and looked at her. Her hair was up in a bun, held in place by a leather hair thing she'd made in art class. Usually she anchored it with a little wooden stick, but today she'd used a gnarly pencil, tooth marks up and down its yellow sides, the segment of metal at the end bitten closed. Her face was pale, the blue of her eyes grayer than usual, doused somehow.

I said, "What time'd you get home last night?" I had turned as I left the SCRA parking lot and seen that the guys had made space for her against the bike rack, and that she was leaning back, Cal on one side of her and Eric Rumsen on the other.

"Ten-thirty."

In my hearing, her parents had said they wouldn't be back until eleven, and I took some comfort in the fact that she'd gotten herself home with time to spare. "So what happened? Did you smoke?"

"Yeah."

"Did you get high?"

She held her hand out, palm parallel to the ground, and tipped it back and forth. "Next time I probably will more."

"Next time?"

"Come on, Richard—we're not just going to let the parade go by, are we?"

I shrugged, but I was relieved she'd used the word "we." I decided then and there: next time for sure. "Did you cough?" I asked, and she gave me an embarrassed grin.

"I couldn't help it."

Soon we were walking through a part of Palo Alto I didn't know very well, full of large old houses and great, leafy shade trees. Palo Alto was our marketplace, our office building—it was where we shopped, went out for pizza, took karate, and saw doctors and dentists—but until Malcolm and Bob I'd never had a friend who lived there, never had a friend whose father wasn't connected to Stanford.

There was a check-in station every mile, where refreshments and first aid were available, and where you had to get your sheet stamped to prove you'd been there. By the third station I was hot and tired, and my water bottle was heavy. I said, "Want to stop for a few minutes?" There was a bench under some trees and near that a lemonade stand.

"Why?" she said.

"To rest."

"Let's rest after five miles, then we'll be a quarter of the way done."

We rested after Mile Five and then again after Mile Eight, sitting side by side on a curb and drinking our warm water. I had a piece of beef jerky each time, just because I could, but Sasha only picked raisins from her gorp, ate three or four, and put the bag away.

The other walkers near us were mostly adults, balding guys with beards, fattish women with tie-dyed T-shirts and hairy legs. Occasionally we'd come upon a group of kids our age and we'd talk to them for a while. At Mile Ten a bunch of high school kids were standing around the check-in station drinking Gatorade, and without talking about it Sasha and I arranged ourselves close enough to them that we could eavesdrop on their conversation. A girl was telling a long story about someone named Cappy, and for the entire time she was talking I tried and failed to figure out if Cappy was an adult or a kid. Then another girl said that someone named Paul was being a real asshole, and a short guy with a big nose said, "That's 'cause he's not balling Kathy anymore."

"Ready?" Sasha said, and though I wanted to hear more I said yes.

"Hang on one sec," she said, and she moved to a low stone wall, sat down, and took off her shoe. "Ewww," she cried. There was a blister the size of a pea on the end of her toe. "Shit, now what am I going to do? I have to pop it. You have to pop it for me. Get a rock or something."

"I'm not going to bang your toe with a rock!"

"You're so scared of everything."

I turned and walked away from her. One of the high school girls wore a purple tank top with no bra, and I let myself stare at her breasts for a moment, almost wishing I'd get hard. Malcolm and Bob had boners all the time and laughed at each other for holding their binders over their crotches and wearing loose, untucked shirts. I had hard-ons in my sleep and frequently woke with one, but that was about it. I'd never even had a wet dream.

The girl caught me staring, and I looked away and then went back to Sasha. Over at the check-in station, two adults sat behind a folding table, and I said, "I'll go ask them what to do."

"No."

"Why not?"

"They might make me stop. You saw that man."

A few stations back we'd seen an older man on a stretcher, his face bright red: a little later we passed someone who told us that the check-in woman had taken one look at him and made him lie down.

"It's a blister," I said. I remembered having one when I was seven or eight, and how my mother had pierced it with a needle and drained it. "If you want to pop it, you need a sterilized needle."

She pulled her sock back on, then her shoe.

"You're just going to walk with it?"

"We'll ask in there."

"Where?"

She angled her head across the street, at a little white cottage set back in a weedy yard.

"You can't just go up to someone's house."

She set off, and I followed, across the street and up the steps to a small porch. A tall, skinny guy answered her knock; he had light brown hair and weirdly pale blue eyes. He looked about the same age as my father's graduate students, maybe late twenties.

"Excuse me," Sasha said. "We're doing the Walk for Mankind, and I have a blister I need to pop. Do you have a needle and a pack of matches?"

The guy frowned. "A what?"

"A needle and a pack of matches. I have to sterilize the needle or I might get an infection."

He had a long neck—very long, and thin. Also long arms, long legs—he looked like what a stick figure would look like if a stick figure were an actual person, except his face was long, not round.

"I've got matches," he said. "I guess I can look for a needle." He stood there for another moment and then headed inside, leaving the door open and heading down a hallway. I saw a dark living room with a sagging couch, a fireplace containing a single charred log.

"Come on," Sasha said, stepping up into the house.

"What are you doing? Stop."

She kept going, crossing the room and looking at something on the mantel before moving to the TV and lifting a framed picture from its surface.

I stepped over the threshold. In addition to the couch there were two huge, disheveled armchairs and several small tables, all piled high with books. I wondered if he might *be* a graduate student—or an assistant professor, for that matter. My father had chaired the History Department hiring committee the previous year, and he said the candidates were getting so young the University was going to have to start requiring the daily wearing of academic regalia, just so everyone would know who was who.

The guy came back in, the top of his head just missing the doorframe. He saw me first. "Whoa. Did I say to come in?"

I looked at Sasha, and his eyes followed mine, in time to see her put the picture back on the TV.

"Whoa," he said again. "Whoa, whoa, whoa."

"Sorry," she said, smiling a big, bright smile like the one she'd given the guys at SCRA. "You seemed cool—I didn't think you'd mind."

He half laughed, half snorted. "Cool? How old are you two, anyway?"

"Fourteen," she said. "Well, I am. His birthday's not till July."

"Man," the guy said—but he went into the kitchen and began rummaging in a drawer, and after a moment we followed, Sasha going in after him while I stopped in the doorway.

He found matches and gave them to her, then rummaged some more and found a needle. She held them both in one hand while with the other she reached down to pull off her shoe and sock.

"You can sit down," he said.

She sat at his table. I thought of going to help her—offering to hold the needle while she lit the match or something—but I just stood there. When it came time for her to pierce the blister I looked away. There was a red Stanford banner hanging on one wall, and I wondered if he'd done his undergraduate work at Stanford, too.

Sasha stood. She unpinned her hair and then redid it, catching the damp strands that had come loose and working to jam the mangled pencil back through the holes in the leather thing.

"OK?" the guy said.

"Um," she said, smiling brightly again. "Could I use your phone?"

He smiled, too, but not in a friendly way. "You want to use the phone," he said, making it a statement rather than a question.

"My parents said I had to call in the middle. They're really overprotective—they almost didn't let me do this. *Their* parents were overprotective. I'll probably grow up to be overprotective myself."

"Or you could break the mold and surprise everyone."

They stared at each other for a moment, and then he swept his arm to the side, indicating a wall-mounted telephone.

"Richard," she said, barely glancing in my direction, "you might as well wait outside."

I turned and left, walking through the dark living room and out the door. She was in a weird mood, and I almost wished we were walking with some other kids. It was strange Dan and Joanie had told her to call, but so what if they had? That didn't make them overprotective. I thought of how she'd complained about Dan's waving us off at the starting point. She had no idea how lucky she was.

The tall guy came out of the house and stood near me, his arms dangling by his sides. I had my gorp open, and I offered him the bag. To my surprise, he reached in and scooped up a handful.

"Thanks, I like the raisins."

"So does Sasha," I said. "My friend. Whenever we stop she just picks out the raisins."

He rolled his eyes. "I'll bet she does."

"What do you mean?"

"Nothing. So how long is this thing, anyway?"

"Twenty miles," I said. "We're halfway done."

He looked across the street. A woman with big sunglasses seemed to be arguing with the volunteer at the check-in station. He said, "If I was going to walk twenty miles it sure wouldn't be around Palo Alto."

"But it's *in* Palo Alto."

"I mean I'd want to *get* something for my efforts. Some payoff."

"We are. A thousand dollars."

"*You* aren't," he said, and then he really looked at me and smiled. "Unless you two are out to defraud some folks. Are you out to defraud people?"

I shook my head.

"You're sure?" he said. "May I see some ID, please?"

I giggled, then coughed to cover the girlish sound. "It was

Sasha's idea," I said. "I just came along for the ride. I'm not much of a do-gooder."

"Do-gooders do good for themselves," he said, "not for the people they're helping. Did you know that?"

"How cynical."

He grinned, revealing big, square teeth. "How about a couple more raisins?"

I handed him the bag and he dumped some more gorp into his palm. He said, "It's none of my business, but do you always do what Sasha wants?"

This annoyed me, and I was about to tell him how wrong he was when the door swung open and she appeared.

"OK," she said as she came down the steps, "let's get going."

The guy put his hands on his hips and stared at her. "You get both birds?"

She looked up at him. "What?"

"With one stone. Wasn't that the whole idea of this stop? Kill two birds with one stone?"

She stood still, on the verge of saying something. I was sure it would be something sarcastic or rude, and I felt nervous. Then whatever it was disappeared and she looked at me. "Ready?"

I nodded.

She adjusted her backpack, then looked up at the guy one last time. "Thanks again, by the way."

"You're welcome," he said evenly. "By the way."

The last two miles were death. We'd thrown away our water bottles—too heavy—and we were hot and thirsty and incredibly tired, each step a trudge, each curb a mountain to descend with another opposite to scale. My whole body was made of sand, a vast desert that could be moved only by time. Sasha's face was the color of a faded bloodstain, her hair almost black with sweat.

"A thousand dollars," she said when we'd entered the last

mile, and the two of us began chanting it, "A thousand dollars, a thousand dollars," over and over again. I tried to think of something I'd buy if I were getting the money, but all I could come up with was grass, I wanted to buy a field of grass to lie on.

The last check-in station was on campus, in front of the Hoover Tower. There were banners congratulating us, tables with free food and drinks, a group of elementary school kids with a row of basins that people were lining up to bathe their feet in. We surrendered our sheets to be stamped one last time, and then we lay down under the closest tree and didn't speak for at least ten minutes.

"I can't believe we said we'd walk home," I said at last, and she laughed.

"Yeah, that was brilliant."

It was almost six, and I pictured my father in the kitchen, starting work on one of the rudimentary weekend dinners he served. I imagined him casting glances at the box of See's Candies, looking forward to the moment after we'd eaten when we'd break the seal on the box and each choose a chocolate.

"Maybe I'll come over," I said.

Sasha looked at me. "What for?"

"I don't know."

She'd been lying there with her eyes closed, but now she got onto her knees and began scanning the area.

"Who are you looking for?" I had an idea she thought Dan might've driven over to ferry us home.

"I'm meeting someone. I don't know when I'll be ready, so maybe you should just go ahead without me."

"Who?" I said, but my voice cracked, and I sounded squeaky and pathetic.

"Just someone."

My stinking shoes lay a few feet away, and I sat up and reached for them. "It's not like I care."

"Yes, you do."

My socks were damp. I had to turn them right side out again, and when I finished I brought my moist fingers to my nose and smelled sweat and rubber.

"OK, it's Cal," she said. "From last night. The guy in the vest."

"I know who Cal is." I pulled on one sock, then the other. "What are you going to do with him?"

"Nothing. Talk."

"*He's* who you called," I said. "God, I can't believe this."

She seemed not to hear me. Still on her knees, she swiveled away from me and craned her neck, and then she saw him; I could tell because she brought her fingertips to her lips.

Now I had a rival. She began meeting him after school, at his apartment, and after the first few times this happened—Sasha simply not showing up for the afternoon bus home—I wasn't surprised when she announced to me that she was going to start riding her bike to school instead of taking the bus. She said it was because it was spring now, and because riding the bus was for losers, but she didn't make the excuses with much energy, and I didn't argue. I switched, too, so we could still go to school together, though of course I had to make the ride home by myself. My afternoons reverted to the old style: a snack, homework, the click of my father's bicycle as he returned from work.

"I don't think you should go to his apartment," I told her, but she didn't care. She said he was teaching her to meditate, that they smoked, pigged out on Fritos when they had the munchies, sat on his balcony and sunned themselves. The pencil she'd used in her hair on the day of the Walk turned out to be the pencil he'd used to record his pledge the night before, and she guarded it like a treasure, keeping it in a special wooden box on her dresser.

"Are you, you know, boyfriend/girlfriend?" I asked her one

afternoon when we happened to meet at our bicycles after school.

"It's complicated," she said, but her face filled with color, and I felt something heavy lodge in the middle of my body.

We still got together, but unpredictably—when Cal was busy. I was at her house one afternoon when Dan said, "So you didn't want to work on the planning committee, too, Richard Appleby?" and Sasha, without giving me time to respond, said, "Richard missed the first meeting and they're being ridiculously strict about attendance." Another time, Joanie told me she was sorry to hear my mother was ill, and Sasha shot me a hard stare and then explained later that in order to get out of the house one evening, she'd said I was upset about a health problem my mother was having, and she was going to take a walk with me.

We were at Tressider when she told me this, the student union on campus—throughout the fall and winter we'd often ridden our bikes over and either bowled a few games at the crummy bowling alley or just bought sodas in the little store and absorbed the scene: guys with long hair, girls with bare feet, the sound of someone beating on a bongo drum.

Today, we sat at a table on the terrace and passed a single can of Coke back and forth. "Why did my mother have to be sick?" I said. "Why did she have to be in it at all? Couldn't you just say we were going to ride bikes?"

"They didn't want me to go out. They're being ridiculous these days. I had to think of something they couldn't say no to."

"Well, now what am I supposed to do? What if your mother starts asking me questions?"

"She won't."

"She might."

"She won't. She's worried about you. She won't ask you questions."

I felt my throat squeeze, and I half stood and pushed my chair backward.

"Watch it," said a voice from behind me, and I turned and saw that I'd nearly run over some girl's toes. She was pretty, with long straight hair parted in the middle and a leather cord around her neck.

"Sorry."

"It's OK, honey. Just be more careful. There are other people in the world, too, you know."

I pulled my chair back to the table and sat down again. My face was on fire, and I looked away from Sasha, focused on a pigeon pecking between the tables, bobbing for crumbs.

"Do you think she's sexy?" Sasha said quietly, leaning forward.

I didn't care. I was furious at her, furious at the girl, furious at Joanie. She didn't need to be worried about me. She had said to me once that I could trust her if I ever wanted to talk—*About your mother,* she didn't say, *about what she did to you*—and I'd thought of trying to explain that it really wasn't that big a deal, my father and I were doing fine. People never seemed to believe me, though—Mrs. Bloom, my science teacher from last year; Malcolm's mother, who'd cornered me once—and so I'd learned not to bother.

Looking over my shoulder, I slid my chair back again, carefully this time, and squeezed out of it. Leaving Sasha with a puzzled look on her face, I went over to the little convenience store where we'd bought our soda. I had a pocketful of change, and I picked up a bag of potato chips and got in line to pay. I looked out at the terrace and saw Sasha sitting at our table with a bored look on her face. The girl I'd almost hit still stood behind my chair, talking to a table full of other girls. She kept flipping her hair away from her face, which I guessed was sexy. Her breasts were on the small side, though. Malcolm had brought a *Playboy* to school a few days earlier, and I remembered the huge breasts on the centerfold, and the way she had her tongue sticking out a little, just enough to lick her upper lip. We spent lunch paging through the magazine, sitting behind the portables so no teachers would see us. Bob liked the women who held their breasts in their upturned hands, but I thought they looked weird, as if they were about to hand them to you, like little pets that wanted to be cradled.

It was almost my turn to pay. The cashier was a middle-aged woman with pale, fat arms. When I was much younger my mother and I sometimes met my father at the faculty club for lunch, and afterward she and I would stop at this store for Wint-O-Green Life Savers, which I would chew at home in front of the bathroom mirror once it was dark out, desperate to see the famous sparks.

I set the chips on the counter and reached into my pocket— and then suddenly I didn't want them anymore. I left them sitting there and went back outside.

"What the fuck was that?" Sasha said when I got back to the table. "You didn't even buy anything?"

I shrugged.

"Look at that guy," she said in a lower voice, angling her head toward the guy at the next table. He had long dark blond hair in a ponytail, and he was bent over a notebook, writing quickly. Spread out on the table in front of him were four or five open books.

"What about him?"

"Daddy is so fucked up. He says the students here aren't serious. 'It's not Yale, that's for sure.' That guy hasn't stopped writing since we sat down. Last year all Daddy could talk about was how the students at Yale don't know anything about living. Now the students at Stanford don't know anything about hard work."

I thought of the afternoon when Dan came home so angry. I'd thought he was mad at his colleagues, but maybe I'd been wrong.

"He has to stop complaining," she said. "He has to relax and leave me alone." She was blushing, and I knew what she was thinking: so she could see even more of Cal.

The next day was a Saturday, and I slept in, not waking until my father opened my bedroom door to tell me he was going to his office. It was 9:42, very late for me; between my inability to sleep all morning and my dearth of boners, I was turning out to be a lousy teenager.

"Sorry," my father whispered. "I just wanted to tell you, I'm going to work."

"I'm awake now," I said, pushing up on one elbow and rubbing my face. "You don't have to whisper."

He glanced at his watch. His voice still low, he said, "There's a chance I'll be late getting home today."

"OK."

"One of my doctoral students is bringing in the first half of his manuscript. Rather interesting work, in fact—he's looking at the Judiciary Reorganization Bill of 1937, the so-called court-packing plan. He said three o'clock, but he's not terribly reliable."

"Dad, it doesn't matter."

He pulled a handkerchief from his pocket and blew his nose. "I thought we'd go to the Legion of Honor tomorrow afternoon," he said. "Around one-thirty? They're exhibiting some marvelous early Rembrandt drawings."

When I heard the front door close I got up and had some cereal and then went to Sasha's, realizing only after I'd rung the bell that my arrival might blow open some lie she'd told.

Peter opened the door. He was still in his pajamas, and I was relieved to see them all at the dining table.

"Come in, Richard," Joanie called. "We're having French toast."

"Not quite the breakfast of champions," Dan said from his place at the head of the table, "but I think I'd rather be in the middle of the pack and eat well, wouldn't you?" He waved me in. "What shall we call it? The breakfast of mediocrities? Doesn't have quite the right ring. Come in, sit, eat, please—I need some help here."

Sasha was picking at her food and frowning, and she glanced at me but didn't speak. Everyone else was more or less finished, but Joanie fetched me a plate heaped with French toast and bacon, and when I sat down Dan slid the syrup in my direction.

I was unscrewing the cap when, under the table, Sasha's foot came down on mine, hard. I looked at her, but her face was unreadable.

"Nice day, wot?" Dan said in a fake English accent.

Sasha let out a barely audible snort, and I realized I'd interrupted a fight. I cut off a bite of French toast and shoved a piece of bacon into my mouth.

"T'isn't cricket," Dan said to Sasha, "your staying behind."

"OK, it isn't cricket."

"It's meant to be gor-juss," he went on, leaning harder on the accent, and now I had it: they were going to Muir Woods. I'd heard about it last Sunday: *We've been in California for nine months and we still haven't seen the redwoods!* I'd been in California for thirteen and three-quarters years and I still hadn't seen them.

"Besides," Dan continued, "if you don't go, your mum will be the only bird along." The way he said "bird" sounded like "bud"—your mum will be the only bud along.

"Stop it," Sasha said. "Stop it with the accent. And she's not a bird. You sound like an idiot."

Dan put his palm to his chest. "Harsh verdict," he said, but in his own voice.

"Would you say 'chick'?" she went on. "It's basically the same thing."

"Joanie?" Dan said. "Care to weigh in?"

Joanie shrugged. "What's wrong with 'woman'?"

"Your daughter," he replied, "is not, strictly speaking, a woman. Yet." He turned to me. "Semantics aside, we have an excellent expedition planned for the day. We're going to Muir Woods, and we'd love to have you join us." He drummed his fingers on the table, then leaned way back in his chair, crossed his arms over his chest, and said to Sasha, "*Why* wouldn't you want to go? That's what I don't understand."

She rolled her eyes. "I told you—I have a French test Monday and I'm really behind."

He looked at me again. "What do you think? It'd do you good. 'For what are they all in their high conceit, When man in the bush with God may meet?' I'm on a quest today, Richard— you can join me."

"You're an atheist," Sasha said to him.

"Agnostic, actually," he said. "But it's a metaphor. And it's less a quest for than a quest away from. As, in many ways, it was for Emerson."

I liked the idea—a lot more than Rembrandt drawings, early or otherwise—but I said I had homework, too, and for the next twenty minutes, as her parents and Peter moved around the house getting ready, Sasha and I stayed at the table and hardly said a word. The French toast was tepid, but I worked on it anyway, methodically sliding each bite through the pooled syrup before putting it in my mouth.

At last they left. "Thank God," she said as we heard the car back out of the driveway. "I thought I might kill them."

She left me sitting there and went to the phone in her parents' bedroom. When she came back she said Cal couldn't come for another hour or so, and did I want to wait with her?

She was wearing the same blouse she'd had on the day she accused me of looking at her boob, and as she reached for her juice glass the slit fell open. This time I did look: she wasn't wearing a bra, and her breast was round and pale and angled outward.

Her nipple was small and tight, the color of an underripe strawberry.

She went over to the sliding door. "Let's go outside."

I followed her to the patio. The sun was high, and the plate glass windows reflected the entire yard: the patio with its wooden furniture, the flower beds full of spiky purple agapanthus and low-lying white impatiens, the high fence that ran along the edge of the property. And Sasha, too: standing near the picnic table with her hands on her hips, dressed in her blouse and cutoffs, her bare legs glowing white in the bright light. I took a quick look at myself: as runty as ever, Richard with his big ears and his slightly too-small brown-and-orange striped T-shirt. "You need new clothes," Gladys had said to me a week earlier, standing in front of the dryer folding laundry.

I wondered: Would Cal park in the driveway? What if the Hoppers, who lived next door, happened to be outside?

Sasha went back in for a deck of cards, and we sat at the table and played double solitaire, the sun climbing higher, an occasional light breeze stirring the highest leaves of the trees on the other side of the fence. For a little while I could hear the Hoppers in their backyard, talking quietly. Teresa Hopper was from Peru, and her voice had a singsong quality. Her husband's was duh duh duh, and hers was d' dee d' dee dee d' day. They were in their seventies. He was a Nobel Prize winner; he'd done something or other in chemistry that about three people in the world understood.

Thirty minutes went by, forty. At fifty I found myself getting nervous. I sort of wanted to leave. Then suddenly there was something at the side of my head, warm and moving, brushing my ear—as if a squirrel had jumped onto my shoulder. "Ah," I said, leaping up and swatting at my head and neck; then I turned around and saw Cal grinning at me.

"Damn," he said. "I nearly had you." He circled the table and stood behind Sasha, who was trying not to smile. He put his hands on her shoulders, then moved one hand to her forehead and pulled her head to his belly. "You were too perfect," he told me. "I had to try."

Sasha had seen him coming—he must have held a finger to his lips. Tiptoed up behind me, stealthy as a thief. I hadn't heard the gate open. Hadn't heard his car door slam.

"So this is it," he said, stepping away from Sasha and looking around. It was the first time I'd seen him since the night at SCRA, and he seemed different. His hair was in a ponytail today, and he had a pack of cigarettes rolled in the sleeve of his T-shirt.

He walked over to the house, cupped his hands at his eyes, and peered through the windows. "Nice setup," he said over his shoulder. "Professor Horowitz has done very well for himself."

"Professor Levine," I said.

"What?"

"I told you," Sasha said. "We're renting. This is the Levines' house—they're in Rome."

"Prego," Cal said. "Of course you did. If Daddy gets to stay at Stanford, you're going to buy a nice, big house."

"He is staying," she said. "But we're not going to buy a house. We're going to rent again—probably in College Terrace."

This was good news to me—that they might move to College Terrace. I'd been wondering where they would live next year, worrying it might be farther away.

"All right then," Cal said. "You ready, baby? We got no time to waste."

Sasha's cheeks turned pink, and I wondered if she was embarrassed by his bad grammar. I looked away, and when I looked back she was climbing onto the picnic bench and draping her arms over his shoulders. "Whoa," he said, laughing a little, "let me get my balance." He reached for her legs, squatted, and lifted her onto his back. His tanned forearms crossing her white thighs: I got up and began sweeping the cards together, gathering them into a loose pile and then into a neat stack.

"What time do you have to be back?" he asked her.

"Five. At the latest."

"Then we better hurry. Going to a party," he explained to me. "In the Santa Cruz mountains."

I wondered if Sasha knew how far away that was: a solid hour in the car each way. "I'll put the cards away and lock up," I told her. "If you want."

"That'd be great, man," Cal said. "Thanks. You're too heavy, baby," he added, and he bent his knees and loosened his grip on her legs. "Get your stuff and let's go, all right?"

She made for the house, and I continued with the cards, giving them a shuffle for good measure and sliding them into the box. Sasha was back in a moment, a shoulder bag of Joanie's in her arms.

"Really, thanks, man," Cal said, and he dug into his pocket and tossed a joint onto the table. " 'Preciate it."

Sasha's eyes met mine, and she looked away.

"No problem," I said, and I waited until they were gone, then pocketed the joint, took the cards inside, locked the doors, and left.

I didn't smoke it. Not that day, not the next, not the next. Sasha asked, and I said I was saving it, and that became the plan. I hid it in a Band-Aid box under the sink in my bathroom. It was in with a bunch of other stuff: a half-used travel-size Crest, a bottle of dandruff shampoo, an inch-thick stack of Kleenex with no box. No one ever opened that cabinet; no one had opened it in years.

Soon, I had to go to my mother's again. This time, my father was going away for the weekend himself, to visit his cousin David in Seattle. I was glad about this: I thought he was lonely. When we left, his overnight bag was on the backseat next to my pack.

My mother was in a good mood when I arrived. There was a vase of pink carnations on the coffee table, and she had gotten her hair cut—just a little, but enough to make it look neater. She had fresh lipstick on, and she smiled as she got dinner ready, asking me to tell her about school, and which of my teachers would I miss next year, and was I glad it was almost summer.

"Did I ever tell you about the job I had picking strawberries?" she asked a little later, once we were at the table. She had, but I shook my head, and she went on. "This was 'forty-eight, maybe 'forty-nine. Usually in the summer I worked at the library, shelving books—my mother had worked there during the war, so the director knew us. But that summer your aunt Alice needed a job, so I had to find something else. I saw a notice in the drugstore downtown, advertising for strawberry pickers, and for some reason I thought it sounded like fun. A hundred degrees out in the sun every day—I don't know where I got that idea. But my father said they'd never take me, so I took it as a challenge."

I was cutting minute steak into pieces and chewing them slowly, half listening to her and half thinking of what Sasha'd told me about the party in the Santa Cruz mountains, how she'd eaten a hash brownie and gotten higher than she'd ever been before. I was worried about what they might be doing this weekend—maybe going to another party where she'd try mushrooms or even LSD.

"Are you listening?" my mother said.

I looked up at her. She had a thin face, thinner now than before. Perhaps because of this, her lips seemed swollen, overfull. The lipstick had worn off; most of it was on her glass now.

"Yes," I said. "You saw an ad."

"So I went out to this farm," she said, "about three miles outside town, and there were already crews in the fields, but I rang the doorbell on the farmhouse, and a grizzly old lady came to the door—I swear, she had whiskers. And I told her what I wanted, and she pointed to the barn, and I went out there and found Mr. Fisher."

Mr. Fisher was the farmer. He had a hundred acres, strawberries and lettuce and artichokes. This was outside Salinas. When I was younger my parents sometimes took me for a drive down there, to where my mother had grown up, and inevitably we would pass what my mother called "Mr. Fisher's"—never "Mr. Fisher's farm" or "Mr. Fisher's land," just "Mr. Fisher's." At some point I learned that Mr. Fisher was a man she'd worked for, the summer she was eighteen, but for a brief period in my very young childhood I'd heard "Mr. Fisher's" as "mist or fishers," and when we drove by I looked hard to see if I could figure out which it was.

The next part of the story was that my mother joined a crew of migrant workers—Mexican—whom Mr. Fisher hired for the season and housed in a long bunkhouse with a corrugated roof. The story was about how my mother worked hard to prove herself, and how by the end of her six- or seven-week stint working with them, the Mexican women all doted on her.

"They cried on my last day," my mother was saying. "They'd embroidered a tablecloth for me, sitting up late after work—I can't imagine what it did to their eyes. And they gave it to me just before I got in my car for the last time and drove off. And do you know what I felt?"

I knew what she felt. I hated this part of the story.

"Nothing," she said. "I felt nothing. Not gratitude, not shame. Nothing at all."

We'd both finished eating, and I pushed back my chair and cleared our plates, hoping we could move to the TV now.

"Would you like dessert?" she said.

I was surprised by this; she never served dessert. "What is it?"

"Cake." She went to a paper bag on the counter and took out

a small pink box, fastened with tape that she cut with a knife. She lifted out a cake, only four or five inches in diameter, iced in white and decorated with yellow swirls.

It was her birthday; I'd forgotten entirely. I was furious at my father for not reminding me. "It's your birthday," I said. "I'm sorry. I didn't get you a present."

She came close and put her arms around me, pulling my head to her neck and holding it there until I began to get a cramp and moved away.

I turned and looked at the flowers on the coffee table. That it was her birthday explained them, but I didn't know if the explanation was that someone had given them to her for her birthday or that she'd bought them herself.

"They're from Patrice," she said.

"Who?"

"My friend Patrice. I met her at work."

"Is she another social worker?"

"No," my mother said. "She comes in at night and cleans." She opened a drawer for forks, reached for plates, and set them on the counter with a clank. When we sat down again, slices of cake in front of us, she looked upset.

I leaned my nose close to the cake. "This smells good."

She edged a bite onto her fork and ate it, chewing and then reaching for her wineglass. She set it down without drinking any. "She shouldn't have spent the money," she said. "She doesn't have an extra cent." She let out a deep sigh and pushed her plate away.

I busied myself with my cake, eating it in one, two, three huge bites. The only milk in her fridge had gone sour, so I was drinking water, and I had the last gulp and carried my dishes to the sink. There wasn't a dishwasher in the apartment, and usually we just left the dishes while we watched TV, but tonight I turned on the water and let it get hot, and I washed our dinner plates, and then the pan she'd fried the steak in, and then the rice pot, a layer of rice hardened to its bottom. She had her chin in her hand, and I took my time, picking at the rice with my fingernails. Sometimes, when she was in a low mood, she would start asking me questions—about how I was doing, how I was *really* doing—and I thought that if I took long enough with the rice pot, if I made sure I got every single grain, maybe I could keep her questions at bay.

That Sunday, my father came for me straight from the airport, where his plane had landed a little after two p.m. There was traffic as we drove by the Oakland Coliseum, but even so we got home before five, a good hour and a half earlier than usual.

We'd stopped for milk and cereal and some pork chops for dinner, and so we used the kitchen door—which is how we managed to avoid disturbing Sasha and Cal, who were in my father's bed, in a room at the opposite end of the house.

My father found them. He left me in the kitchen eating an apple, and I heard his steps as he headed away, and then I heard them again, quick, as he returned.

"Your friend," he said, standing in the doorway, fumbling with the buttons on his sport coat. "Ah, your friend is here. In my room. I'm afraid you'll have to . . ."

Somehow I understood immediately. I set the half-eaten apple on the counter and edged past him.

They were mostly dressed when I got there. Cal sat on the edge of the bed putting on his shoes, his disheveled hair hanging to his shoulders, while Sasha stood with her back to the door and buttoned her blouse. She wore shorts, and I noticed a blue vein running up the back of one knee.

"Richard," Cal said.

She turned, and when she saw me a look of dread came over

her face. She bent for her sandals and brushed past me, muttering, "Don't say anything," under her breath and continuing down the hall.

Cal stared at me. "Bad scene," he said, and he gave me an indifferent shrug and strolled out after her.

I was terrified to return to the kitchen. My father looked up when I got there and then returned his attention to the box of instant mashed potato flakes on the counter in front of him. He poured some potato flakes into a measuring cup and leaned over to read the markings on the glass. At last he straightened up and said, "That was wrong."

"I know," I said right away. "I'm sorry."

He pulled his lips into his mouth, and his chin took on the square, immobile look of wood—the ventriloquist's dummy. He let go of them. "Coming into the house without permission," he added.

"I know."

He turned to the stove, and for a while he focused on dinner, starting water for the potatoes, taking carrots from the fridge and peeling them over the sink. I went to the silverware drawer and began setting the table, making a separate trip for each utensil to stretch out the task.

"It was wrong," he said again.

I turned and saw that he'd set the peeled carrots down. He had a dazed look on his face, and I thought this was the moment when he'd decide to call Sasha's parents.

"But in point of fact," he went on, "they didn't do any harm."

I waited. The idea seemed to get traction in his face; his features settled, and he looked calmer.

"If you could tell her," he said. "If you could let her know I'd prefer that it not happen again . . ."

"Of course," I said.

"Good, that settles it."

He got back to work, and I turned to the table and fidgeted the silverware, unable to believe that this was it, the sum of his reaction. Had he not noticed that Cal was an adult? I wanted to laugh, but at the same time I had an urge to say something about it, to *make him understand*. I became so scared I'd do this that I left the kitchen, and I stayed in my room until dinner was ready.

Sasha's face looked pinched when we met the next morning, her hair drawn back so tightly that the skin at her temples seemed stretched. "Don't say anything," she said right away again, but then her eyes filled with tears and she told me her parents would kill her—*kill* her—if they found out.

"We didn't fuck, anyway," she said as we mounted our bicycles and pushed off. "Is your father going to tell them? Can you talk to him for me?"

"Why not?"

"Thank you so—" She looked over at me and saw what I was really saying. "Because we couldn't. God. It's none of your business."

"Why couldn't you?"

"Richard."

"My father was pretty freaked out. I don't know if I can stop him. But your parents won't be upset, what are you worried about? Your parents are cool."

She stared straight ahead, hands clenched around her handle-bars.

"Why weren't you at his apartment?"

"You are so nosy."

"Sasha, you were in my house."

She broke ahead of me, leaning forward, her calf muscles bulging as she pedaled harder. In a little while she was the length of a football field away, and then she was out of sight.

I didn't see her at school all day, but once the bell had rung and it was time to go home, I hid behind a hedge and then followed her on my bike, staying back so she wouldn't see me. At one point she stopped suddenly, and I made a quick turn onto a side street and stood next to my bicycle, panting. I had no idea what I'd say if she spotted me. I counted to thirty, and when I ventured back to the main road she was moving again, sitting up straight and riding no-handed.

Just then a German shepherd lunged at her from behind a chain-link fence. It barked and barked, leaping at the fence, and Sasha wobbled and grabbed the handlebars and righted herself and then wobbled again and was suddenly on the ground.

I stopped again, and from the shelter of a manzanita tree I watched her stand and brush herself off and right her bicycle, with glances every few seconds at the barking dog. She got on her bike and took off, pedaling hard. "Dogs and vomiting," she had said once, when we were playing Truth or Dare and I'd asked her what she was most afraid of. I'd forgotten about it until this moment.

Getting back on my bike, I rode after her, flipping off the German shepherd when it barked at me. In a little while Sasha came to El Camino, the wide, commercial roadway that ran up and down the Peninsula, and I hung back while she waited for the light to change. I let an entire light cycle go by before following after her, but I had seen her turn onto a side street and knew where to go.

Once I was across, I got off my bicycle and walked it, not sure I wouldn't suddenly need to dodge backward. At the corner where she'd turned, I put my kickstand down and crept forward.

On one side of the street was a row of shabby little houses, on the other were four or five small apartment buildings, each with its own carport. The apartments were on the second story, in a line facing the street; they reminded me of a motel. Sasha was halfway up a flight of stairs, and I jerked back and stood just out of sight.

What to do now? I'd had an image of myself in a heated confrontation with her and Cal—an image of prevailing somehow in this conversation and then riding home with a chastened but grateful Sasha just behind me. I sat on the curb and reached into my backpack for the Oreos I hadn't eaten at lunch. I'd passed the Old Barrel, the huge, cavernous liquor store where my father bought the special Scotch he liked, and once I'd eaten the cookies I rode back, went inside, and found myself a Coke. After I'd paid for it I wandered around the dark store, breathing in the strong alcohol smell, looking at the hard liquors and thinking it made sense that the brown ones could knock you out but wondering how something that looked exactly like water might make you happy and then drunk and then sick.

Outside again, I drank my soda and then rode my bike past Cal's street, continuing on until I'd reached the railroad crossing. The light was green, and I raced across the tracks and then across the busy road running parallel. It ran alongside the tracks all the way through Palo Alto, and I headed north, pedaling fast, hugging the side of the road.

The next morning, she was already at our meeting place when I got there, but this time there was a contrite look on her face. She began talking before my bike wheels had stopped moving.

"Richard, I'm sorry about yesterday. And Sunday. I really am. Let's do something this afternoon, OK? Like old times? Go to the Union after school?"

"Maybe I'm busy."

"Are you?"

"Well, what about Cal?"

"I'll see him tomorrow," she said. "Come on, it'll be fun. I want to student-watch, we haven't in so long."

And so at the end of the school day we rode home together, detouring to leave our backpacks at home before continuing on to the Union. It was late May, and the terrace was packed with students, four or five sitting at each table, dozens more milling around. Circling the area, looking for somewhere to sit, I smelled marijuana and incense. Finally we found a place on a low wall, and we settled there, next to a guy who looked like Jesus. His dark brown beard reached past his collarbones, and I noticed a grain of rice in it before I looked away. He strummed a guitar, his fingernails ragged and lined with dirt.

At my side, Sasha reached over her shoulder and scratched her back, dipping her hand under her shirt to get at the itch. Lying in bed the last two nights, I'd imagined her and Cal rolling around in my father's bed, and I'd gotten hard thinking about it. Seeing the two of them in my mind, naked in the twisted sheets, I'd rubbed my hand up and down my dick, but I couldn't find what I was looking for.

I elbowed her and tilted my head toward the guitar player. In a low voice I said, "Maybe you should break up with Cal and go with him."

"Richard," she said. "God."

"He's not so bad."

"Don't be an asshole. And I'm not 'going' with Cal." She looked at me, then quickly looked away. "Come on, I said I was sorry."

This was true, but what could I say? Not sorry enough?

"You have to understand," she went on. "It's not really a sexual thing. I mean, we kind of had to try, but that's not the point. It's this deep connection. I can't describe it."

I snorted.

"What?"

"I can. Ever hear the word 'pervert'?"

She rolled her eyes. "He's twenty-five."

"Exactly. Go tell your dad you don't have to read *Lolita*, you're living it."

Dan had taught a seminar on Nabokov the previous quarter, and he'd told us that *Lolita* was the best novel written in English in the last forty years and that we should read it as soon as possible. It was the only time I'd seen Joanie seriously disagree with him. "No, they should not," she said. "Prude," he said, and she said, "No, not prude. Parent. There's a difference."

Sasha pushed off the wall and faced me. "So what do you want to do now?"

"What do you mean? We just got here."

"It's boring."

"It's the Union. It's the same as it always is. You were the one who wanted to come."

"I'll be back in a sec," she said. "I'm going to buy a Coke."

"Fine," I said, and I watched as she headed for the convenience store and then veered into a phone booth.

I looked around. More than a month had gone by since the day I almost ran over the pretty girl's toes, and soon the school year would be over. What then?

Across the way, two guys at a table caught my eye. They weren't students, I didn't think—they were too old, too neat. The one facing me had sandy brown hair and a handlebar mustache, and he kept making hatchet motions with his hand. The guy with his back to me was nodding. He was tall and slender, with short light brown hair and a long, thin neck.

Suddenly I knew who he was. The guy from the Walk for Mankind—the tall guy whose house we'd barged into. It would be funny, I thought, if Sasha and I were to appear at his table and say hi. I hopped off the wall and casually strolled past him, pretending unawareness. Then, when I was far enough away, I bent down to tie my shoe and from the safety of a crouch stole a look at his face.

And it wasn't him. This guy had a beard, for one thing, but beyond that his face was too round, and he had dark, hooded eyes behind horn-rimmed glasses.

I was disappointed. I was more than disappointed, actually: I was crushed.

Sasha kept up the apologetic behavior, enough so that I wanted to say to her: Look, you don't have to do this, my father isn't going to tell. She rode home from school with me every two or three days, and she invited me over so frequently that I was suddenly seeing Dan and Joanie more than I had in weeks.

But it wasn't the same. In the fall, when the Horowitzes were new, every day I was there something fun happened. Now the house felt different. Dan annoyed me, lurking on the edges of anything Sasha and I were doing, saying, "What are you reading for English, *My Side of the Mountain*? You two are smarter than the average Stanford undergraduate—why do they underestimate you with this crap?" Sasha chalked up his mood to the grief he felt over Watergate. "It's like he's personally injured," she told me, rolling her eyes. "It's like he's a little kid who found out there's no Santa Claus."

One Friday night I stayed for dinner. It was a week before the end of the school year, June, an evening when the light hung on and on until at last there was nothing but a pale yellow-green rim of sky visible at the horizon. "Come wish on a star," Joanie called into the house at around nine o'clock.

She and Dan were on the patio, wrapped in blankets against the cool evening air. Sasha and I were at the dining room table playing Scrabble, and Peter lay on the floor reading comic books.

"Go," Sasha said to Peter.

"You go," he said without looking up.

I could no longer see Dan and Joanie, though I could just make out their shapes.

"Richard Appleby, are you still there?" Dan called.

"Yes."

"Don't break my wife's heart. Come wish on a star."

Sasha was rearranging the tiles in her tray, and she gave me a quick glance—shrugging, rolling her eyes—and looked down again. I had an "a," an "e," three "i"s, and a "q"—about the worst selection of letters imaginable. I got up and went to the door, sliding open the screen and then sliding it closed again behind me.

"Is it getting cold in there?" Dan said. "Close the glass door, too, will you?"

I had to reopen the screen door, reach for the handle on the glass door, and slide it closed. When I'd done this he gestured me close. "Have a seat, Richard," he said in a low voice. I looked at Joanie, her entire body wrapped in the blanket so that all I could see was her hair and her high-cheekboned face.

I sat on a bench.

"Does Sasha seem different to you?" Dan said.

Joanie made a little noise in her throat, a whimper. "Don't."

He stood up and walked to the fence, jiggling the change in his pocket. He came back. "Richard, if there were anything going on, you'd tell us, wouldn't you? Anything we should worry about, anything we should know."

I was speechless, couldn't have gotten a word out if I'd had a script in front of me.

"Richard?"

I struggled to find words. "Yeah. I mean, I guess."

Dan stiffened. "There is something?"

"He meant he'd tell us," Joanie said. "Right? You'd tell us."

I looked into the bright house, saw pots and pans stacked by the kitchen sink, Sasha at the dining table with her chin in her hand, Peter on the floor with his knees bent.

"No, I think there is something," Dan said. "Richard. What is it?"

Joanie was on a lounge chair, reclining, and now she sat up. "Dan, stop it."

He snorted and walked away again. He bent over and picked up some object I couldn't quite make out—it was small enough to fit in the palm of his hand. He tossed it up and caught it.

"Richard, it's OK," Joanie said. "I apologize."

"Christ!" Dan said, and he threw the thing at the fence, where it hit with a thud and fell to the ground and broke.

In a moment Sasha was sliding the glass door open, asking what had happened, what was that noise, what was going on?

"Nothing, nothing," Joanie said. "Daddy tripped on something."

"A clay pot," Dan said evenly. "What's happening in there? Is Peter still reading comics?"

"I don't know." Sasha stepped out and closed the door behind her. "It's freezing out here." She looked at her father and mother, and I had an idea she knew we'd been talking about her.

"Come sit with me, love," Joanie said, and Sasha went over and sat on the edge of the chair and let Joanie wrap her in the blanket. Inside the house, Peter had sat up and was sitting cross-legged, looking out at us—though of course he couldn't see us, he could only see himself.

"So what did you wish for?" Sasha asked me.

"Nuh uh uh," Dan said. "Richard Appleby gets to have some secrets, Sash, it's only fair."

"I haven't wished yet," I told her. "I'm going to now." And I looked up at the sky and held still for what seemed like the amount of time it would take to make a wish.

. . .

My father graded his last final exam on my last day of school, and that evening he announced that he'd booked a room at a lodge in the Trinity Alps: to celebrate the end of the year he was taking me on a surprise fishing trip. We'd never gone fishing before, and I was thrilled. When I was much younger I'd had a period of wanting to try fishing, based on a photograph I'd seen of a boy holding a fish the length of his torso. I'd pestered my parents for a while, but when the three of us went on trips it was always to cities with museums, or places where my father needed to do research.

We left early Friday morning, a box of food Gladys had prepared sitting on the seat between us. We had a long drive ahead, and I tried to read for a while, but I was too excited thinking about the fish I was going to catch—big ones that would be so heavy I'd need help holding them up for the picture. Restless, I decided to find license plates from all fifty states, but after four I gave up and asked my father to play Twenty Questions with me. I got him up to twenty-nine questions with Mr. Murphy, my math teacher, then had him grumbling minutes later when I guessed Franklin Roosevelt's wheelchair in seven.

We ate ham sandwiches at ten o'clock and stopped at a Denny's at noon. By three we were in the foothills, and I stared out the window, noticed how the trees changed as we climbed, pine and fir taking over, keeping the highway in shadow for long stretches.

"I presume the house will be undisturbed," my father said out of the blue.

Sasha had used a key we kept hidden under a flowerpot just outside the kitchen door, and before leaving the house this morning I'd moved it inside, just to be safe. I looked over at him: my father with his gray hair and his short-sleeved plaid button-down shirt. He was getting soft at the middle: his stomach spilled over his belt like a baking cupcake bulging over the side of the tin.

"It will," I said.

I asked about the fishing lodge, and we talked about the kinds of fish we might find and whether there'd be some way to eat our catch; and then we drove for several minutes without speaking. There was a California state map in the door pocket, and I opened it and ran my finger along the route he'd shown me at the Denny's. We were getting closer.

"So," he said. "I guess things are a little iffy with the Horowitzes."

I looked over at him. "What do you mean?"

"About whether or not Dan will stay at the University next year."

"He is staying."

With his right hand my father felt for the box of food and without looking found the plastic bag of gingersnaps Gladys had tucked between the sandwiches and the apples. He pulled a couple of cookies out, put one in his mouth whole, and held the other between his thumb and forefinger as he put his hand back on the wheel. He chewed and swallowed the cookie in his mouth before he spoke.

"My understanding," he said, "is that there have been several conversations, and there's a chance . . . by mutual agreement . . ."

"They're renting a house in College Terrace," I said. "Sasha told me."

"Hmm," my father said, and I turned away from him and stared out the window. In the next lane there was a station wagon with its backseat full of kids, and I could tell from a glance that they were having a lot more fun than I was. If I were on this trip with the Horowitzes, it would be me and Sasha and Peter in that backseat, passing around *MAD* magazine and arguing about who was going to get the windows after the next gas station stop. From the front, Joanie would hand us slices of apple, and Dan would make up silly rhymes based on the road signs we passed.

Instead, I was alone with my father. "They are," I said, but I was still facing the window, and he might not have heard me.

It was sundown when we reached the lodge, a redwood structure about a mile from the highway, its "No Vacancy" sign blinking in the dusk. My father went to the desk and got our key, and I followed him up a narrow flight of stairs to the second floor. "Here we go," he said. "We made it."

A strong flowery smell assaulted me as he opened the door, and I covered my mouth and nose. "Let's let in some air," he said, and he crossed the room and pushed open the single window.

The light switch was just inside the door, and I stepped in and flipped it. The beds were covered by flowered bedspreads in shades of pink, red, and purple. The pillows were draped with giant squares of lace. There were pitchers of dried flowers on every surface, sitting on top of lace hankies. A line of china sheep paraded across the dresser, followed by a single china shepherdess. And, maybe worst of all, there was a row of pink hearts above each bed.

"I thought this was supposed to be a fishing lodge," I cried.

"It's not so bad," my father said.

"It's terrible."

"I'm sorry," he said with a sigh.

"Everyone's sorry," I shouted, and I hurried back down to the lobby, went outside, and started walking. There was enough light for me to follow a path around the side of the building, and I moved quickly, crossed a clearing with picnic tables, climbed over a low fence, and headed into the trees. It was cold and smelled of pine, and of damp earth and something a little rotten that I couldn't identify. An animal skittered away, and I froze, imagining a skunk but then figuring if it were a skunk it would've sprayed already. I thought there might be deer nearby, maybe antelope. What were antelope, anyway, a kind of deer? I knew nothing. The idea that my father and I could just drive into the mountains and catch fish revealed itself in all its absurdity. The whole thing was doomed, pathetic. I imagined Cal laughing at us. The inn building was close, lights from the guest rooms shining down from the second story. I pictured my father in our frilly room, wondering whether or not to come after me. Let him wait, I thought, let him wonder. How could he have brought me to such a ridiculous place?

But now that I was thinking about him, I began to feel bad. It wasn't fair to leave him there, when the whole reason we were here was me. I made my way toward the building, crossing the fence at a different point, outside some kind of office, a room with a desk and several fish mounted on the wall. I moved closer and identified a rainbow trout, a brown trout, and a salmon. There was a door to the outside, and I tried it: unlocked. I stepped in and made for a door just opposite, which let onto a hallway that smelled of cigarettes. I got my bearings and found the lobby, and I moved through it as fast as I could, breaking into a run when I reached the stairs. I opened our door, and my father was stretched out on one of the beds reading, looking as relaxed as he might have at home.

"There you are," he said. "I'm glad you're back."

In the morning the proprietor fixed us up with equipment and a guide, a slow-talking man of about thirty-five who drove us in a pickup truck to a wide, rushing river, where he kept a boat tied to an old wooden pier. It would be nice to say that the day was a great success, that I was an angler from that weekend on, someone whose spirit came alive when he held a rod in his hand, someone whose every encounter with a fish told him who he was. It would even, in a different way, be satisfying to say it was a disaster, one mishap following another, not a fish caught after eight hours on the water, and that my father and I drove back to the Bay Area united by failure, laughing together or entirely silent.

In fact, I learned to thread a worm onto a hook, to hold a

fishing rod in the correct way; I discovered that catching a fish was hard work, and that the satisfaction—because I did catch a couple—was fleeting and tinged with dismay. My father and I both got sunburned; for dinner Saturday the innkeeper served us the tiny trout I'd caught that afternoon; Sunday morning we went back out ready to repeat the entire thing; and by one or two that afternoon we were both finished.

"I guess we probably won't do that again," I said at some point during the long drive home, while we were on a particularly dreary stretch of Interstate 5.

"We could," my father said.

"No, we don't need to."

We didn't say anything more for a few minutes, and then he cleared his throat and announced that there was something he needed to tell me.

I looked at him, thought about how skinny his shoulders were, about how our fishing guide had such big shoulders that the sleeves of his T-shirt barely reached the tops of his arms.

"What?" I said.

"It's about your mother."

She was sick. I thought of Joanie telling me she was sorry to hear my mother was ill, and I had an idea that she knew, that Sasha knew—that the lie Sasha had told had been not for her benefit but for mine, to hide my mother's illness from me. My mother's thin face: she'd been sick for a long time.

"We'll be divorcing," my father said, and for an instant I was disappointed: she wasn't dying.

"I'd hoped we could avoid it," he went on. "When she left I thought she'd realize she'd made a mistake."

She'd been gone over a year now; I couldn't believe he'd been thinking that this whole time.

"She'd like more time with you," he added. "Every other weekend."

"No."

"It's a new idea. Things like this take some getting used to."

"I won't."

We entered a terrible smell, cow manure or cow carcasses or something, and I held my hand over my mouth and nose, breathing in the scent of worms and the river.

After a while the smell faded. We approached a cluster of gas stations, the arches of a McDonald's springing up among them.

"Would you like to stop for a milkshake?" my father asked.

"No, keep going," I said, and for a long time after that neither of us spoke.

The house was untouched. It was long after dark when we arrived, but I left my father poking around the kitchen and went to ring the Horowitzes' doorbell.

A full minute or two passed, and then Joanie answered. "Richard!" She was wrapped in a bathrobe, but I could see the outlines of her nipples through the thin material. Bare feet, her yellowish toenails longer than they should have been, which made me feel weird. "Sasha's not here," she said. "They're both—"

"Who is it?" Dan called from their bedroom.

"Richard," she called back.

He came up the hallway, naked except for a towel he pinched closed at the waist. The hair on his chest was sparse, ginger going white.

"I'm sorry," I said. "I thought—"

"We farmed the kids out tonight, Richard Appleby," he said. "Married couples need time alone."

"Dan, for God's sake." Joanie tucked her hair behind her ear, then untucked it and spiraled a lock around her finger. "Sorry, Richard. How was the fishing trip? Did you catch a lot of fish?"

"Oh, that's right," Dan said. "This was the great fishing weekend. Don't you have a speckled trout for us or something?"

I wanted to ask him about what my father had said. And "by

mutual agreement"—did that mean he and Joanie both thought he should leave? Or he and the University? That would be embarrassing, the University wanting him to leave. Though Yale had.

He was holding the towel between his thumb and forefinger, and now he pinched it tighter, gathering the material into his fist. "No speckled trout, then," he said. "Too bad."

"I'll bet you had a nice time, though," Joanie said. "You and your dad."

I looked past them, saw empty wineglasses on the coffee table, discarded clothing on the couch. "Where *is* Sasha?"

"They're both with the Wilsons," Joanie said. "They'll be home tomorrow morning."

Sasha hated the Wilson kids, fifteen-year-old twin girls who attended a private school and played field hockey.

"Come back tomorrow," Dan said. "We like having you around—you know that, don't you?"

I mumbled something and got out of there, running down their driveway and out into the street, and then running all the way to my house for no good reason.

I took the Band-Aid box over to Sasha's the next day, and I had my first taste of marijuana in a tiny park near our houses, the two of us sitting on adjacent swings that creaked every time we moved. I coughed, of course, and didn't feel a thing, but, unlike fishing, smoking pot turned out to be something I was very good at, and each encounter with a joint told me exactly who I was, a guy who preferred the dazed-out float of a good high over everything else.

"*Now* do you get it?" Sasha said one hot afternoon when we'd gotten stoned and were on our bikes in search of food. "It took you long enough."

"Give me a break," I said. "You loved being the only one. Well, no more, sister."

She laughed at this and then couldn't stop laughing and had to get off her bike. We were headed for JJ&F, a little grocery store on the far edge of College Terrace, but she was laughing so hard I got off my bike, too.

"Well, no more, sister," she sang, and now we both cracked up, laying our bikes on the sidewalk and crouching next to them, laughing the ocean-wave laughter of the stoned, up and down and down and up, and it was incredibly intense and at the same time locked away from the real world, safe behind a wall of glass.

At last we got back on our bikes and continued. In the store we walked back and forth between the ice cream display and the shelves of chips, finally settling on an enormous bag of Cheetos. Once we'd paid, we walked our bikes down College Avenue, taking turns holding the bag open so the other person could scoop out a giant handful.

"Beware the orange fingers," she said at one point, waving her stained fingers in my face, and we cracked up again, Sasha laughing so hard this time that she had to cross one leg in front of the other.

"OK," she said after a time, standing normally again but shaking her hands as if she were trying to air-dry them. "I have to maintain." She ran her fingers through her hair, leaving a trace of Cheetos dust on the edge of her face. "Let's go. Just don't say anything funny."

We walked half a block in silence.

"I didn't say don't say *anything*," she said, and a giggle edged its way into her voice.

I bit the inside of my cheek so I wouldn't laugh and set her off. I thought for some reason of my father, chuckling a little the previous night as he glanced at the comics page. "I like Beetle Bailey," he'd said, looking up at me. "Do you?"

She was a little ahead of me. She wore a halter top, and on her bare back there was a sunburn line from the string of her bathing suit. I wondered if she'd been lying out. Joanie liked to sun herself on the patio, recline on one of the lounge chairs with the *New York Review of Books* and an iced coffee. I pictured the contours of Joanie's wide belly, the bits of pubic hair that escaped from the leg holes of her bathing suit, making me want to look and not look at the same time. That sunny patio: soon it would belong to the Levines again.

"So when are you moving?" I said. "Where are you going to live next year, anyway?"

Sasha was licking her fingers, washing off the orange dust. "College Terrace."

I stopped walking. The whole of College Terrace was just College Avenue and the dozen or so streets that crossed it, each only two blocks long. We had just passed Princeton Street and were on our way to Oberlin. Wherever their new place was, it couldn't be far away. "You mean you found a house?"

"Yeah. It's going to be great."

"Where is it?"

She was silent for a moment. "Dartmouth. Have we passed Dartmouth yet?"

"Duh."

"What?"

"We're at Oberlin. They're in alphabetical order. It's like five more blocks."

"They're in alphabetical order?"

"Well, not completely. Cornell is between Wellesley and Princeton, so—"

"So the person who named the streets was a stoner," she said, and we both laughed again, though not so hard this time.

"Well, let's go see it," I said.

"What?"

"Your new house."

"Oh. We can't. Other people still live there."

"The outside."

She seemed to give it more thought than it needed—torturing me a little, I thought. "OK," she said at last, and we continued down College, across Oberlin and Harvard. Dartmouth was the weird one: you couldn't drive through because there was a little park right in the middle; the street stopped and then started up again after the park. Unfortunately, it wasn't the kind of park you could smoke in; it was open to all the houses surrounding it, nothing like the private park near our houses.

We got to Dartmouth Street, and Sasha stopped in front of a one-story stucco house with a huge palm tree in the front yard and several terra cotta pots of cactus sitting on the front stoop. "Voilà," she said.

It looked small, but I could see why they'd chosen it. The sand-colored stucco, the terra cotta, the palm—it was as Western as you could get. I wondered if there'd be a band of light on the floor for Dan to lie in.

"There are only two bedrooms," she said, "but I'm going to take the garage. See?" She pointed at a small structure at the end of the cracked concrete driveway. "Daddy says it'll be hot in the summer and freezing in the winter, but that makes it better, don't you think? I'm going to have a ceiling fan and mosquito netting, and a woodstove for when it's cold." She glanced at me and then looked away again, trying to suppress a smile. "And a separate entrance."

I didn't really want to think about Cal or how much easier it was going to be for her to see him, so I said we should go, and we got onto our bikes and rode home.

Cal, I learned, was a dealer, though he preferred "supplier," as in "I'm a supplier of goods and services," the services being delivery and, where indicated, co-consumption. He'd met Eric Rumsen and Kevin Cottrell at a party at Lake Lagunita, on the edge of the

Stanford campus; the night Sasha and I saw them in the field behind SCRA was the night of his first sale to Eric and the others, two ounces of pot homegrown by a friend of his on a small farm up near Cloverdale. Two ounces was all he'd sell them at a time. "He's concerned about them," Sasha said about this, and I thought: Yeah, concerned they'll turn around and start selling it themselves and he'll get none of the profit.

I also found out, during those early weeks of the summer, why Sasha and Cal had been unable to have sex. "It hurt too much." This wasn't unusual for a fourteen-year-old girl, she told me with confidence. They were going to try again sometime soon.

And there was this: they'd used my house that Sunday afternoon because Cal couldn't wait. They were hanging out at the Union, and they decided yes, they should, they should do it; and Sasha only had an hour before she had to be home, which wasn't nearly enough time to get all the way to his apartment and back, given what had to happen in between. My house was perfect: nearby and empty.

This information came to me slowly, in bits and pieces, usually when Sasha and I were high. Days when she wasn't with Cal, we rode our bikes into the hills: we lay around under giant oak trees, smoking and laughing and sometimes falling asleep in the heat, so that we might wake in the late afternoon with our skin marked by the twigs and bits of dried grass we'd lain on. Gladys always wanted to know where I was going, and so I invented a friend in Los Altos Hills with a swimming pool in his backyard. That I never brought home a wet suit or towel seemed not to occur to her—or maybe she felt she was carrying out her part of things just asking the question. Sasha told her parents the same story, and so we had to name this friend, and we came up with Harry Henry. Saying "Harry Henry's house" over and over again was quite a sport for us when we were stoned. Harry Henry's parents kept a mini-fridge in their cabana, and there were Cokes available all day, and cookies and chips galore. Hillary Henry was Harry's magnificent older sister, who could often be seen sunning herself on a lounge chair.

One afternoon we leaned against the rough trunk of our favorite oak, passing a pipe back and forth and talking about how sad it was that Harry Henry's pet iguana had died.

"Hillary planned the funeral," Sasha said. "She wrote an elegy. 'What ocean contains water enough to feed our tears this day?' "

I snorted. "That's terrible."

She socked my shoulder. "No, it's not. Hillary writes beautiful poetry."

"Harry hates her for it."

"Harry adores her for it. He illustrates her poems. Didn't he show you the pictures?" She said the last word with a slight English accent: the *picshuhs*?

"No," I said.

"No? That sad sketch of poor Iggy with his head on the ground?" She upped the accent. "When she goes away to collidg next year, he'll be desolate. Fortunately, she'll cut off a lock of her heh for him to braid into a wristbaund."

"A 'lock,' " I said. "Don't you think that's weird? And talk normal."

"It should be a key of heh," she said.

"Talk normal," I said, "and give me that." I took the pipe and sucked in a burning throatful of spicy Cloverdale dope. I held it in my lungs, keeping the pipe in my far hand so she couldn't take it from me.

"A key of heh," she said again. And then, dropping the accent, "God, I just realized, I sound like Daddy."

" 'If you don't go to Muir Woods with us, your mum will be the only bud along.' "

Sasha laughed. "Very good. Hey, what are you doing, give me the pipe."

I took another toke and handed it to her.

"Speaking of birds," she said, "do you have a crush on her?"

"Who?"

"Hillary."

My picture of Hillary was mostly a picture of the girl I'd seen when we were stopped at Mile Ten of the Walk for Mankind, the braless girl in the purple tank top. Hillary had that girl's breasts and her long, smooth legs, but in truth she had Sasha's hair.

"Does the pope shit in the woods?"

Sasha snorted and said, "Yes, and all bears are Catholic."

I sang: " 'Get down on your knees and genuflect, genuflect, genuflect, genuflect.' " This was from the Tom Lehrer song "The Vatican Rag"; the Horowitzes were great fans, and I had learned the lyrics to all of his songs.

"Think of a bear kneeling," she said.

"Don't think of an elephant," I said, and she laughed harder.

She sucked on the pipe and then handed it to me, saying, "Anyway, do you?"

It took me a moment to figure out what she was asking. "I want to bed her," I said, and she bent forward at the waist and shrieked, her shoulders shaking with laughter; and then, in a moment, she was on my lap, her shins on the ground outside my thighs, her face inches from mine.

And so I kissed her. A quick lean in, my lips pressed against hers for an instant, and then I pulled back again.

I looked into her face. Saw her long nose and pale eyelashes and pink-rimmed eyes. I had an urge to put my tongue on her eyelid. I cupped my free hand behind her head and pulled her close again, keeping my mouth on hers, lips moving, until I needed to break away for air.

She was smiling. "Look at this," she said, and she leaned in with her mouth just open and ran her tongue across my upper lip.

The next day was the Fourth of July. For a week or more we'd been trying to figure out how to watch the fireworks stoned, and at last we'd come up with a plan. Rather than riding our bikes to the spot where most Stanford families watched, we would meet Cal on campus and have him drive us into the hills, where we'd get privacy—and a better view.

But we hadn't planned on having kissed the day before. I woke up that morning thinking I couldn't go anywhere with Sasha and Cal, and then that I had to see her right away, and then that I had to make sure she never saw Cal again, and then that I should go along with the original plan because otherwise it would all be so obvious. What would be obvious? I started to wonder, but then I was off chasing pictures: Sasha's face, that glimpse I'd gotten of her nipple a few weeks back, the sight of her butt as I pedaled home behind her at the end of the day yesterday.

I hung around the kitchen with my father for a while, agreeing with him that I'd be really careful tonight, saying yes, I'd checked my bike lights, they worked. He was going to a barbecue, and he said again that I was welcome, and I said again that I thought I'd just go ahead with my original plan.

The phone rang late in the morning, and I leapt to answer it, but it was just the barbecue people, asking my father if he had any extra lighter fluid he could bring.

I ate lunch, lay on my bed for a while, went back to the kitchen and found a Popsicle. At last, I called her.

And: Of course we were still going. Why would I ask? She was so nonchalant I wondered for a moment if it had even happened. But it had—I knew it had. I remembered the faint lime taste of her mouth, flavored by the candy she'd eaten earlier. I remembered how her tank top revealed the shapes of her breasts.

We met at seven, rode to the meeting place, and locked up. She didn't say much, and I wondered what was going through her mind, whether yesterday was all she could think of or the furthest thing from her mind. At last a car pulled up, an aging dark orange Mustang with all the windows open. There was a place on one fender where someone had tried to conceal damage with flat paint, and the car looked as if it had a long, thick scab. Cal smiled at us from the driver's seat, and Sasha got in next to him. I sat in back.

She said to him, "I brought food."

He said, "Right on."

"Fritos, your favorite."

"You know how to take care of me."

I studied him as he pulled away from the curb. His hair was loose tonight, a little greasy. I stared at his hands, surprised to find that his fingernails were well trimmed and clean. At a stop sign, he reached over and with his forefinger turned Sasha's chin so she was facing him. Immediately she scooted close, and he put his arm around her and drove with just his left hand.

I couldn't believe this was happening to me. But of course it was—what had I expected? That our kiss yesterday would change things? I felt in my pocket for my pipe and clenched it in my hand, so hard that the metal ridges on the bowl dug into my skin.

After a while Cal turned onto a narrow one-lane road. He took his arm off Sasha and held the wheel with both hands. We drove up a steep tree-thick hill, over potholes, past a run-down house with several old cars parked in a clearing. It was close to seven-thirty, still plenty light out but dimmer, the sky holding on to its last bit of blue. The road turned and got narrower, and a few branches broke as we scraped past some overgrown shrubs.

"Where are we going?" I said. Sasha had told me we'd go to our usual place, smoke, take in the fireworks, head home.

"Little Richard," Cal said, and he turned and gave me a quick grin. "Heh. I like that. Little Richard."

"Where *are* we going?" Sasha asked him.

"Stopping at a friend's house. That OK?"

"Who?"

"Jeremy."

She stiffened. After a moment she got onto her knees and turned to face me. She said, "We can stay in the car."

"What?"

She put a knee up on the seatback and without warning launched herself into the back. She landed with her head on my thigh, one of her knees down in the leg well. She righted herself quickly, scooted over, and sat near the window, behind Cal.

"What was that, babe?" he said.

"I want to sit back here."

She had a stricken look on her face, but though I looked and looked at her, trying to get her to look back at me, she stared straight ahead.

We approached another clearing, another house. This one had a porch, with an old rocking chair right next to the front door, and in the yard a clothesline hung with faded towels. We kept going. Cal flipped the radio on, moved the dial through static and voices. There was a guitar playing what sounded like Spanish music, and then he turned it off.

Now I saw a pair of mailboxes, one with its arm raised. Cal turned onto an unpaved road, and the car bounced as we made our way through a tunnel of wild, branchy shrubs. It was suddenly almost dusk, the sky the color of cheap binder paper, that thin grayish white. I heard a dog bark, glanced at Sasha, saw that her hands were clasped together so tightly that her biceps strained against her skin.

"Here we go," Cal said, and he made another turn, down a pitted drive and into a clearing, where three guys were sitting on

old aluminum lawn chairs in front of a rusted RV with no tires.
Two Dobermans were tied to a tree, and they stood at alert as our
car came into view. They had that tight Doberman look, short
black hair and brown muzzles and stand-up ears.

Cal shut the car off, and one of the guys came over and leaned
in the window. He was bare-chested and smelled of wine. He
shook hands with Cal and then grinned into the backseat, revealing a gap between his front teeth.

"Hello, Sash," he said to Sasha. "Hello, boy," he said to me.

"Jeremy, meet Richard," Cal said. He sat still for a moment
and then got out of the car, shook hands with Jeremy, and
stretched from side to side. His jeans were so old they were worn
through at the butt, and I saw pinkish skin between the last fuzzy
white threads of the denim.

He turned around and leaned in the window. "Climb on out,
kids," he said, but Sasha shook her head, and I didn't move either.

Cal and Jeremy walked over to the other men. One was about
Cal's age, with blond hair to his shoulders, but the other looked
old, maybe sixty: he was mostly bald, with gray wisps above his
ears and a scraggly gray-white beard.

"Who's Jeremy?" I said.

"Cal's friend."

"Where did you meet him?"

"That party," she said. "In the mountains."

"Is he a dealer?"

"No, Richard. Just be quiet, OK?"

I looked through the windshield at the four men. Cal and
Jeremy were talking, but too quietly for the sound to reach us. I
was about to say something about Harry Henry, something about
what he and Hillary might be doing tonight, when Sasha gasped.

I looked out her window. The dogs were moseying toward
the car, sniffing the ground, raising their heads as they came
closer. One of them had a spiked collar around its neck.

"You're in the car," I said. "Nothing can happen."

"Shut up."

I stared at her. She wore hip-hugger shorts and a plaid shirt with the tails tied in a knot several inches above her belly button. As I looked at her pale skin, and the outlines of her ribs, and the faint roundness of her abdomen, I felt a twinge, and then my dick was like a rock. This had never happened in her company before, not even yesterday, when we kissed. Something possessed me then, and I leaned across her and whistled out the open window, and the dogs came trotting forward.

"No," she whimpered, and she pushed me back and dropped into the space behind Cal's seat, pulling herself into a ball and putting her arms over her head.

I moved over to her window, keeping my knees on the seat so I wouldn't bump into her. I leaned out the window, and the dog with the spiked collar came closer. I wasn't sure, but it seemed he didn't have enough rope to reach the car.

"Boris!" the bald man called, suddenly looking over.

The spike-collar dog growled.

Now all the men turned. "Boris," Jeremy said in a harsh voice. "Candy."

Suddenly I saw a loop of rope lying at the base of the tree, a good ten feet of rope I hadn't figured on. I heard a sniffing sound, and I looked down and saw that Sasha's shoulders were shaking. Slowly, I pulled my upper body back into the car. Candy had turned and was walking back to the tree, but Boris was tense with readiness.

"Down and stay," Jeremy yelled, and Boris trotted back to the tree, where both dogs lay down.

I turned toward Sasha. "It's OK, they're gone."

She didn't move, and I leaned down, my head near hers. I put a hand on her back, and immediately she pushed my hand away.

"Don't. Stop it. I never should've invited you."

"Sasha."

She raised her head enough to look me in the eye, her face wet with tears. "I can't stand you. Get away from me."

I straightened up and looked at the men, but Cal and Jeremy had disappeared. The door to the RV was open, and I wondered what they were doing in there. Cal was buying drugs from Jeremy, but what kind? I didn't want to drive home in a car full of drugs. Highway patrolmen would be out tonight, looking for kids with illegal firecrackers; they might pull Cal over just because his car looked crappy.

Cal came out of the RV empty-handed. He saw me looking and gestured at me with his chin, then he shook hands with the bald guy and gave the blond one a thumbs-up. Getting back in the car, he said, "You guys missed out. They had blueberry pie in there." Then he laughed and started the engine, and because there wasn't room to turn the car around he backed all the way up to the road, and the men and the dogs slid away.

We bumped down through the tunnel of shrubs, turned onto the paved road, and drove past the house with the rocking chair and the clothesline. Sasha was sitting up again, her face streaked and dirty. "What's the matter, little one?" Cal said, but she didn't respond.

We came to the main road. "No, go right," she said, and Cal shrugged and turned toward home.

He said, "Don't you want to watch the fireworks?"

"No." She slumped down, putting her shins against the back of his seat. I saw him adjust the mirror to look at her, and it was just like Dan on the morning of the Walk for Mankind, checking in on Sasha, trying to understand Sasha. Spoiled brat, I thought. I looked out my window. It had been a mistake, kissing her. I'd really been kissing Hillary, anyway.

Back on campus, I got out of the car. Sasha got out, too, then circled it and got in again next to Cal. I unlocked my bike, sat on the seat, and toed myself over to her window. It wasn't fully dark yet.

She stared at me. "What are you waiting for?" she said in a nasty voice. "Go home."

I avoided her for several days. I spent a weekend in Oakland, and when I got back I called Malcolm and Bob, for the first time all summer. Bob was away, but I got Malcolm to meet me at Lake Lagunita, where I initiated him into the mysteries of smoking weed, thanks to a small supply of pot Sasha had given me. There were Stanford students hanging around the lake, too, and a couple of girls came and sat with us, told us we were cute, and mooched several hits each from my pipe.

We did it all over again the next day, and then I was out. Money to buy more wasn't a problem—my father handed me cash whenever I asked for it, and sometimes when I didn't—but I had no source.

And so I biked to Cal's, aware Sasha might be there but feeling I had no choice, nowhere else to go, and I needed some pot. If I saw her, I saw her. It had to happen sometime.

It was day two of a heat wave, 101 degrees according to the bank I passed, and I pedaled along the streets with a mouth so dry I might as well have been stoned out of my mind. To fortify myself, I bought a Coke at the Old Barrel and drank it inside the cool, dark building. Back outside, I shielded my eyes from the sun, felt the heat lay across my face again, felt it drape over my arms and legs. I left my bicycle where I'd locked it and walked the rest of the way.

The street was quiet, cars gone from the driveways of the little houses, most of the apartment carports empty, too. I saw Cal's car down at the third building, its scabby fender half in shade. I headed that way, pausing before taking the stairs up to the second story. There was a row of doors on one side of a concrete walk-way, a spindly iron railing on the other. Most of the doors were closed, but I made my way past them to the last one, which was open, with just a screen door blocking access. I pressed my face to the screen so I could see in: matching sofa and chair with gold stitching on the cushions, a china lamp on a little table. Not Cal's, in other words. I turned and headed back. The first door I came to had a "Welcome" sign on it, and at the next, several pairs of little kids' sandals lay near a mat. This left the door at the end of the row, a solid white door with a tarnished brass knob. I knocked, hoping Sasha wouldn't answer.

I heard steps, and then there was Cal, in cut-offs and nothing else, a bleary look on his face. He saw me and said, "Little Richard."

I stood there, unsure how to begin.

"If you're looking for Sasha," he said, "I don't know where she is."

"I'm not. I want to buy from you."

He seemed amused, but he said, "How much money do you have?"

"Forty."

He looked over his shoulder, looked at me again. "Well, come on," he said, and he stepped back to make room for me to enter.

I'd had such pictures of this place—bare mattress, piles of clothing, a general and all-encompassing mess—that for a moment I couldn't quite take in what I saw: a tidy striped couch, a pair of bamboo chairs at a small round dining table almost exactly like the one at my mother's. The kitchen was in the same room, on the other side of a Formica counter, and there were some Chinese food containers and a couple of plates near the sink, but otherwise it was spic-and-span.

"Have a seat," he said, gesturing at the couch as he went into the kitchen and opened a cabinet. He brought out a large stew pot, set it on the counter, and pulled out a plastic Baggie containing about a half an inch of pot.

He brought the bag over and tossed it on the coffee table. Turning one of the bamboo chairs around, he reached into his pocket for his rolling papers.

"I don't care," I said.

"About . . ."

"If it's good or not. I'll just buy it."

He raised his eyebrows, crossed his arms over his chest, and looked at me hard. "Little Richard," he said. "Oh, my."

"Is Jeremy the grower?" I said, nodding at the bag.

Cal chuckled. "Guess you thought that was a drug deal going down the other night, huh?"

"No."

"A little innocent blueberry pie, and Cal's a criminal."

You're a criminal anyway, I wanted to say. I thought of Jeremy's bare chest and wine breath, of his harsh voice when he yelled at the dogs. And of the dogs themselves, of Boris's growl. I felt a wave of dread—intense fear of what might have happened that night, even though the night was long over.

Cal gestured at the pot. "It's on the house. Take it."

I reached for the bag, then stopped myself. Was he playing a trick on me?

"Go on, take it. And tell your friend to call me."

I grabbed the bag and dashed out of there. Stuffing it in my pocket, I ran down the stairs and out into the bright, stinging sunlight. I ran up the street, kept running until I'd reached the Old Barrel and my bike. My fingers shook as I dialed my combination. I was looking at the lock, but in my mind I saw myself pounding the seat with my fist, over and over again.

Once I was on my bike I headed in the direction I'd taken

after my first trip to that neighborhood, toward and then across the railroad tracks, and then along the busy road parallel to them. In about five minutes I'd reached the underpass to the Stanford side of the tracks, but I kept going. I was in the older part of Palo Alto now, and the mature trees offered shade, but I was too hot for it to make much difference. Sweat stung my eyes, made my shirt stick to my back. Abruptly, I turned onto a residential street and stopped. I patted my pocket, making sure the bag was still there. I could be home in ten minutes, in time for Gladys to make me a milkshake before she left for the day, but when I set off again I headed deeper into Palo Alto, aiming, I was starting to realize, for the street where the Mile Ten check-in station had been. Where the tall guy lived.

I found the street, then wasn't sure which of two little white houses was his, one with a fence around the yard or one without. The house with the fence had a station wagon in the driveway, while the other had a two-door sedan, a Chevelle the blue-green color of the ocean. I got off my bike in front of that one. The yard was familiar, the steps up to the porch, the faded black of the front door. Standing there, I thought for some reason of the charred log I'd noticed in the fireplace, and I wondered if it was still there. My father's area of interest was between-the-wars America, Prohibition, the stock market crash, the Depression; he'd told me that in the early thirties fuel was so scarce people would burn a log halfway and then smother the flames so they could get a fire going again the next night without having to use more wood. I imagined that the tall guy would do that, not to be frugal but because he was alone.

The Chevelle's windows were open, as if he'd used the car recently and planned to go out again soon. I left my bike on the sidewalk, went up to the porch, and knocked.

Footsteps, and then the door was opened, but not by the tall guy: it was a woman with mousy brown hair in a ragged cut and, oddly, braces on her teeth, which she revealed in a broad smile that disappeared as she took in the sight of me.

"Sorry, I was expecting someone else. Can I help you?"

I looked past her: it was the guy's house, with the guy's saggy couch.

She cocked her head, waiting.

I said, "Is anyone else home?"

"You mean Karl? Are you looking for Karl? Karl," she called over her shoulder, "there's a boy here for you."

She was a little ugly: "plain," they would say in a book. She was flat-chested, and her eyebrows were so pale it was almost as if she didn't have any. I hoped she wasn't his girlfriend. I preferred the idea of him alone to the idea of him with her.

The tall guy appeared in the doorway, and I could tell he had no idea who I was. He was just the same, though: the lean, lanky frame; the light blue eyes.

"Yes?" he said.

Suddenly worried my bike might be gone, I swiveled around, but there it was, leaning against the tree where I'd left it. I faced them again, the woman with her hand on the doorframe, Karl towering over her.

"Can I help you?" he said. The way he spoke was soft, easy— very different from how he'd talked on the day of the Walk. "Are you selling something?"

"Gorp," I said, and then I began to laugh. I backed down the steps, then turned and made for my bike.

"Hang on," he said, coming after me. "You're that kid, aren't you?"

I kept going.

"You're that kid who wanted to sterilize a needle. You were with that crazy girl."

Now I turned around.

"You gave me some gorp."

"You ate the raisins."

"I probably did." He lowered his chin, gave me a closer look. "What are you doing here?"

"I just—" I tried to think. "I just wanted to thank you," I said, and I reached into my pocket and pulled out the bag of pot. "For helping us. Sorry it took me a while."

His eyes widened. "What is that, marijuana? You can't do that, put that away. Here, come inside." Glancing around, he reached for my shoulder, and I let him pull me toward the house. The woman was still in the doorway, and he beckoned her inside and then closed the door behind us.

"What's going on?" he said. "What is this?"

I looked around. It was dark after the bright afternoon, but I could tell it was different from the other time—definitely tidier, but also cleaner. The air seemed fresh, and the fireplace was empty.

"What's your name?" he said.

"Richard." I glanced at the woman; she was leaning against a wall, watching me. I knew I should talk. "My friend was Sasha. That day. We were doing the Walk for Mankind, the twenty-mile walk. There was a check-in station right across the street."

"That's right," he said.

The woman cleared her throat, and he glanced over at her and then looked at me again. He said, "Richard, you shouldn't give marijuana to a stranger. Not as a thank-you and not for any other reason. You shouldn't do that."

I stayed still, the Baggie slippery in my hand.

"I mean, what if I was a cop," he went on. "Did you think of that? I could be an off-duty police officer." He hesitated. "Are you in trouble? Do you need help?"

"No." I started for the door, shoving the pot into my pocket as I went.

"Wait."

This was the woman. I turned, and she'd moved away from the wall and crossed her arms over her chest. Now I was scared. I got the feeling he didn't care, but she wanted to do something bad—call the police or worse. They were looking back and forth at each other, trying to talk with their eyes. Dan and Joanie sometimes did this, except Dan usually ended up blurting out whatever he was thinking.

"It's hot out there, Richard," she said at last. "Don't you want to have a drink of water before you go? We don't want to hurt you or get you in trouble. Really. Come have some ice water."

My eyes got hot, and I held them wide to keep myself from getting teary.

"Yeah," Karl said. "Good idea. Come on."

He headed for the kitchen and I followed after him. He filled a glass with ice water and gestured for me to sit at the table—in the same chair where Sasha had popped her blister. He sat opposite me and held his hand across the table. "I'm Karl—did I already say that? It's nice to meet you, Richard." We shook, and he said, "Oh, and that's Mary Ann."

The woman had come after us but stood in the doorway. She said, "Mary Ann who's going to wait outside, OK?"

He shrugged.

"I mean, should I stay?"

They exchanged another look, and then she headed for the front door.

I picked up the glass and drank.

"Look, Richard," he began.

"Thanks for the water," I said, and I set the glass down and pushed my chair back.

"Hang on, hang on." He got up and brought a jar of peanuts to the table. "Have some of these before you go, the salt'll do you good."

I took the jar and shook a few nuts into my palm.

"So how old are you?" he said.

"Almost fourteen."

"Once you *are* fourteen you'll be half my age. So, guess what, I'm twenty-eight."

"OK." I wanted to leave, but I didn't want to have to pass Mary Ann.

He said, "I'm twenty-eight, I grew up in Sunnyvale, I'm a manager at the PayLess in Mountain View."

I was surprised by the third statement; I'd been sure he was an academic. A scientist—that was what I was expecting. I'd been all ready to tell him I was a faculty brat.

"You want me to keep going?" he said. "You know what managers do, right? I'm the guy they call when there's a problem. 'Karl, Karl to register three, please.' That's me."

"Do you wear a red vest?"

"White shirt and tie," he said with a smile. "My red vest days are behind me."

Right after my mother left, my father thought we should stock up on household stuff, and we went to the PayLess in Menlo Park and filled two shopping carts with toilet paper and Ajax and family-size boxes of breakfast cereal. Since then we hadn't ventured farther than JJ&F.

His eyes were still on me, and I looked away. I imagined him as a teenager—a tall, skinny high school kid in a red vest. I wondered if he'd even gone to college.

There was a stack of photos on the table. The top one was a green blur, with some dark spots on one edge. Karl saw me looking and slid the photos to the middle of the table. He held up the top one so I could see it. "Guess what this is."

I shrugged. "Something green."

"Yeah, but what? Guess."

"I don't know."

"You're no fun. It's a frog. Part of a frog. Didn't come out too good, did it?" He tossed the picture aside and swiveled the stack so I could see the next one right side up. It was the same idea—blurry green—but I got it this time: the dark spots were bumps on the frog's skin, and there was a grayish white thing that might've been part of its eye.

He tossed that one aside, too. "Here we go," he said, and he held up a picture of the frog as a small green blob on the muddy edge of some water. "He wasn't a close-up kind of frog," he said. He turned the photos around again and slid one after another from the top of the pile. "Now we're talking," he said and tossed a photo at me.

It was a picture of snow-capped mountains, like something you'd see on a postcard. He tossed another, and a third, and they were all like that—mountains with forest, mountains with the sky pink behind them.

"Here's us," he said.

He and Mary Ann were standing together on a narrow trail, each wearing hiking boots and a huge backpack. She had on sunglasses, so her eyes didn't have that naked look, and I had to admit she had pretty good legs. They were both smiling like crazy.

"And here's me," Karl said, and he passed me a picture of him sitting against a boulder, sticking out his tongue and crossing his eyes.

"Where is this?" I said.

"Cascades. It takes forever to get there, but it's worth it, it's beautiful. Does your family backpack?"

I shook my head.

"Well, maybe when you're grown then. We spent ten days—it was pretty great."

I put the picture down and slid the whole mess back to him. Like I was going to start backpacking when I was grown. I was pretty sure that when I was grown I'd be like my father, doing something that involved desks and table lamps. I hadn't even gone to Muir Woods when I had the chance.

"So what's going on, Richard?" Karl said.

"You mean with Sasha?"

"I mean with you. Is something going on with Sasha?"

I thought of how he was with her, the day of the Walk. Kind of mean. "She's my best friend," I said.

"But something happened. She's in trouble. Or she got you in trouble?"

Suddenly I was furious at him. He'd taken one look at her and decided she was—what? A scammer. Just because she wanted to make a phone call. "No!" I said. "You're wrong about her," and I pushed away from the table and ran for the front door.

"Richard!"

I bolted out of the house, brushed past Mary Ann, hopped on my bike, and took off. I pedaled as hard as I could, my legs pumping, my breath coming so fast that soon I'd convinced myself it wasn't misery making my eyes so wet but just the hot, dry air. Why hadn't I seen her since the Fourth of July? I didn't know anymore if I was avoiding her or she was avoiding me. What was I supposed to do? When I got home I left my bike in the garage and went around the corner, but when I imagined standing at their front door I convinced myself I should wait until tomorrow. I'd go over first thing, before she had time to go to Cal's. "Want to go to the Union?" I'd say. Or, "Hey, I've got some weed, let's get high." No, that was stupid. "Want to ride bikes?" No, I'd just stand there and say, really deadpan, "Do you want to play?"

Our doorbell rang early the next morning. I was still in bed, and I let my father get it, then scrambled into shorts and a T-shirt when I heard Sasha's voice. *She'd* come to *my* house? At first I was mad, but this was actually much better.

She knocked on my door as she opened it, saying, "Wake up, wake up," and walking right in.

I stood in front of my bed, my face still chafed from the too-tight neck of my T-shirt. Her hair was in braids, a style I'd never seen on her. They made her look younger.

"Oh, good, you're up," she said. "We're going to the beach, you can come."

I wondered if I'd heard her right. "What?"

"We are going to the beach," she repeated, enunciating each word. "And you can come."

I was dumbfounded. Did she have no memory of the last time we saw each other? Or the time before that?

"Don't you want to?" she said. "I'm not mad anymore."

"About what?"

"The dogs."

The dogs! *She* was the one who'd been obnoxious. I said, "Maybe I'm mad."

"About what?"

"I said *maybe* I am. If I'm not then there wouldn't be an about."

"What is it?" she exclaimed. "What? I want you to come to the beach." She seemed genuinely puzzled—as if she couldn't fathom a reason why I wouldn't want to go. I thought of the last look she'd given me, that sneer through the open window of Cal's car. Had she truly forgotten?

She said, "Come on, it's a special trip. We'll bury Daddy in the sand like we did that other time."

She was referring to a trip the five of us had taken ten months earlier, in September: my first trip to the beach with the Horo-witzes. We'd buried Dan so deeply that from the back all you could see of him was his coppery hair, growing like some fantastic sea plant near the beach grass.

"It's going to be really hot again today."

It probably was. And going to the beach with them—I felt myself giving in. At the beach we raced up and down the tide line, built sand dungeons, competed to see who could get their s'mores the perfect caramel color fastest, without having them go up in flames. One overcast afternoon at Half Moon Bay I won, and Dan nearly had a fit. Looking at my golden marshmallow, he sputtered, "Well, but you . . ." "I mean, the angle . . ." Then he got hold of himself and said, "Richard Appleby is a young man of exceptional talents," and Joanie said, "Dan Horowitz is a middle-aged man of exceptional restraint," and he laughed this huge, happy laugh.

Sasha was waiting. I was about to say yes, I'd go with them, when I thought of Karl—not Karl yesterday, but Karl on the day of the Walk, standing outside his house waiting with me for Sasha to come out. Asking me if I always did what she wanted.

"No," I said, "I have stuff to do."

"What stuff?"

"Just stuff."

She turned, and in a moment I heard her Dr. Scholl's clacking down the hallway. I waited for the sound of the front door and then made my way to the kitchen.

My father was at the table eating cereal and reading the newspaper. He looked up as I came in. "She's quite the early bird today."

I got out the Raisin Bran and poured myself a heaping bowlful, then took the milk from the refrigerator and flooded the flakes. I ate standing, spooning up the cereal and barely chewing, and then tipping the large quantity of excess milk into my mouth.

"It's still hot," my father said. "But I don't think it'll be quite as bad as yesterday. I heard it was ninety-eight in the city. Unheard of."

Don't say it, I thought.

"You know what Mark Twain said, don't you?" he went on. "He said, 'The coldest winter I ever spent was a summer in San Francisco.' Not this week."

"Yeah, well," I said. "I'll bet it was hotter here."

"Oh, no doubt," my father said. "No doubt." He took a sip of his coffee. "Oh, Gladys will be off next week. Did I already tell you? We'll have to fend for ourselves. I hope you're in the mood to have pancakes for dinner."

"I'll try to be by then," I said, and I left him sitting there and went back to my room.

And realized I'd made a terrible mistake. It was definitely going to be hot today—a beach day if ever there were one. I raced out of the house and up the street, but their car was gone. Now what was I going to do? The day would be endless. I trudged home, got on my bike, and rode down the hill to SCRA. It was only about nine o'clock, but it was crowded like midday, mothers clustered in the shade or in the baby end with their toddlers, the rest of the pool crammed with older kids. I had to pee, and I went into the men's locker room, locked myself in a stall, and let the smell of mildew take me back eight or nine years, to the first few times my mother sent me in here by myself because I was old enough not to need to go into the women's with her. The men's side was much smellier, I'd found, and it was too crowded—less with people than with the suits some men left from one visit to the next, hanging from hooks, their voluminous legs drying in folds.

It was empty this morning; all the men were at work. Even in the summer they worked all the time, doing research or writing. My father was trying to finish his book by the end of August so he'd have the next few weeks to prepare for fall quarter. I didn't know what Dan was doing. Taking the day off today.

I went outside. A couple of my friends from elementary school were playing Ping-Pong, and I decided against a quick dip in my shorts and headed for my bike. That night in the spring, when Sasha and I walked down here and she first met Cal: why had I left?

Gladys would have arrived at the house by now, and so I headed for campus, thinking I'd buy something at the Union, a candy bar or maybe a box of Jujubes. Halfway there, the notion of going to Harry Henry's house popped into my mind, and there was a split second when I thought it was something I could actually do. I thought of the way Sasha had laughed when I said I wanted to bed Hillary, and then of the way she'd twisted onto my lap as if it were a place she knew well. Those kisses, and then the final one, around the corner from her house late that afternoon, the lime candy taste lingering, her lips soft and sweet and wet.

She came over again that evening, ringing the doorbell during a game of Scrabble my father and I were playing. Her hair was pinned up in a bun on the back of her head, and her shoulders were sunburned. She followed me back to the table and pulled up a chair, and for a while she whispered word ideas to me while on the other side of the board my father glanced at us from under his eyebrows as he moved his tiles around.

"I guess it's not fair," she said. "Two against one."

My father raised his head. "Oh, that's OK. Richard's happier when you're here."

My face grew warm, and I kept my head lowered, my gaze directed at my tray. "Ha!" I heard my father say, and he laid all seven of his tiles on the board, reaching a triple word score with the last letter.

"Ouch," Sasha said.

I turned and looked at her. "How was the beach?"

"Crowded. I went in up to my ass." She glanced at my father. "Sorry."

"What about everyone else?"

"Peter only went to his knees. Daddy went to his shoulders and then dunked, the freak. Mom went about mid-thigh."

"Was it cold?"

"Freezing. Which is one of the reasons I'm glad we decided to go back to Connecticut. You can swim when you go to the beach there."

I didn't move, but I felt my pulse pounding in the back of my throat. I couldn't look at her. I couldn't look at my father. I looked at the Scrabble board, letters marching meaninglessly here and there.

"When do you go?" my father said.

"Next Tuesday morning. Well, Mom and I go Tuesday morning—we're flying. Daddy and Peter are driving the car back." She turned to me, and I forced myself to meet her gaze. "We were going to tell you," she said. "At the beach today."

I shook my head, not sure I could speak.

"Are you going back to the same house?" my father said.

"We aren't even going to New Haven—we're going to Hartford. Daddy's going to teach English at a boarding school near there. You actually have more of a chance to really *teach* with high school students—they don't think they already know everything." She looked away, her face stained with embarrassment.

My father was watching me. He cleared his throat and pushed his chair back. "I think I'll leave you two," he said. "Is that all right? We can finish another time? I have a little work I wanted to do tonight, anyway."

When he was gone, I took the board and dumped the tiles on the table. Then I got up and went into the kitchen. I found an unopened box of cookies and tore the flap, taking some satisfaction in the fact that because of the tear it wouldn't close neatly.

Sasha came in after me. "Give me some."

I fished out a handful for her, then grabbed as many as I could for myself. "Let's go outside."

We went out front, down to the foot of my driveway. The heat today had been nothing like yesterday's, and it was almost cool now. Sasha sat first, and when I sat I left several feet between us.

"I'm going to high school," she said.

We'd finished eighth grade, but our school was a junior high that went through ninth; I had another year before high school.

"Freaky."

"There are two thousand kids there."

"God, two thousand?"

"Tell me I'll make friends."

I turned and looked at her. There were tears in her eyes, and her lips were red with the effort of not crying. "You will," I said. "Of course you will."

She put her hands in front of her eyes. Her shoulders shook a little, but after a moment she sighed and wiped her palms across her cheeks. She said, "You know last week? The Fourth?"

I didn't respond.

"We finally fucked. After you left. We went to his apartment, I didn't get home till almost midnight. I was so lucky—my parents were outside. When they came in I just pretended I'd been in my room."

I had heard the words—*we finally fucked*—but I had kept them at a distance. Now they came close. I didn't want to think about Cal's dick pushing into her, but I couldn't stop myself: the picture was insistent, unstoppable, he went in and in and in. I couldn't stand it, and I blinked fast, but it stayed with me.

"I haven't seen him since then," she said. "I kind of—I kind of decided I didn't want to. So it's good we're moving."

Across the street, Yvonne Mazar held a garden hose over her flowers. She was a classicist, married to the dean of the medical school. She waved, and I waved back. Elegant—that was what my mother always said about her. She wore her hair in a sleek bun that reminded me of an apple turnover.

Sasha leaned down and scratched her ankle. "Why *did* you whistle at the dogs? I was thinking about doing it with you until then."

I didn't know where to look: at her, away from her, at Yvonne across the street. I stared at my knees. I was embarrassed and astonished, both at once.

"I really wanted to leave it here," she said. "My virginity, you know."

My heart was beating fast, which made it hard for me to follow what she was saying, to figure out what wasn't making sense. "Hang on," I said. "You knew you were moving last week? On the Fourth?"

She gave me a concerned, even a surprised look. "I knew a month ago. Six weeks. Before the end of school."

"But the house on Dartmouth Street . . ."

"Richard."

I stood up and walked a few paces. Across the street, Marvin Mazar had come outside and was standing on the doorstep, watching his wife. He was in his pajamas, it seemed. Striped shirt, striped shorts. Though maybe they weren't his pajamas. Maybe they were just what he wore after work in the summer.

Suddenly I was incredibly tired. I felt the way I had when I'd tried to stay up till midnight on New Year's Eve, back when I was little. This intense, almost dizzying tiredness, a tiredness that was like floating on a raft in a swimming pool. Snapping back to alertness was like having someone bump your raft—your arms and legs would flail for a moment.

"Richard?" Sasha said.

"I'm going to go in now. I have to go to bed."

"It's eight o'clock. Ten of eight."

"I have to anyway," I said, and I left her sitting there.

. . .

For the first time ever, a weekend arrived when I wished I were going to Oakland. On Saturday, I got Malcolm to ride up into the hills with me, and I spent the day stoned out of my mind, the two of us smoking every last particle from the bag of weed Cal had given me. Sunday morning I convinced my father to take me to Santa Cruz instead of the city, and we rode the roller coaster together, my father heaving a great sigh when our car finally came to a stop. After that, he watched while I went on the other rides, waving at me when I flew or twisted into view. He disappeared for a few minutes while I was on the pirate ship, and when I saw him again he was holding something in front of his chest, pale and indistinct like a bundle of fur. I wondered if he'd gone to a duck-shooting booth and won a stuffed animal, but it turned out to be cotton candy, a big cloud of it that he ate very slowly, small bit by small bit dissolving in his mouth while I went on several more rides.

At last we headed home. Pine trees soared on either side of the road, and the sky was visible only in jigsaw fragments, deep blue behind the dark green. I looked over at my father, thought of the moment during the drive to the Trinity Alps when he told me Dan might be leaving. I was a fool. This last month—the smoking, the laughing, the kissing, *the house on Dartmouth Street*—my heart raced at the extent, at the sheer length of her lie.

I spent Monday alone in the house, relieved Gladys was on vacation. I cleaned my room, throwing away schoolwork from the last two years and then, for good measure, all the work I'd saved from elementary school, too.

But Tuesday morning I couldn't stay away. I walked up their driveway and took note of the car, its trunk open, several suitcases lying inside.

"Richard Appleby!" Dan said when he answered the door. "I knew we'd see you again."

I went in and looked around, at the empty shelves and moving boxes, at the two carry-on bags sitting in the entryway. "Hate to be leaving, Richard," he said to me, his lips curved in a wry half-smile. "You know how it is, though. The academic life."

The sliding glass door was open, and I went and pressed my nose to the screen, looked out at the patio.

He came up behind me and stood there without speaking. At last, his voice low, he said, "Do you think we should have made her tell you sooner?"

I stood still.

"I can't decide," he went on. "I can see it both ways." He put his hand on my shoulder. "But she's our daughter. That's what it came down to."

"It's OK," I said.

"There, I knew you were sensible." He turned back to the room. "Didn't I always say Richard Appleby was sensible?"

I turned, and there were Sasha and Joanie, standing near the front door with their bags in their hands.

I followed them out the front door. In a moment Dan was behind the wheel, and Peter and Joanie were side by side in the backseat. The front waited for Sasha, but she lingered.

"Here," she said to me, "hang on a sec," and she got a notepad and pen from her purse. She bent over, raised her knee a little, and used her leg as a surface for writing. Finished, she tore off the paper and handed it to me. "It's dumb, but I didn't know you were coming over."

Dan gave the horn a little toot. "Sash," he called through the open door. "Parting may be sweet sorrow, but missing your flight is just plain old sorrow—and a few hundred bucks to boot."

"O-K," she said over her shoulder. She offered me her hand. "We started with a handshake—maybe we should finish that way, too."

Her note was in my right hand. I switched it to my left, but then Peter rolled down his window and yelled goodbye, and I leaned down so I could see across him to Joanie and wave at her, too, and somehow in the middle of all of this Sasha got into the car.

I looked at the note. "See you at Harry Henry's house," she'd written. "Out back near the cabana."

She closed the door and rolled down the window. "Bye," she called, and Dan tapped the horn twice and pulled away.

That's not the end of the story—not quite yet—but I'll say now that I never saw her again, and I've often wondered what happened to her. Where would she have landed, in academia or as far from it as possible? Close to Dan and Joanie, or as far from her parents as I ended up from mine?

I am married now, and the father of three, and while I do have a career that involves desks and table lamps, I also take my family backpacking every summer, and at night, in the mountains, when our campfire has burned low, we lie flat on our backs and stare at the vast, starry sky, until one of the kids complains about a rock under his shoulder or another says she needs to pee, and then we get up and settle in our tents for the night.

How do people do it, pry themselves from their pasts? "Pry" makes it sound dramatic, but it isn't. I wish I could say my life in the natural world began with a transformative experience: like the fishing weekend with my father, only successful. An epiphanic trip to the mountains, a hike along a rushing river that taught me how I wanted to live. But that's not how it happened. The course of true progress is boring. You don't just suddenly become an outdoorsman, just as you don't just suddenly become assertive and independent, ridding yourself forever of your shabby victim rags. It's incremental. Think of that frog, the one in Karl's picture. There wasn't a single moment when he passed into maturity, a single instant when an observer could cry, "Look, he's a frog now!" No, it happened slowly, beginning with four tiny bumps, four promises of the legs that would widen the world for him beyond anything he could conceive of in his watery tadpole dreams.

Sasha left on Tuesday; by Friday the hot weather was back. It was time for another weekend with my mother, and Friday evening, when I arrived, she presented me with three flavors of ice cream to choose from, her way of acknowledging that we were on our new schedule now, with my visits occurring every other weekend, as she'd wanted. Her apartment was an oven, and she said we'd find a swimming pool tomorrow for sure, or else spend the day in a nice, cool movie theater.

But in the morning she said there was somewhere she wanted to go first, and I wasn't surprised when she drove us to the ghetto again. I thought of asking why, but I didn't want to hear her earnest lecture. I decided to be stoic and keep my mouth shut.

This time she parked, and we got out of the car. "Let's just walk," she said. "I want you to get comfortable here," and we started up the sidewalk, the day warm already though it wasn't yet ten o'clock. A couple of men stood in front of a drugstore, and they stopped talking and openly sized up my mother as we went by.

At the corner up ahead of us, a skinny young woman stood with three children, two of them clutching her leg and wailing. The third was older, a girl two or three years younger than I. As we approached, the woman slapped one of the crying children and pushed the other away, snapping, "Pick him up," at the girl, "come on, do," and giving the little boy another push for good measure. The girl bent over and picked up the boy, held him under his bottom as he flailed and screamed, and by now we'd gotten close enough that I had to look away to avoid eye contact with her.

My mother went right up to the woman. "Do you need any help? Can I do anything for you?"

The woman reared back and stared at my mother, an incredulous look on her face. "No, I don't need no help. Who you think you are? Come on," she said to the girl, and she grabbed the forearm of the child still at her feet and strode away, the other two following behind her.

My mother looked at me and then looked away. "It's not easy to accept help," she said. And then, a little defiant: "I'm not sorry I offered."

"I didn't think you were." I stole a glance in the direction they'd gone; the older girl was looking over her shoulder at us. This time I let myself meet her gaze: a moment's seeing each other and then she faced forward again.

People walked past us, the two men from before, an old woman pushing an even older woman in a wheelchair. There was a yellow dog on the other side of the street, trotting back and forth and looking at us but not barking. Cars went by, some slowing as they came abreast of us, the people inside giving us long curious looks.

My mother began walking again. "I thought we could stop and say hi to a friend of mine."

"Who?"

"A woman from work. Patrice."

"Oh, right," I said, remembering the flowers from my mother's birthday. "The cleaning lady."

"Richard!"

"What?"

"Nothing. Never mind." She opened her purse and pulled out a small spiral-bound notebook. "I think it's this way," she said, flipping through the pages. "Around that corner."

We went around a corner onto a street lined with run-down clapboard houses, each with a steep flight of steps leading to a front door. Checking her notebook, my mother slowed down, studied the front of each house before continuing on. "We're looking for forty-seven," she said. "But I haven't seen any numbers, have you?"

I'd seen a small 23 on one house, but I didn't say so. On we went, my mother scanning, me keeping quiet. Across the street, three teenage boys lounged on a flight of steps, two side by side and the third a few steps up, his face tipped to the sky. Behind him was the ghost of a number, 52. I looked at my mother and saw that she'd lost some of her resolve; she'd put the notebook away and pulled her purse strap higher on her shoulder.

"I just don't know," she said.

"You could call her. If we could find a phone."

My mother frowned. I saw she didn't want to call; I saw she wanted to leave.

"Couldn't you?"

"I don't have her phone number."

"You could find a phonebook."

"You've got a lot of your father in you," she said. "Did you know that?"

I did; she'd said so many times. I could remember being a very small boy and feeling hugely proud of it. I didn't know when it had changed from being a good thing to being a bad thing—for her but also for me.

I looked over at the boys. They couldn't have been less interested in us, this white lady and her kid. They were waiting for something, looked as if they could wait all day.

"I'm sorry I said that," my mother said. "Your father is a good man."

I looked away from her. "I thought we were going swimming."

"We are. And listen—I was thinking we could go out for dinner tonight."

"OK."

She looked into my eyes, and I knew I should be more enthu-siastic. "That sounds good."

"We'll make it an early birthday dinner," she said, and she reached over and let her fingers brush my neck. "It'll be nice. A nice dinner for a nice boy."

We started toward the main street again. A siren sounded somewhere nearby, just the one initial rising sound and then nothing. A small rubber ball lay on the sidewalk in front of me, and I kicked it into the street.

"Good morning," said a stout older lady as she approached, and my mother said good morning back. The lady wore a shiny lavender dress and carried a white purse over her forearm, and she beamed at me as she got closer.

"Richard," my mother whispered, "say hello," but it was too late, the lady had passed us.

I put my hands in my pockets, and my right fingertips touched paper. What's that? I started to wonder, but then I knew. It was Sasha's note. I'd solved the problem of what to do with it by doing nothing. If Gladys had been around this week, it might have ended up a hardened wad in the lint trap of the dryer. Instead, I'd accidentally brought it to Oakland, in the pocket of an unwashed pair of shorts.

On we walked. Back at the main street, I spotted my mother's car, up ahead of us in the next block. We'd been walking only twenty or thirty minutes, but I knew it would be a furnace.

We approached a little grocery. I saw an old man sitting in the doorway, half in the store and half out, the lower part of his face covered by a patchy white beard. A wretched smell reached me as we came abreast of him: urine and whiskey and something rotten-smelling that made me gag. My mother stopped. The man was asleep, or close; his eyes were yellow slits, his body slumped sideways. She took her wallet from her purse and pulled out a twenty-dollar bill. She glanced at me and then stepped closer to him. "Here you go," she said, and she reached her hand toward him, but he didn't move. She bent down as if she were going to set it on his lap, but at the last minute she let go of it, and it fluttered sideways, brushed his leg, and then, caught by a gust of air, turned over once and landed a few feet into the store.

She looked at me and then looked into the store, where a middle-aged man stood behind the counter and watched us. There were shelves of canned food, open crates of vegetables, containers of milk in a refrigerator with a glass door. My mother was still, the counterman was still, the drunk at our feet was still. I stepped over his legs and picked up the money. When I turned around again, my mother was gone. I shrugged at the counterman, stepped back over the drunk's legs, and followed after her. I caught up with her at the corner, where she was waiting for the light to change, and I held the bill out to her.

"Keep it," she said.

The light changed, and she stepped off the curb and started across the street. I looked at the bill, started to put it in my pocket, changed my mind and followed after her. On the other side of the street, I held it out again.

"I said keep it."

I put it in my pocket as we arrived at the car. It was incredibly hot inside, and I rolled down my window and leaned my head out. My mother turned the key, and the engine revved but then fell silent. She sighed and turned the key again, and now it caught, and she put the car in gear and pulled away from the curb.

The traffic light was red. The grocery was the fourth or fifth business in the next block, and I could just see the drunk's shoe poking out. A pair of teenage girls came out of the store, both with their hair in afros. I wondered what it would feel like, hair like that, if it would be soft or scratchy.

The light changed. "Stop," I said to my mother as we crossed the intersection and gathered speed, and she pulled over and jerked to a stop at the curb.

"What?"

"Wait a sec," I said, and I got out of the car and approached the grocery. Inside, the counterman was ringing up a purchase, but I saw him see me. I stopped at the drunk. He had slumped a little more, and now his mouth was open, his lower lip revealing some missing teeth. A faint snore whistled out of him. His pants were black, and I could see the outlines of his thin legs under the cloth. He wore a jacket despite the heat, and under that a shirt of the kind my father usually wore: collar, buttons, breast pocket. I reached into my pocket, felt the heavier paper of the twenty, the slightly crinkled surface of Sasha's note. I glanced over my shoulder: my mother was watching from the car, a look of pride, maybe even wonder, on her face. I turned back. The counterman had stopped what he was doing and was watching openly now, his hand resting on a brown and orange can of Yuban. I took the scrap of paper from my pocket, leaving the twenty behind, and, taking shallow breaths through my mouth, I leaned down and slipped it into the man's breast pocket.

It would be years before it occurred to me that with that one gesture I managed to kill two birds with one stone. And I do mean kill. And I do mean birds, though perhaps I should say it with an English accent, *buds*. It isn't easy, admitting your murders.

Molten

. .

At four-thirty Kathryn chose a last CD and put it into Ben's stereo. Low, gritty guitar chords burst from the speakers, the speed of a terrified heartbeat. She eased herself onto his bean-bag chair, her head knocking time. *I have a present: it is the present. You have to learn to find it within you.* She loved this song, the hard, repeated chords, the singer's hoarse voice. Usually she couldn't really enjoy the last CD, she was so busy dreading the moment when she'd have to stop for the day: five-fifteen, five-twenty at the latest in order to be downstairs before Lainie got home from track practice, followed just a little later by Dave returning from work. Today was different, though. Both of them were going out tonight. Kathryn would be back up here by seven-thirty, and then she'd have hours. A vast opportunity. A bonus. A reprieve.

The verse went on, building to a glorious burst of sound, guitar bright and dirty at the same time, the fierce rat-a-tat of the drums. *If you could save yourself, you could save us all. Go on living, prove us wrong. Your leap of faith could be a well-timed smile. Survival never goes out of style.*

A philosophy of life. A philosophy of life in a rock song, a wake-up call of a rock song! Kathryn might have been surprised, before. Now she knew. Ben's music contained everything.

She sang along to the next song, impatient without knowing why until the third one started and she understood she'd been waiting for it. It was her favorite on the album, the one she was always happiest to hear, although "happy" wasn't really the word—"ravished" was more like it. She was ravished by the opening torrent of sound, by the way it thinned into a rocky stream of notes, and then into the vocals: *Dreamed I was a fireman. I just smoked and watched you burn.* (The first time she heard it, she thought it was "*Jingo* was a fireman." Like the opening of a children's story! Ben would've found that hilarious.) *Dreamed I was an astronaut. I shot you down like a juggernaut. Dreamed we were still going out. Had that one a few times now. Woke up to find we were not. It's good to be awake.*

Actually, the first time she heard it she couldn't tell *what* the words were. It was just noise, across the board. Racket. This band and nearly every other. (Of course, that was only about a week after the funeral—she could hardly understand her husband then.) Still, horrible as most of it sounded, she kept listening: first to ten-second bits, then to whole songs, whole albums. And it took. There were still bands she couldn't stand, but others: the way one singer sort of half screamed and half laughed; the deep, velvety dee-dee-dee-doo of a bass; the clatter and roll of a drum set.

And the guitars. There'd been a moment early on when she suddenly stopped and asked herself just what instrument she was hearing, and when the answer dawned on her, obvious and shocking, her face actually filled with heat. Guitar. Electric guitar. What had she thought it was, a trumpet? How could she have arrived at the age of forty-five without knowing how an electric guitar sounded? She loved guitar now, the edgy off-sounding chords, the quick up-and-down wail of a line of notes, the occasional sweet, high, shimmering trill. Guitars could sing, cry, whisper, growl. Awesome, as Ben would have said.

Dreamed I was a dream. I stole you away in your sleep. Saved you from a fire, a gun for hire, I introduced you to a vampire.

A song was a dream. That's what Kathryn thought now. A song was someone else's dream, and when you listened to it you became part of it, and you were linked to all the other people who had listened to it and all the people who would listen to it in times to come. In a phantom space somewhere, she and Ben floated behind dozens of songs together, hundreds of songs—separated by an enormous crowd.

Forty minutes later, the CD was over. She went down to the kitchen. Outside, the sky was the dreary gray of old whites: socks and T-shirts thrown in too many times with a load of jeans. The breakfast dishes were still piled by the sink. She bit into a toast crust, then threw the tail end away. She arranged the dishes in the dishwasher and sat at the table. Just before five-thirty she heard Lainie stowing her bike, and then the front door opened and Lainie passed by the kitchen doorway on her way to the stairs.

"Hi," Kathryn called, and she heard Lainie stop and pause, then turn back.

"Hi." Lainie wore navy blue nylon running shorts and an old T-shirt of Ben's, black with the word "Superchunk" written on it—the name of a band, obviously, though Kathryn remembered trying for a joke when she first saw him wearing it: *What's that, a kind of peanut butter?* And Ben . . . well, he gave her a smile, of course. A forbearing smile.

Lainie's muscular legs were red from her workout, and her face was still splotchy. Standing in the doorway, she dropped her backpack, then pulled her ponytail elastic out and shook her head.

She'd wash her hair and come down with wet spots on the shoulders of whatever T-shirt she put on next, smelling of the apricot stuff she used as conditioner, an oddly disturbing smell to Kathryn lately—musty somehow, like the inside of a rarely opened closet.

"How was school?" Kathryn said.

Lainie shrugged, though somewhere in her eyes there was a bit of surprise at being asked—Kathryn was a bit surprised, too.

"The usual," she said. "Mr. Nadler's definitely got a screw loose. He had us spend half an hour looking at each other's palms and then writing descriptions of them."

"Of each other's palms?"

"It was about metaphors. Describe the palm in terms of something else. He's a few flowers short of a bouquet."

Kathryn felt a smile pull at the corners of her mouth. A few boards short of a fort. A few letters short of a Scrabble game. A Ben and Lainie thing. How had it started? With Dave, now that she thought about it, saying someone was a few hot dogs short of a picnic, to the kids' endless amusement.

"What did you use?" Kathryn said.

"Huh?" Lainie reached up her sleeve and scratched her shoulder, an absent look on her face. At odd moments Kathryn was amazed by her, by her athleticism—her tiny breasts and rough, manly habits. Lainie burped out loud, sat with her legs splayed. Kathryn sometimes thought of her as an emissary from some foreign place, sent to spy on the locals. She imagined Lainie composing her report: "And the mother was so soft. She sat around *thinking* all the time. Plus I never saw her run—not even when she was in a hurry."

"For your metaphor," Kathryn said.

"Oh." Lainie rolled her eyes. "A desert. Real original, right? Allison did a tree for my hand." She held out her palm and Kathryn looked, but she couldn't really see the lines, just the tawny pads at the base of each finger. "It was all about branches," Lainie went on, "because, like"—and here she switched to a high, flutey voice—"life can go in so many directions, you know?"

A heaviness fell over Kathryn, like a lead apron—on her shoulders, her arms, her heart. Color rushed into Lainie's face, and something passed between them for an electric moment. They were thinking of the same thing. So many directions, meaning so many wrong ones. The fallout of a moment's choice—of an impulse. Kathryn put her chin in her hand and looked away.

Lainie reached for her backpack and stood there for a moment, a shape in Kathryn's peripheral vision. She said, "I guess I'll get in the shower."

Kathryn sat. The heaviness sank through her: traveling her bloodstream, outlining her bones. Her body had become a scale, a device for measuring grief. The shifts could still catch her by surprise.

Something orange flashed through the backyard, and she looked up in time to see a tabby cat alight on the fence and then dive into the neighbor's yard. Next she became aware of Lainie moving around in her bedroom. There were footsteps across the upstairs hallway, and the shower came on with a sudden burst. On the other side of the bathroom was Ben's room. Just two more hours and she could go back up. She glanced at the clock: *less* than two hours. The few other times both Dave and Lainie had been out in the evening she'd sat in there with Ben's windows open—his windows open, his lights off, the night mixing with the music until the combination all but carried her away. Coming back downstairs afterward she'd felt a dark, empty exaltation.

In a few minutes the front door opened again, and Dave appeared in the kitchen with a cautious, measuring expression on his face. He ducked his head a bit, then looked back up at her. "Hi."

She swallowed. "Hi."

There was no reason not to get up and go kiss him, no reason for him not to come over and kiss her, but neither of them moved. Whenever they kissed now she felt that they were kissing either because of Ben or despite him.

Dave set his briefcase down and stretched, then glanced over at the sink. Don't bother, she wanted to say, there's nothing there: no pile of washed vegetables, no Styrofoam tray of meat.

"Hungry?" he said.

"Not really," she replied, although all at once she was, a curved, off-center hunger deep in her stomach.

"Lainie?"

"Taking a shower."

"I could go get Indian."

She nodded.

"Or Chinese. Will you eat if I get something?"

She nodded again.

He sighed, his face tired around the eyes, grayish. He looked rumpled, in an unironed plaid shirt and khakis that suddenly appeared too short, bits of his dark socks visible between hem and shoe. "My engine's smoking again," he said. "I've got to take it in tomorrow."

"Oh." She tried again: "Too bad."

"What'd you do today?" Before she could answer, he went to the cracker cabinet and fished in a box of butter thins. She figured he was afraid of her reply—afraid she'd say, as she usually did, Nothing. In fact, she'd even left the house for a little while, for the first time in days. Then spent seven hours listening to music.

"Errands," she said. "I picked up your gray suit for you."

"Oh," he said, brightening a little. "Thanks."

Lainie's door opened with a slight creak, and a moment later her footsteps sounded on the stairs, bam, bam, bam, until the final few steps, which she took in one leap, ending with a great thud.

"Hey, Pop." She came into the kitchen with long strides, her hair wet on her shoulders as Kathryn expected, but wearing her new crocheted black sweater over a short burgundy dress.

"What's this?" Dave said. "You look like a movie star, what's the story?"

"Dad," she said, giving him a look. She hated being complimented, had since early childhood, when she was always telling Kathryn and Dave not to make too big a deal when she did something well—rode her bike without training wheels, added numbers in her head.

Kathryn looked more closely. Lainie's cheeks were flushed, and her lips—was she wearing lipstick? A pale matte shade obviously chosen to look like no lipstick at all.

"I told you," Lainie said. "I have that study group tonight."

"Oh, yeah," Dave said, nodding. "I'd forgotten."

Kathryn drummed her fingers on the table. "You'd better call for that Indian so neither of you'll be late."

Dave scratched the side of his neck. "Indian food OK with you, Laine?" He opened a drawer and riffled through the assortment of takeout menus inside, finally pulling out a light green one. "I guess I'll skip it tonight," he said over his shoulder to Kathryn.

Her heart pounded. "Your meeting?"

"I'd forgotten Lainie needed a car."

"She can take mine, you can take yours."

He gave her an irritated look. "I told you, the engine's smoking."

Her mouth went dry. This wasn't happening, it couldn't be. She'd even figured out what she was going to play first: X, this loud, off-tone band with a screechy female vocalist. *Your phone's off the hook . . . but you're not!* "That's ridiculous," she said as evenly as she could. "You drove home with it smoking, you're going to have to drive it to the shop . . ."

"It's thirty minutes on the freeway. I don't feel like standing on the side of the road waiting for Triple A if it dies."

"Well, then you should take the Trooper and Lainie can get a ride."

Across the kitchen, Lainie opened her mouth and closed it again. "I told Allison I could drive," she said in a small, shaky voice. "I already know, she can't get a car tonight."

"It's fine," Dave said. "You can take the Trooper as planned." He faced Kathryn. "I don't mind missing it this week. It's no big deal."

Kathryn struggled to maintain her expression, but it was too late: a series of questions was forming on his face. Why did she want him to go? Why did she prefer to have him gone? Why beyond the fact that it was now impossible for her to be with anyone?

She didn't want him to know—ever. *I've been listening to Ben's music. Constantly. And* nobody *gets to ask me about it!* "Well," she said. "It just doesn't make sense, that's all."

He shrugged. "I'm not going to keep going forever, you know."

She looked away, a feeling of desperation coming over her. Of course he wasn't, but it had barely been six months, he couldn't be ready to stop yet. As much as she didn't want to go, she wanted him to. Why? "It makes me feel better," he'd said early on. And she wanted him to feel better. And she wanted herself not to.

She'd gone once. Had let him drive her to the place, the room where even the arrangement of chairs was respectful and solicitous, not too close but not too far apart. She chose one with glossy wood arms, but then she looked around at the other bereaved parents, and the meeting started, and *she couldn't do it*. She felt molten. She didn't want friends, compassionate or otherwise. She wanted to scream in a padded room, scratch her arms until they bled.

"So?" Lainie said. "Are we having dinner? Because I could pick up food somewhere on my way."

Dave looked at Kathryn, his deep-blue eyes bloodshot with fatigue and grief and worry. And impatience: that, too. He hesitated for a moment and then reached for the phone. "No, no," he said. "We're having dinner."

After Lainie left, the evening inched along glacially. Dave was in the kitchen while Kathryn was in the bedroom. Then Dave was in the TV room while Kathryn was in the living room. That's how it was now. After a while she picked up her library book, a novel about a woman falling in love with a minister in contemporary rural England. As if she cared. As if she *gave* a fuck. What a word, what a good word—what an *essential* word, and how surprising. She used to try to shame Ben out of using it. Not by saying it was bad or dirty—God no, she had subtler tactics than that—but by trying to appeal to his sense of pride. It's clichéd, she told him. But—and here she took some belated pleasure in his willfulness, or his indifference, whatever it was—*he* didn't give a fuck about that.

All evening his stereo called to her. His room called. At one point she got up and went to the bottom of the stairs and just stood there, looking up into the shadows. Dave appeared at the other end of the hallway and they stared at each other for a long moment. Then she turned and walked away.

In the morning she could hardly wait for them to leave. Lainie's spokes finally twitched through the side yard, but Dave hemmed and hawed about his smoking engine and how the garage guy would take him to work but he might need her to pick him up. Whatever, she wanted to say. What*ever*.

Finally, up the stairs to Ben's room. Each morning she entered it with the guilty conscience of a snooper. Each day she had to reclaim it. She wondered about this. Could you snoop on someone who'd died?

Died. It sounded so peaceful. Ben had *been killed*. Huge, straining train engines haunted her dreams now: movie trains hurtling through tunnels, steam engines puffing around ominous bends. Ironic, because the train that had killed him was your basic commuter, a five-car double-decker shuttling back and forth between San Francisco and San Jose. It was an irony perhaps only Ben would have appreciated, with his finely honed sense of the ironic. "It's an ironic beanbag chair," he'd said when he dragged the bright orange vinyl thing in from a garage sale. "It goes with my ironic studiousness." Which was a reference to something *she'd* said, a little too naggingly, a few weeks earlier: that she felt like he studied from a distance—that he didn't so much study as watch himself study. At which point he'd given her an ironic smile and put on his headphones.

She did what she always did to start. Crossed to his dresser and opened his drawers. Socks and underwear, shirts, shorts. Sweatshirts at the bottom. She could no longer bear to smell them, but she patted the bulky shapes, old blues, grays, greens. "This girl said I look good in dark green," he'd said once, and she'd smoothed his shoulders and smiled, thinking he always had, since he was a baby.

Back across the room to the closet. She slid open the door, knelt in front of his worn old backpack, and unzipped the front pocket. There was the envelope. Some mornings it was enough just to see it there, but today she took it out and opened it, a security envelope with a scratchy black pattern on the inside. It contained the article from the *Chronicle,* folded awkwardly to accommodate the uneven lengths of the columns.

Her friend Susan had suggested a scrapbook. "It would be a place you could keep the article, and the note from the little boy's family, and some recent photographs . . ." Kathryn had demurred politely, but she'd been incensed. Like she'd want bookends for his life, his baby book on one end of a short shelf and a book about his death on the other. Ha.

She pulled the article out, still soft and smudgy, not yet passed into the brittle yellow stage that was the destination of all newsprint. Unfolding it, she didn't read the words so much as take in the shapes of the paragraphs. She had it memorized. Just as she had the note memorized.

Her chest tightened. She hated to think of the note. The loopy handwriting, the little bouquet of flowers on the return address label. She hated to think of it but she wanted to think of it. Sometimes she felt she needed to think of it.

Dear David and Kathryn and Lainie: We are so sorry for your loss. Ben must have been a wonderful son and brother. The death of a family member is always hard. What happened Tuesday fills our hearts with grief. No one but a hero would have done what Ben did. We know that he gave up his life so our Tyler could live. When he is old enough we will tell Tyler that he owes his life to a hero.

The nerve. That was all Kathryn could think: the *nerve*. Because to hell with how it was heartfelt and all that crap—where was *We know that our negligence caused this*? Where was *We will blame ourselves forever*? Nowhere, that's where. Nowhere. And *The death of a family member is always hard*? *What happened fills our hearts with grief*? It was too bad they were so sad! The thing that got Kathryn most, though, was *We know that he gave up his life so our Tyler could live*. As if he'd made a conscious choice! Me or this little kid? OK, the kid. It was enraging: they seemed to expect her to be *proud* of him—to share their admiration of what he'd done.

Well, she wasn't. She didn't.

They'd actually gone so far as to enclose a photograph of little Tyler, a mottled-background shot from Sears, with the kid looking wet-lipped into the middle distance, a tiny toolbelt strapped around his waist. Dave had agreed that there was no reason to save the note, and after a few weeks Kathryn had thrown it away. He didn't even *know* about the photograph. It hadn't been in the house an hour before Kathryn had put it into a metal bucket and thrown a lit match in after. A lovely gesture.

She looked down at the article again. "Youth Saves Child, Loses Life." Some days the headline had an almost poetic power over her, but today she just felt sour. Youth—it made him sound like an Eagle Scout. And *loses* life? He hadn't *misplaced* it. Where is my life? Shit, it must be around here somewhere!

Where is my mind? Where is my mind? That was from a song, but which one?

She put the article back in the envelope, the envelope back in the backpack. The closet was crammed with his stuff—papers, old clothes, his one blazer flattened between ski jackets. *Mom, I look like an idiot!*

She closed the closet door and went to the stereo. There were hundreds of records, lined up in milk crates. Shelves and shelves of CDs and tapes. He'd spent a fortune, driving up to San Francisco, Berkeley, Oakland. Record stores sometimes called and left messages for him—*Tell him we just got a used copy of blah blah if he's still interested*. Kathryn would tell him—then overhear him sheepishly asking Lainie if he could borrow twenty bucks, his own wallet long since empty.

What to play? She didn't know what she felt like today. Actually, she did: everything. She began pulling out CDs until she had twenty-five or thirty in a pile on the floor. She pinched open the cases and put the discs into the carousel, which had slots for something like a hundred CDs. In theory, that meant she could listen to music nonstop for about four days. If only.

She pressed Random and sat in the beanbag chair.

Hips like Cinderella. She adored this song! The voice was insinuating, lascivious, close to a whisper. *Must be having a good shame.*

That whispering voice and the bass and drums, full of tension. *Talking sweet about nothing.* Getting ready for: *Cookie, I think you're TAME!* And the guy screamed it, and the guitar rushed in, and Kathryn's head knocked around so much she could have ended up with whiplash.

Sometimes her neck ached afterward, downstairs.

Ben twitched his foot. She used to pass his room and he'd have the headphones on and be twitching his foot like a madman, and in her mind she'd be like, Go running! Let off some steam! What a fool. *Listening* was letting off steam. Listening was like sex and eating and screaming, all at once. It was so physical. Looking at a painting, reading a book—you could forget you had a body. Rock and roll existed to remind you of your body. It existed to make your body into an instrument, to play you.

Fall on your face in those bad shoes.

The headphones thing destroyed her. She couldn't count the number of times she'd asked him to wear them, saying something asinine like "It won't matter to you and it will matter to me." Aargh. She'd tried them and it mattered—God, did it matter. Listening through headphones was like talking on the phone long distance to someone you were dying to see. To touch. All that nagging was just one of the things she'd like to kill herself for.

Dave would sigh and turn away if she said that to him. That she'd like to kill herself. He'd sigh and turn away if she said it, and she'd say it so he'd sigh and turn away.

The song ended. What would be next, what next? Random always gave her a nervous feeling, her heartbeat up in her throat. Aching anticipation.

The morning sun moved slowly across Ben's room, and she followed it, ending up sometime after noon on the floor by the closet, her lower body flooded with light while her face and shoulders grew cold. The songs washed over her, jazzed her, ignited her, and put her out in the space of three or four minutes. She was hungry but she waited and it went away. Thirsty—that usually lasted. Whatever. It didn't work to bring stuff to eat or drink in with her. She zoned out, and for a while she didn't even really hear the change from one song to the next. Peace.

A song ended and the next began, and she sat up. A ringing, shiny like bells—she absolutely loved the guitar on this. She'd gone through a phase of listening to this band over and over, one album after another. *I fell in love with a hooker, she laughed in my face. So seriously I took her, I was a disgrace. I was out of line, I was out of place, out of time to save face. See the open mouth of my suitcase, saying leave this place. Leave without a trace.* Here was her favorite part, the guitar winding. *Leave without a trace.* And winding tighter, cinching a string around her heart: she actually saw this, white kitchen string around a fist of muscle, blood turning the white to red, and it didn't disgust her at all, it just—went with the song. *Leave. Without. A trace.* And there was a dazzling burst of chords, and God, it was sublime, sublime and ordinary, sublime because ordinary—it was rock and roll. She imagined Ben in here, damned headphones on, listening to this—its antic energy, the questioning defiance of its lyrics. *I tried to get a good job, with honest pay. Might as well join the mob, the benefits are OK.* What was it like to be seventeen, eighteen, and to hear that? Last fall, maybe a week or two before the accident, Ben had joked that he'd go to college next year unless he got a better offer. "It's usually *after* you've gone to college that you get the better offers," Dave said, and the two of them laughed the thin-lipped Stephenson laugh.

Ben was a Stephenson, no question. Kathryn's strain of high-cheekboned Slavic seriousness barely registered in either kid. Summers in North Dakota, visiting Dave's parents on their farm, Ben fit right in. Tall, rangy. He looked good with a piece of straw poking out of his mouth. He *looked* good: then he opened his mouth and the illusion pretty much fell apart. "Oh, no!" he cried.

"I forgot to worry about *nasty microorganisms*," and he made a big show of spitting the straw to the ground. Dave's father gave him a slightly irritated glance as he passed by in his work pants, off to fix the tractor.

Still, Ben was good-natured on those visits. "Bologna salad sandwiches for lunch?" he'd cry. "Yay, Grandma." He even made one at home once: chopped bologna and relish mixed together in a bowl and spread on white bread. Kathryn walked into the kitchen and couldn't believe her eyes. "I'm cultivating my roots," he said. "Also a slight stomachache."

A new song came on and her chest tightened. She stood up but then didn't move. She couldn't stand to listen to it, but once she'd heard the first chords, how they organized themselves into the beginning of the song, she couldn't really not listen, either.

Lay down Rosey. It's the blue and the orange time, a water and a twist of lime. I had so much to tell you, I raced through the sky, to touch you for the last time. So much to tell you, I raced through the sky, to whisper a message into your morphine drip.

Then a heartbreaking violin passage, an embroidery on the idea of loss.

And: *Not a dark boy. A sparkle and a mark boy. Making cake out of trashcan afterthoughts. Death is a spinster, mortally whacking the funny boys. Till they're not laughing anymore.*

She didn't know what it was about. Someone lost to drugs? Cancer? It didn't matter. It was about her, her feelings. The next part was the hardest, and she went over to the stereo, ready to turn it off, then stopped. *Don't cry, don't cry, don't cry, don't cry. I'm having fun driving, I'm riding, riding, riding . . .* It was the same singer, a woman with a low, scratchy, fervent voice, but now she was singing the boy's part. *No need for you to cry.* Full-throated, Kathryn pressed the Stop button.

It was too painful, but so gorgeous. Gorgeous music. In the silence, staring at the green light on the stereo, she could almost hear how the song would end, with the single sustained note of the violin wavering over the fading guitar. And how, if she were listening to the CD straight through, the next would begin moments later, deceptively simple: *Won't you look inside and see, what's inside a girl like me? Rivers of blood pour from my eyes, your careless heart I do despise*. The singer's voice placid, making its way through the verse, growing. And then, entreatingly, full of feeling: *Swim back to me*. The cry of a spurned lover, Kathryn supposed, but what did that matter? There was no word for what Kathryn was. No word like "widow" to convey the exact shape of what was gone.

Her eyes hot, nausea climbing to her throat, she took the disc out and put it away. She couldn't. Sometimes she wanted to, but not today. Not today.

Ben must have been a wonderful son and brother.

She took a deep breath and let it out again. Even. An even keel was what she needed. She hit Random again. Tat, tat, tat, tat. Thank God. This was easy, this next song, starting with a sprightly tapping of drumsticks. She moved away from the stereo and sat down again. Ben had had a drum once. Little drummer boy, four or five years old, marching around the house. It had been a birthday present—a hostile gesture from the other kid's parents, she joked to Dave. Eventually she'd made it disappear.

The *mistakes* she'd made.

The song got under way, the drum awfully insistent. Then she realized: someone was at the front door. She stood and looked out Ben's window, but there was no car, just the sidewalk and the empty street. And the strip of earth between them where, this year, nothing was planted.

Tap, tap, tap. She left the room and made her way down the stairs, her pulse going fast. She didn't like to have to talk to people without warning. The phone was easy, she just let the machine get it, but the door . . . Once, maybe just a few weeks after it happened, someone knocked, and it was this woman Kathryn barely knew, a mother from Lainie's school, and she'd come over to see if Kathryn *wanted to talk*.

She reached the door and put her hand on the knob. Her mouth was dry. She wiped her palms on her jeans and then pulled the door open.

It was Kaz—Ben's friend Matt Kazmann. Tall, black-haired, heavy, pale. Dark plastic-framed glasses, a silver stud just below his lower lip. His black T-shirt fell loosely from thin shoulders and then went taut at his plump belly.

He looked past her as he spoke. "Um, I was driving by, and, like, did you know your sprinkler's going over there?" He pointed over his shoulder to the side of the house Kathryn couldn't see. "It's sort of, like, flooded. I mean, I wasn't sure if you knew."

The minute he spoke she became aware of the sound of water running through pipes. Dave had said he'd turn it on as he left; she'd forgotten to turn it off. Which meant it had been going for—what?—five hours? Oh, well.

"Thanks," she said. "You're right, I've got to turn it off."

She moved past him onto the porch, crossed the grass, looked around the corner of the house. God, a pond. She squished through the sodden grass and shut the water off. Much too wet to retrieve the sprinkler now, but she should try to remember before Lainie or Dave got home.

Kaz was still on the porch. He was so pale—as if he never went outside during the day. Not that she should talk.

He tipped his head toward the open front door, a confused look on his face. "Is Lainie home?"

The music. He could hear it tumbling down the stairs. *Why can't I get. Just one fuck. Why can't I get. Just one fuck. I guess it's got something to do with luck, but I . . .*

Heat filled her face, a line of sweat on her upper lip. Of all songs. "She's at school," she said. "Shouldn't you be?"

He lifted a shoulder. "Not really. Whatever."

Go. Go. She needed for him to *go away*. She said, "So you were driving by?" It was a tiny street, no one just drove by.

"Yeah, kind of." He looked out toward his car, parked halfway down the block, and the cluster of pimples on the side of his neck darkened to crimson.

Well, *she'd* go. She'd go in. She took a step toward the door, but poor Kaz: he carried something around with him, and it wasn't just that big gut. He was always lumbering, psychically lumbering. Lumbering after Ben, lumbering downtown: you'd see him from a distance, black hair and a slopey body, some vaguely reluctant determination to keep on. At the cemetery he'd stood with his arms crossed tightly in front of his chest, hands tucked into his armpits. Slightly away from where the other kids huddled, not quite ostracized but almost.

He and Ben had been growing apart. That's what it was. Ben had been in the middle of a kind of shift, toward a different group of kids. Happier kids? Or just interested in appearing happy? Ben had always worn his darkness lightly. *Not a dark boy. A sparkle and a mark boy . . .*

She stepped up into the entry hall. "Well . . ."

Kaz squinted. "Are *you* listening to that?"

"I'm just . . . sorting."

His eyes widened a bit but he didn't comment. Then: "Ben loved this album."

"Really?" A rush of something through her chest. "Did he talk about it a lot?"

"He *played* it a lot. He wore out the vinyl and had to buy the CD. I mean 'wore out'—it got a little scratched."

"He didn't like that?"

"He hated it. Dude was *beyond* uptight." Kaz bit his lip and looked away for a moment. "Sorry."

"It's all right," Kathryn said.

More. She wanted more. "Would you like to come in?" she asked brightly. "I think there might still be some water if you're thirsty."

He smiled. "Uh . . ."

"Come in," she said. "Really." She stepped backward and held the door open wide, and after a moment he came in and looked around uneasily.

It was no wonder: the living room was appalling. The blinds were still drawn, and there was dust everywhere. Old newspapers all over the hearth, empty Diet Coke cans cluttering the coffee table, a pair of dirty socks peeking out from under a chair. And was that a *smell*? Maybe so. Maybe it was coming off her.

The kitchen was a little better. She filled a glass for him and watched thirstily as he drank it standing in front of the dishwasher, his stud glinting below his lip. Gulp, gulp, gulp: a kid hoping to outwit the neighborhood witch. Why had she invited him in? This was all wrong. She wanted to be upstairs again, alone. She could hear the beginning of a new song: *Candy says, I've come to hate my body* . . .

"Could I go upstairs?"

"To *Ben's* room?" Her mouth was drier than ever as she searched his pale face.

He nodded.

No, no, no, no, no. He certainly could not. She didn't want anyone in there. Some days she could sense Dave's presence—a whiff of early morning, shaving cream and coffee—and it made her crazy.

Lainie never went in, she was sure of that.

"Mrs. Stephenson?"

Kaz stared at her. Matt Kazmann. It was his loss, too, she knew that—she knew all about that. But now, today, this moment in her kitchen: Matt Kazmann suffered, too. No less because he'd been losing Ben anyway. Just like Kathryn.

It was too fierce, the pain of having children. It hurt just to love them, let alone this. It hurt to be impatient, bored, entranced. Always knowing they were on their way away. How could you so much as kiss their tiny toes knowing that? The pain was the exact size of Kathryn's own body. Feeling it was simply feeling the inside of herself.

Kaz set his glass down. "Sorry," he said. "I'm going to take off."

"No," she said. "Go upstairs. Take some time in there, take as long as you need."

She sat at the kitchen table. She heard the stereo go off, then nothing. He wasn't moving, wasn't making a sound. Just sitting on the bed, maybe. Looking through the CDs, remembering. "Kaz thinks they're rad," Ben had said once, about a band the two of them were going to hear in San Francisco. *Kaz thinks they're rad*. Meaning Ben didn't, or wasn't sure, or didn't even know the band. Meaning Kaz's wanting to go was enough.

Ten minutes went by, fifteen, twenty. The house was silent, the sun-filled silence of two o'clock in a suburban house on an empty suburban street. Outside were all those lawns to be fertilized, watered, mowed, edged. There was nothing sadder than a little rectangle of lawn on an empty suburban street at two o'clock in the afternoon.

Footsteps on the stairs. Kathryn reached for a section of newspaper, then shoved it away. Why pretend?

He stood at the entrance of the kitchen. Face still pale, belly pushing at the thin black T-shirt. What, she expected him to look different? Or was it that she wanted him to?

"Thanks," he said. "I've been wanting to do that. I mean, I wasn't sure if it would be OK."

He hadn't just been driving by, he'd come over on purpose. That's what he meant.

"Sure," she said. She'd wanted more from him earlier, but not now. What question was there? What single question?

Kaz reached under his glasses and pinched the bridge of his nose. "OK, then," he said. "Thanks." He gave her a funny little wave and walked away.

As soon as the front door closed she stood up. She hurried to the stairs, then took them two at a time and raced into Ben's room. But: nothing. Not a sign of disturbance, not a lingering smell. Neatly made bed, beanbag chair, records, tapes, CDs. Dresser. She went over to the closet and slid open the door. Backpack. She pressed the front pocket and felt the crinkling of the envelope.

I've been wanting to do that, he'd said.

Wanting to do that. She knew what he meant.

Blood hurtled through her body, and she stood still for a moment, then headed for the kids' bathroom. That nausea. She used Lainie's brush on her hair, set it down again, and opened the medicine cabinet. Nuder Than Nude: that was the name of the lipstick. She uncapped it and rolled some across her lips, then yanked some toilet paper off the roll and rubbed it away. Her mouth looking red, blurry.

The death of a family member is always hard.

Back in Ben's room she plucked a disc from the CD carousel, dug out its case from the pile on the floor, and hurried downstairs. "Without a Trace," that was the song she wanted to hear, but why? Grief rose up inside her and she knocked it back.

She fetched up in the kitchen, suddenly unsure of herself. Beached. The breakfast dishes, the toast crusts . . . It was the same as yesterday, the same as the day before. It would be the same forever. An oppression of breakfast plates. That should be the collective noun, like a school of fish, a herd of cows.

She felt—*dry of mouth and spirit.* She liked the phrase, and as she mustered the energy to push off from the counter, locate her car keys, and head out to the driveway, she muttered it over and over to herself. Dry of mouth and spirit. Dry of mouth and spirit.

The Trooper was a furnace. She got the engine running and immediately lowered all the windows. It reminded her of going to pick up the kids from school, being in the car at this time of day. People driving around in cars, mothers driving children around in cars. It weighed on her, the idea of so many people in so many cars.

She *couldn't* do what she wanted to do. But she wanted to do it.

She turned onto El Camino and drove alongside the railroad tracks. Mountain Mike's, Baskin-Robbins, Lyon's. All virtually empty right now. A few old people shuffling into Walgreens. A good time to buy Depends!

God, what a bitch.

She came to the crossing. RR. Ben, who'd adored trains as a little boy. A sob heaved upward but lodged in her chest. It made her dizzy to think about it. It made her dizzy and it made her crazy.

On the other side she passed the car wash. The other side of the tracks—it wasn't lost on her. Smaller houses, smaller yards. Well, they had to play somewhere, didn't they? If they had tiny yards they were going to wander away, weren't they?

She drove alongside the tracks but then braked at the turn, because really, this was too awful. Monstrous. What was she doing? She glanced at the passenger seat and saw the CD lying there. In her mind she leaned toward the refrain she wanted: *Leave. Without. A trace. That* was a trace, the song itself. Wholly inadequate, and yet . . . She put the disc into the car stereo and pressed the button.

The guitar rang, and she looked at the house. One in from the corner, she knew from having driven by once, just after it happened.

She couldn't do this.

Shouldn't do it.

Couldn't, shouldn't, couldn't, shouldn't.

He stretched for the child, grabbed him, and threw him away from the tracks. Slipped and was struck.

So said the witness, a man who'd pulled over to see what was going on, why a tall, dark-haired teenager was scrambling from a car to race for the tracks when a train was coming . . .

She stared at the tracks now. Sunlight reflecting blood-brown on steel. A howl through her mind: *Don't.*

She was so thirsty. She set her blinker though no one was coming, then turned onto the street and pulled to the curb in front of the house.

It was small, white, neatly kept. She cut the engine and the stereo fell silent. Maybe no one was home. There was a metal garbage can empty at the curb, which might mean no one was home. Or might not.

She walked up the edge of the driveway. A mass of Johnny-jump-ups grew against the porch: blossoms of dark purple and pale purple and yellow, tiny and so tender.

She stepped onto the porch and the door knocker galvanized her: brass molded into the words "Bless Our Home." Bless it yourself, she thought nastily.

She rapped once, hard. It was two-thirty in the afternoon, maybe little Tyler was asleep. Down for his nap. *Do you want me to put him down?* Dave said, taking the baby Ben from Kathryn and setting him in his crib. Then, murmuring to the baby: *Now why did I say that, hmm? We certainly don't want you to feel put down.*

The door opened, and there stood a woman, thirtyish, narrow-shouldered. She furrowed her brow and stared at Kathryn, then looked out to the curb, where Kathryn had parked the Trooper—the car Ben had been driving that day. Kathryn saw it dawn on the woman, the understanding of who she was.

She peered past the woman into the house. Beige carpeting, a sectional couch in front of a giant entertainment center. The woman's eyes were wide now, her hands knotted together just below her bustline. She still hadn't spoken.

"I came," Kathryn said, but then she stopped. Her mouth was a desert. She sucked her cheeks for some saliva, a way to talk. "I came," she said, "to tell you that I'm sorry he did it." She leaned closer to the woman. To Janette McCormick. Round blue eyes, wispy eyebrows, putty pink skin.

"I'm sorry he stopped," she went on. "I wish he'd kept on driving."

The woman opened her mouth, then closed it again. Blood sloshed around inside Kathryn's head. The skin around her mouth tingled. Time passed, a second or a minute or ten.

Behind her the day sat still, waiting. Deep blue sky beyond the shade trees. She looked down and saw the woman's feet in flowered Keds, the toe of one shoe covering the toe of the other.

Kathryn turned and walked back to her car. Her big, expensive silver Isuzu Trooper. A train of a car. She was still being watched, but then she heard the door close, and she imagined the woman pressing her back against it, sobbing into her hands.

Settled in the driver's seat, Kathryn started the engine, and the CD started, too, right where it had left off. *I tried to dance at a funeral, New Orleans style. I joined the grave dancers' union, I had to file. Standing in the sun with a popsicle, everything is possible. With a lot of luck and a pretty face, and some time to waste. Leave without a trace. Leave without a trace. Leave. Without. A trace.*

And the instruments burst into conversation, bright and brave and onward, even knowing they'd soon stop. Kathryn pulled away from the curb. She reached for the volume knob and turned it up. No: she *cranked* it.

For DSD

Jump

. . .

Alejandro was thin like a teenager, with skinny shoulders and skinny legs and no butt. His black hair lay against his scalp in long, wavy strands and hung so low on his forehead it almost reached his eyes. "I got cables," he cried in response to Carolee's announcement, his hand up and waving like a school kid's. "I can help you."

It was a little after midnight, and her car was dead. Beggars weren't supposed to be choosers, but did she really want Alejandro's help? Here at work he messed up all the time, making a hundred fifty copies when a customer wanted fifteen, jamming the self-service machines when he tried to add paper. She couldn't believe he hadn't been fired.

"What's the matter, Carolee?" one of the other guys said. "Alejandro said he can help."

Alejandro turned away, eyes downcast, front teeth pulling at his lower lip. She'd trained him when he first started, almost a year ago, and she felt sort of responsible for him. It wasn't just that she'd been around longer than he had—she'd been around longer than anyone, including her boss. It was more, he was the runt of the litter and she hated watching anyone get bullied.

She gave him a swift nod and they headed for the exit, Alejandro trotting beside her and then darting ahead to push open the door. "Yo, Chavez," someone called after them. "No funny business."

The moon was high and bright, and a cold wind blew bits of debris around the nearly empty parking lot. Carolee turned up the lapels of her flimsy jacket and clutched them close. She hated her heavy coat so much she'd ditched it at the first false note of spring.

They began walking. An empty VitaminWater bottle lay in their path, and Alejandro paused, raised his foot high, and gave her a huge grin when he saw he'd flattened it. He said, "You're lucky I'm even here tonight. Usually on Fridays I'm wit my friends doin' airsoft."

"Airsoft."

He stared at her with disbelief, his thin face pinched from the cold. He had smooth olive cheeks and the beginnings of a fine, silky mustache that never seemed to grow. He said, "Carolee, you gotta be kiddin'. It's guns— Not real— It's so fun, you gotta go wit me sometime."

He told her about the empty shopping mall where he and his buddies played late at night, its businesses shuttered, a giant "For Lease" sign facing the highway. There were recessed doorways perfect for ambushes, vacant loading docks. He said, "My boy Gordo's a security guard, he lets us in."

"Hope he doesn't like his job," Carolee said.

"Why, cuz he could lose it? Gordo's smart, he ain't gonna get caught."

He was parked at the far end of the lot, his boxy old Nissan just a few spaces from her battered Hyundai. By the time they got there she had to pee, though she'd peed right before she clocked out, like ten minutes ago.

He swung open his trunk. "Fuck me."

Inside were a bicycle wheel lying on its side, a mess of dirty clothes, a six-pack of off-brand cola. No jumper cables.

"I know I had 'em," he said. "Somebody musta stole 'em."

She turned to go. She had a theory that any one bad thing made it likelier more bad things would happen. Her dead car had set her up. She said, "I'll figure something else out."

"Carolee, no, we can go borrow some. Gordo has some."

"It's fine, Alejandro."

"Or I can drive you home and go get 'em after, bring you back tomorrow. You workin' tomorrow?"

She wasn't. And she really had to pee, the feeling like a knife slice now, which was not good. Plus it was incredibly cold. In the morning she could probably find someone with cables at her apartment, get a ride back up here and deal with her car then. All she was supposed to do tomorrow was stop by her mom's. There was some project her mom had in mind for the two of them, labeling photos, reorganizing a closet—the kind of thing Carolee thought of as playing with the past, as if the past were a doll and the two of them were putting dress-up clothes on it, combing its hair so it would look pretty.

She said to Alejandro, "I live in Sunnyvale."

He shrugged and opened the passenger door for her, and she got in, the car smelling of old French fries and air freshener. He settled into the driver's seat and wiggled his eyebrows at her. "Finally I get you in my car."

"Do *not* do that."

He held up both palms, then backed away from the curb and drove straight across the painted lines of a dozen parking places.

Leaving the lot, he gave her a worried glance from under the fringe of his hair and faced the road again.

Now she felt bad; he was just doing what guys did. And he looked so hangdog, slumped in the seat, steering with the heel of one hand.

She said, "So this airsoft war. It's teams?"

He looked over and grinned. "Every man for himself."

"But you help Juan."

"I help Juan and Iggy. Gordo helps me."

"Gordo helps you but you don't help him?"

"He don't need help."

And on he went, like the little kids she used to babysit, who talked and talked, and then talked more as bedtime got closer. He basically was a kid: twenty-two at the most, whereas she'd turn thirty in less than a month, and what a good time that was going to be. Her mom kept saying they'd go out somewhere really nice, just the two of them, like that was the solution and not the problem.

They drove past a gas station, and Carolee wondered if she should offer to buy him some. "You got a full tank?"

"Yeah."

Another gas station, complete with a big bright mini-mart.

"Can we stop for a sec?"

"I said I'm good."

"Not for gas."

He turned to her with wide eyes. "Carolee, no. You're my role model, you can't smoke."

"I don't smoke. You can keep it running, I'll only be a sec."

The cashier was an old guy, sitting on a stool with his neck arched so he could watch a TV mounted to the ceiling. Carolee ducked into the bathroom. It was dank and freezing, with scattered puddles on the concrete floor. There was nowhere she wanted to put her purse, so she held the strap between her teeth as she lowered her thighs to the frigid seat. At first it felt good letting the urine out, but as she finished it burned, a sure sign, and she knew she had a bad night ahead.

The store light was bright and ugly. She found the grocery aisle and scanned the shelves, hating the way boxes of food looked in these places, the yellows and cardboard reds.

Alejandro stood empty-handed at the register, leaning on one elbow. When he saw her he straightened up. "What you got, juice?"

She flashed the label at him.

"Cranberry juice. Guess you got a infection, huh?"

"Alejandro!" She set the juice on the counter and fished in her purse. In the mirror behind the register she saw how she towered over him, all 5'10" of her. She felt like his mother.

She opened her wallet, and he reached across her to a plastic tub of Slim Jims. He said, "On you? Thanks, boss."

"I'm not your boss."

"You are. You're my boss lady."

It seemed even colder when they got back outside. She hated "boss lady." She was shift manager, which—despite the flowchart she'd made for the online business class she took a few years back—meant next to nothing. Shift manager at the idiotically named Copy Copy, her thirtieth birthday coming soon—she was kicking ass.

Back in the car, she unscrewed the top of the cranberry juice and drank from its too-wide opening, the juice sweet-sharp, with that drying effect. She wiped her mouth with the back of her hand.

He said, "Carolee, I hate to tell you, cranberry juice ain't gonna fix it."

She looked over at him, sitting behind the wheel, a serious look on his face. "You're a doctor now?"

He shrugged and sat there nibbling on the Slim Jim. Another

car pulled in next to them, and the driver got out, a man in his fifties with thick, disheveled hair and the ruined nose of an alcoholic. He spoke through his open door, waving his hand like he was excited or upset, and when he moved away Carolee got a quick glimpse of his passenger, a black and white mutt with floppy ears.

She'd left clothes in the washer, she just remembered. Put them in last night when she got home from work and forgot all about them. Evenings she worked late, she was sometimes so fried she didn't even eat, or she ate crap from the freezer, Hot Pockets, Bagel Bites, stuff she bought for emergencies. Her laundry would've been taken from the washer by now, left wet in her basket if she was lucky or just dumped on the floor. She hated her apartment. Every now and then she thought of trying to move north, closer to work, but it was like the idea of signing up for some classes again—it wouldn't make a big enough difference, so why bother?

She turned to Alejandro. "So are we going?"

He didn't respond, his expression glazed, the Slim Jim drooping from the corner of his mouth.

"Yo," she said.

"What?"

"Are we going?"

He shook, or shivered—it was like a wet dog trying to dry off. Moving slowly, he started the car, put it in reverse, and pulled out of the gas station, but when he came to the on-ramp for the freeway he turned right.

"Wait, what're you—"

"Shortcut."

There was no shortcut to Sunnyvale, and her pulse picked up a little. Was this going to turn into one of those horrible stories, woman killed by coworker on deserted street? She thought of a Monday morning when she'd gotten to work early, and Alejan-

dro and the other night-shift guy were sitting on opposite coun-
ters, tossing a roll of packing tape back and forth. When he saw
her he hopped down and gave her a big smile. "Hey, Carolee," he
said, "come and kiss me, just right here"—he tapped his cheek
twice—" 'cause I know you love me."

He wasn't a maniac. A fuck-up but not a maniac. And maybe
not such a fuck-up, either—for him he was probably doing well,
just having his job. She was pretty sure he was first-generation,
with parents who didn't speak English.

She was in pain again, and she shifted in her seat, trying to get
comfortable. She had swiped some sleeping pills from her mom's
medicine cabinet, and this was definitely the night to try one.
Either that or lie awake watching the clock. She was pretty sure
Kaiser opened at 9:00 on Saturdays. At 9:01 she'd call for some
Cipro.

He said, "What you doing tomorrow?"

"Nothing. Dealing with my car." Maybe she'd skip the stop
at her mom's, though then she'd have to hear the usual moaning,
What's the point of having you close by if I never see you?

"No, after that," Alejandro said. "Later. We should go out.
You wanna go to a movie? I ain't hittin' on you, I swear."

She glanced over at him, sitting there all thin and hopeful.
Did he really think she'd go out with him, even as friends? They
were so different: age, race, everything. What would they talk
about, airsoft wars? She said, "You've got to be kidding."

He stared straight ahead, hands tight on the steering wheel.

She said, "What?"

"Why are you such an icicle, lady?"

"I'm sorry." She hesitated. "It's late. Don't listen to me."

On they drove, past heavy trees on one side of the road and a
big wall on the other. The streetlights were far apart, and they
were the fancy kind, with curly iron things spiraling on top of the

globes. At a T intersection, she looked in both directions and saw more walls, more trees.

"Where are we?" she said.

"Atherton."

"Why are we in Atherton?"

The light turned green, and he made a left and passed through a giant stone gate. Now they were somewhere residential, but quiet, wealthy, spread-out residential, with smaller closed gates at driveways every hundred yards or so and, way back from the gates, the smudgy outlines of giant houses. Atherton was where the rich people lived, the richest people, richer even than the kids Carolee had gone to school with in Palo Alto. Atherton kids went to private schools. They drove brand-new cars and walked in gilded groups through the pricey Stanford Shopping Center, where Carolee had her first job, cashiering at a gourmet hot dog stand. In those days, Carolee's richest friend was Tamara Bevin, and she said her parents had chosen Palo Alto over Atherton or Woodside because they wanted her and her brother to learn about the real world. Carolee and her mom lived in the thin strip of south Palo Alto that ran between El Camino and the railroad tracks, where the houses were small and close together and you could hear shouts many nights, and cars roaring up and down the streets—and she knew that was about as real as Palo Alto ever got.

Alejandro stopped at a driveway. He reached up to his sun visor, and the gate swung inward.

"What the fuck?" Carolee said.

"*Mi casa.*"

The car crunched over gravel and slowed as a huge white cake of a house came into view, with pillars and a covered entryway, and a massive double door flanked by glowing lanterns. He cut the engine, and they looked at each other.

She said, "You live here."

"My mommy and daddy do. Come on, I gotta make a stop."

Inside the house it was dark, though there was a light on somewhere near the back, so dim it might be nothing more than a night-light. He moved fast, and she picked up her pace and trailed him through an enormous living room, twice the size of her entire apartment, and through a corridor that led to a vast kitchen, with stoves and ovens and sinks and refrigerators at one end and couches and easy chairs and a huge flat-screen TV at the other, where a small, dark-haired woman sat watching some show with the sound off, her tiny body enveloped by a splashily flowered robe, white with giant red and orange flowers that gleamed in the near dark.

"Sandro," she said, leaping to her feet and switching on a lamp. *"Madre de dios."*

"Mami." He crossed the room and kissed her cheeks.

Her hands fluttered from her face to his face to the pockets of her robe. Her skin was a darker olive than his, her eyes deeply black and ringed with shadows.

"Sandro, you almost gave me a heart attack. What's wrong, what is it?"

He said something to her in Spanish, and they went back and forth, speaking rapidly. Alejandro gestured at Carolee, and the woman came over and held out her hand. She was maybe 4'11", and she had tiny, almost nonexistent breasts; she could have passed for a child if it weren't for the blurriness of her aging face.

"You are most welcome," she said. "How do you do? I am Alejandro's mother."

Carolee took the hand, which was cold and soft and seemed to slip from her grasp the moment she touched it. Was she the maid? No, she wasn't the maid, and Alejandro was not the person he pretended to be. All these months Carolee had assumed he was from the Latino part of Redwood City, near the taquerías and bodegas. He obviously *wanted* people to assume it, with his cholo talk.

"Carolee," the woman said. "In Spanish we have Carolina. Are you for Carolina?"

Carolee shook her head. She'd been named for her mom's parents, Carol and Lee. It was embarrassing, she never told anyone.

"You work at the photocopy shop?"

"She's the queen there," Alejandro cut in, speaking in perfect, unaccented English. "The queen of photocopies and expedited shipping services."

Carolee felt her face grow warm, but he turned to his mom and said, "*¿Dónde está Papi?*"

She gestured at the ceiling, and he left the room, his footsteps sounding on a flight of stairs.

Carolee looked at his mom. She used to know how to deal with people like this, rich and in every way out of her league; she got through school dealing with them, charming them, making sure she was *that nice girl Carolee* to all the parents she encountered because that was how she got to go places. "Mrs. Chavez," she said. "I'm sorry to intrude."

Alejandro's mom smiled. "It's Mitchell—Chavez is my maiden name. My son borrows it because he does not like Mitchell. But please, call me Raquel."

"Raquel," Carolee said. She repeated the apology, explaining about her dead car, but all she could think was what a liar Alejandro was. He'd faked this Latino homeboy thing and he'd changed his name to go with it? She was going to kill him. Her days of protecting him from the other guys at work, trying to sand the edges off their teasing? Over.

His mom was waiting.

"He was giving me a ride home," Carolee said, "and then suddenly we were here. I don't know why we stopped."

His mom's arched eyebrows went up. "For medicine. He didn't tell you?"

"Medicine?"

"He has a soft heart. He always has."

Carolee forced herself to smile, but things were going from bad to worse. What did Alejandro think he was going to do, dig up some old pills from an infection he'd had? He was a liar, and he was out of his mind.

She had to pee like crazy, and she looked around, wondering where the bathroom might be. Bathrooms. The sitting area was full of furniture, everything covered with flowers, gold tassels, big silk buttons. Even the lampshades were flowered, and the lamp bases were painted with ladies holding parasols.

"May I use the bathroom?" she asked. "The restroom?"

Alejandro's mom showed her the way, reaching into a small pink-and-gold room and turning on a light. When she was gone Carolee closed the door. It hurt, and then it hurt a lot more as she finished. There were tiny linen hand towels, ironed, and rather than use one she dried her hands on her pants. She thought of a boy she dated in high school, from a rich family in Crescent Park, and remembered going home with him for dinner one night: soon after they arrived the boy's mom suggested he show her *the restroom* so she could *freshen up*. She didn't know what that meant, freshen up, but she figured she must look dirty, so in the bathroom she took a small fringed cloth—terry, not as fancy as this one—and wetted it thoroughly to scrub her face, realizing only afterward that it was a hand towel and not a washcloth. "They sound very la-di-da," her mom said when she got home and described the evening. Carolee had liked the boy: David Connell, with his straight dark hair and his voice that still cracked sometimes. He ran track; she met him after practice most afternoons, and they made out behind the tennis courts until it was time for him to go into the gym to shower. She remembered loving his intense sweat smell, the damp of his shirt. But after that dinner with his family she broke up with him, saying she needed more time to study. It was a good excuse: it was junior year, everyone was working like crazy. No one had to know the truth, which was that it made her too nervous, the threat of being found out.

It was after one a.m. She decided that when she got back to the kitchen she'd excuse herself to Mrs. Mitchell, call a taxi, and just eat the fare, thirty bucks, forty, whatever it would be. Alejandro she would deal with later.

But when she returned she found not just Mrs. Mitchell but also Alejandro and a short, stocky white man with thick eyeglasses, standing there in blue pajamas and a bathrobe, looking recently awoken and very disgruntled. Someone had turned on the room lights, and it was bright now, almost like a stage set.

"Dees ees her, dees ees Carolee," Alejandro said, diving back into the accent. He came and put his hand behind her elbow. "You OK, lady? You wanna sit down?"

She glared at him. "I'm fine. I need to get home, I'm going to call a taxi."

"No, no. *Mi padre* is gonna help you."

"Now listen—" the man said, casting a furious look at Alejandro's mom.

" 'My father,' " Mrs. Mitchell said.

"My father," Alejandro said, switching now to the low, robotic tone of an automated phone system. "My father. Is going. To help you."

His father was going to help her. His father was going to help her because . . . he was a doctor. *You're a doctor now?* she'd said to Alejandro, mocking him. Would she have believed him if he'd said, *No, but my dad is*? He'd set her up, brought her here to expose her prejudice. Her assumptions. He was showing her.

Or was he? She looked at the three of them, Alejandro and his beautiful Latina mother and his angry white father. She didn't think so. She didn't know what he was up to, but his eyes were brighter, his stance was straighter, his whole being was focused in a way she'd never seen before.

"I'm going to call a taxi," she said. "What's the address here?"

"*Chica,* no," he cried. "I ain't lettin' you pay for no taxi. You the boss lady."

"That's *enough,*" his dad said.

But Alejandro ignored him and headed off toward the dark end of the kitchen, leaving the three of them just standing there. His dad gave his mom a furious glare, and, as if in response, she turned from him and called to Alejandro, "What are you looking for? I wish I'd known you were coming, I would have put some Limonata on ice."

Carolee saw a cluster of family photos on a table halfway across the room. They were mostly too far away to see clearly, except for a large one of a much younger Dr. Mitchell—still with a full head of hair, his face partly masked by a pair of aviator sunglasses—holding a small boy in a swimming pool, both of them lit up with delight, the boy with his arms wrapped tight around the man's neck.

Alejandro came back with two beers. He handed one to Carolee and twisted off the cap of the other, leaning his head back for a long gulp.

"You're drinking," his dad said.

"Believe it or not, I can have a beer."

"Not in this house."

Mrs. Mitchell pulled a tissue from her pocket and dabbed at her eyes. "Robert," she said to her husband. "Please, I am begging."

Dr. Mitchell flushed. Under his eyes were pads of flesh the size of Carolee's baby toes.

Alejandro said, "You always told me I could come to you for help."

Dr. Mitchell turned and walked a few steps away. Watching

from behind, Carolee saw how tense he was, his shoulders rising and then dropping heavily as he exhaled. He turned to her and said, "What's going on?"

"I'm sorry?"

"With your urinary tract. What are you experiencing?"

Heat filled her face as she explained her symptoms. She was furious at Alejandro for putting her through this, but she stayed on her best behavior, voice calm and polite, careful not to give offense. Dr. Mitchell said it sounded like a UTI but she'd need to be tested, and she said, "They're kind of chronic. I'm pretty sure. I don't want to trouble you, I can call my doctor in the morning, that's what I was planning."

"Why don't you write a prescription," Mrs. Mitchell said to her husband. "Sandro can drive her to the twenty-four-hour Walgreens, everyone is happy."

"Uh-uh," Alejandro said quickly, shaking his head. "Papi don't work like that. He got principles, he need to give her a pee-pee test first."

The room went so silent Carolee could hear a clock ticking somewhere, and outside, in a backyard she knew would be vast, some small night animal passing with a rustle of disturbed branches through a shrub.

Dr. and Mrs. Mitchell remained mute, staring at each other with what Carolee took to be easily revived hatred.

"*Es complicado,*" Alejandro said happily.

They rode in Dr. Mitchell's Mercedes, Carolee and Alejandro both in the backseat like kids. The streets were dark and deserted. Dr. Mitchell drove with his hands at exactly ten and two o'clock. Alejandro was quiet, and out of the corner of her eye Carolee saw him picking at his cuticles. Saying goodbye to his mom, he had bowed his head and let her kiss him over and over again.

Dr. Mitchell's office was in Palo Alto, in a medical complex about four blocks from where David Connell's family had lived—maybe still lived. Carolee had no idea what had happened to him, besides the obvious. Everyone had gone to college except her.

It used to bug her, but it didn't anymore. Growing up, she'd always thought she'd go to college, and her mom sure thought it: Carolee was going to make her proud, reverse the family history by *not* getting pregnant in high school, *not* dropping out before graduation, *not* getting married and divorced in just eleven months. Carolee was going to go to college and maybe even graduate school . . . but she broke her arm at the first volleyball game of her senior year, and after that everything went to shit. She had a cast over her elbow, so she couldn't do her homework, couldn't write her applications, couldn't work the cash register at her job, and when spring came and everyone else was figuring out where they were heading for the next great thing, she had nowhere to go and no money to get there. The first year or two were hardest—she tried community college classes, hopped from one bad job to another, found some other losers to hang out with until she realized two of the guys were dealing meth—but things fell into place after that. Her mom said there was no shame in scaling back your plans, and most of the time Carolee believed her. Or tried to.

At the exterior door Dr. Mitchell flipped through the keys on his ring, and she shivered as she waited. He looked over at Alejandro. "Your friend is cold. Where are your manners?"

Alejandro looked as if he'd been struck, the sting of surprise making him go still for a moment. He shrugged off his peacoat and handed it to her, and though she didn't want it—a rough wool thing with chipped plastic buttons—she draped it over her shoulders and avoided looking at either of them.

Inside, Dr. Mitchell led the way up a flight of stairs made of pebbled driveway concrete. He unlocked his suite and began flipping light switches, first in a small waiting room, then in an open area with a reception desk and file cabinets and a long counter with computers, and finally in his office, with its fancy furniture and large framed picture of Mrs. Mitchell on the wall, a beautiful twenty-five or thirty years old, with perfect golden skin and masses of black hair, but sad eyes, even then.

He came back into the open area and stopped abruptly. Looking hard at Carolee, he said, "He hasn't been to see his mother in a month. Did you know that? A month!" He stared for a long moment and then headed down a corridor and unlocked another door.

Alejandro shrugged, a kind of exaggerated, helpless, what-are-you-going-to-do? shrug, and she shrugged back. A moment later, his dad returned carrying a cup sealed in a plastic bag and a little foil envelope that looked like a condom. "Come on, genius," he said to Alejandro. "Show her the bathroom."

The toilet was the handicapped kind, extra high, and there was a huge bottle of pink soap mounted to the wall. When she was finished she had to hand the cup to Dr. Mitchell and watch as he carried it away.

At the reception desk, Alejandro had taken a seat and was eating foil-wrapped chocolates from a glass bowl, unwrapping them and popping them into his mouth one after another. She leaned against the wall and closed her eyes. She thought of the way his mom had leapt from her chair when he first appeared, and she wondered if Mrs. Mitchell sat there every night, in the same spot, waiting for him. Carolee's mom sort of did that, but with her it was a ratty mustard velour couch and a box of wine. Classy, the last guy Carolee dated had said when they stopped by one evening. Then: Hey, I'm only kidding. But whatever, he was pretty much of an asshole, and she dumped him a week or two later. Which had its benefits, since not having sex meant a lot fewer UTIs. How she'd gotten this one, she didn't know. It was her dead car. Or maybe it started with the UTI and the dead car followed from that.

"*Chica,*" Alejandro whispered. His phone was in his palm; she was half aware he'd been texting someone.

"What."

"You wanna go by the mall after? The guys are still there."

She stared at him, Alejandro with his hair in his eyes, his shoulders swamped by a baggy black T-shirt. He looked clueless: ready to forget the last two hours and power on.

She said, "Are you serious?"

His eyes widened. "I thought you were interested. You can play, Gordo has an extra gun."

"Do you not understand how mad I am? You don't just kid-nap people."

He sighed and looked away. "I know." He reached into the bowl of chocolates and fingered through them as if there were a particular one he wanted to find. "I didn't think you'd go if I told you."

"You were right about that. You should keep your family shit to yourself."

"What? I wanted to help you."

"Right, and crawling up your dad's ass was just—a side thing."

He pushed his hair away from his face and seemed even younger, his mustache a series of faint lines made with a tiny paintbrush. "It ain't a big deal. He just don't like how I live."

"Alejandro, stop talking like that! You blew your cover, how dumb do you think I am?"

His face colored. "Not as dumb as me."

"How dumb are you?"

"Pretty fuckin' dumb."

"Well, that's one true thing you've said. What's with the cholo act, anyway?"

He kept his eyes on her for another moment and then looked away again. She wanted to walk out of there. She could hear his father pulling open a drawer, sliding stuff around like he was searching for something, trying to help her . . . and still, she was tempted to walk out right now.

Alejandro Chavez. Alejandro Chavez who was really Alejandro Mitchell, rich and only half white, which meant an extra advantage because you got to check a minority box on ethnicity questionnaires. He'd had everything, and where had he ended up? Working a shit job, driving a shit car, playing war games late at night in a shit shopping mall. What a waste.

She heard a sniff and looked up. He was staring down at the desk, eyes wide like he was trying to keep tears from falling. She said, "Oh, come on."

He shook his head and cupped his hands over his eyes.

"What?"

He bowed his head farther and pressed his palms to his face. His shoulders began to shake, and she realized he wasn't faking. She hurried across the room and crouched next to him.

"Alejandro, please."

He shook his head.

"Your dad'll be out here any second. What's wrong, what's the matter?"

"Nothing."

"Something is."

He looked up with his eyes streaming. "I fuckin' *hate* him."

She tried to think of something to say, but somehow she was remembering David Connell again, that weird dinner with his family, and how his older sister was there, visiting from wherever she was in school, so there were too many of them to sit at the kitchen table and they had to eat in the dining room, with its heavy velvet chairs. Maybe because of the atmosphere, the talk was slow and painful, with each topic squeezed dry before anyone was willing to let it go. Near the end of the meal, David started saying he should take Carolee home, it was getting late, and suddenly his dad stood up, pulled his keys from his pocket, and tossed them to David, saying, "Take my car if you want—it's roomier." Thinking back, Carolee had a total blank in her mind about what happened next, how the goodbyes went, which car they took, any of it. What his dad said, though: that she remembered. Maybe that was why she'd broken up with David—not the wealth itself but the way his dad more or less offered her up to him, like she was some random trinket he'd acquired somewhere, a little more of the plenty he used to prove what a good father he was.

Carolee looked at Alejandro. "Of course you hate him—he's a dick."

Alejandro stared at her.

"What?" she said.

He pulled up the neck of his T-shirt and wiped his eyes. "Did you just call my pops a dick?"

"He isn't one?"

"Say it again."

"Dick."

"Say 'Your dad is a dick.' "

From the end of the hallway came the sound of water running and the lid of a hinged wastepaper basket swinging up. Alejandro grabbed his phone; Carolee jumped to her feet and moved away from the desk.

His dad appeared, heading past the reception area toward his office. "What are you doing?" he said to Alejandro over his shoulder. "You can't sit there."

She had an infection—but she already knew that. She had an

infection but she was in luck because he had an antibiotic in his office, and he gave her six tablets in a blister pack, to be taken twice a day for three days. "Don't stop just because you feel better," he said gruffly, and she thought, I know, I'm not stupid, and then felt a tremendous pity for Alejandro, to be this man's son.

They retraced their steps, down the pebbled stairway, through the lobby, out to the car.

Dr. Mitchell said, "Where do you live?"

Alejandro waved him off. "I can take her."

"Where," Dr. Mitchell repeated. "Do you live."

He drove out to the freeway, past David Connell's street, through a neighborhood of large old houses where she'd been to parties when she was younger—children's birthday parties with petting zoos brought in for entertainment, sweet sixteen parties with special themes: *Carnaval!* Hollywood in the thirties! She always had her mom drop her off a block away, so no one would see their car.

In the Mercedes they sped south, the heater blowing, no one saying a word. Her exit came up, and she directed Dr. Mitchell to her apartment. He didn't even turn around when she said thank you. "See you at work," she told Alejandro.

She was on the sidewalk when Dr. Mitchell powered down the passenger window. He leaned across and spoke to her. "Excuse my son. He should be seeing you in."

Fury rose up in her, and she said, "Actually, he's being polite. He's being a gentleman, pretending we aren't fucking. Come on, babe, you're coming in with me, aren't you?"

Dr. Mitchell's eyes widened ever so slightly.

Alejandro got out of the car, grinned uncertainly, shut the door behind him. He came and stood in front of her. "Are we making out?" he whispered.

She rolled her eyes at him and then took each of his forearms and pulled them around her. At the curb the Mercedes idled, and she pulled Alejandro closer and waited, willing the car to leave. She wanted to keep hating him—Dr. Mitchell—but it was fading, and she found herself thinking that they all, all three of them, knew one thing: that wanting to be gone was one thing, but going was another.

For SJH

Dwell Time

· · · ·

He was late, which wasn't like him. Laura kept her eye on the clock as she moved around the kitchen, unpacking groceries, starting dinner. Her first husband had been late all the time, and early on with Matt she had arrived at restaurants and been amazed to see him there ahead of her; had even been taken by surprise, still choosing her outfit, when he showed up at her front door at precisely the time he'd said he would. He joked that she had the divorce equivalent of PTSD and needed cognitive restructuring. "Am I Adam?" he would say. "No. So there's no reason to think I'll behave like Adam."

It was forty-five minutes now—only forty-five minutes, but still. She looked at the face of her cell phone to make sure she hadn't missed a call, then tried calling him again for good measure. There would be an explanation: an unavoidable delay combined with a cell phone breakdown. "I'd've stopped at a pay phone," he might say, "but I couldn't find one. What ever happened to pay phones?"

It was a Monday, which meant tonight it was just the two of them and her girls—his kids were with their mother. Laura was making enchiladas, a good compromise in the complicated culinary calculus of this family: simple enough that she wouldn't feel she was making nicer meals for her kids than for his, but also sure to please them, or at least Charlotte, who in all foods preferred things folded or rolled to things lying flat on a plate.

Once the baking dish was in the oven she made her way upstairs. Charlotte was in her room, and Trina wasn't due for another five or ten minutes. Laura wandered into the master bedroom, took off her shoes, and looked at the bed. Neither she nor Matt had bothered with it this morning, and the bedclothes were invitingly messy, coaxing her to lie down for five minutes. But no, she was too jittery—she'd be up again in thirty seconds. Where was he?

"Mom?" Charlotte called from behind her closed door.

Laura went back to the hallway. "Yes?"

The door opened, and Charlotte poked her head out, her waist-length hair in a different style from the one she'd worn not an hour earlier: her waves straightened by the plug-in hair iron she'd requested for Christmas, her part moved from the side of her head to the center. She was thirteen, newly involved with the mirror. "What?" she said to Laura, running her hand down the smooth length of her hair.

"What what?" Laura said. "Didn't you call me?"

Charlotte stared for another moment, a dreamy expression on her face, and then shrugged and closed the door.

Back in the kitchen, Laura checked the landline again: still no messages. She called his office again and again got his voice mail. She heard a car in the driveway and hurried to the window, but it was just Trina, being dropped off; she watched as Trina climbed out and went to the trunk for her backpack. This house was in the middle of nowhere, five miles from downtown Auburn, near the end of a long road bounded on both sides by orchards. It was a nice house, and it had made far more sense for Laura and the girls to come here than it would have for Matt and his three kids to cram into her little post-divorce cottage, but there were times—like now, as she peered into the darkness—when she wished she'd pushed for a new place for the new big bunch of them. Somewhere with neighbors. Somewhere in town.

Trina came in, dumped her things on the kitchen floor, and shrugged her bomber jacket on top of them. "I'm starving," she said as she opened the pantry door. Over her tiny, barely developed frame she was wearing an even tinier black T-shirt. She was fifteen, but in her tight top and heavy makeup she looked like a ten-year-old who wanted to pass for twenty-one. Hand in a bag of potato chips, she turned to Laura and said, "I need better eyeliner."

"Hello to you, too."

"Mom, I'm serious. You buy department store stuff for yourself and Walgreens crap for me. It's like, do you *want* me to look like a ho?" Sometimes she waited for a response, but tonight she just headed off, calling, "Where's Matt, anyway?" as she disappeared.

"I don't know," Laura said. She was alone in the kitchen, neither child within hearing distance. She said, "I don't know, I don't know, *I don't know.*"

The room smelled of tomato and melted cheese. She turned off the oven and cracked the door. Maybe he'd gone for a drive (he wouldn't do that) and his new Jeep had broken down (it was three months old) and he was out of cell phone range and couldn't call.

Had he mentioned an evening meeting? She knew he hadn't. She'd spoken to him in the middle of the afternoon as she sat waiting in her car for Charlotte, nothing to do but call and bother him.

"You're not bothering me," he said. "I'm glad you called,

actually. I've been trying to remember, I know you'll know this: Who was that guy in that movie, you know, the one about the people, who lived in the place—"

"Stop," she said with a laugh. "I'm not that bad."

And they said bye, see you at home, and now he was over an hour and a half late.

I ran into an old friend and we got to talking. I lost track of time . . .

He didn't, ever. So, an accident: she pictured smashed front ends, engine fires, holes in the guardrail. She imagined a fire truck pulled over at the side of the road, firefighters walking up and down in their black coats, draping blankets over the dead.

To stop herself she summoned the girls. At the table she talked so she wouldn't seem worried, then fell into silence as they barely picked at their food.

Trina laid down her fork with a clank. "These enchiladas are disgusting. They're soupy."

"I think they're good," Charlotte said. "But I'm not really hungry."

"Why," Trina said, "do we always have to have Mexican? I don't even like it."

"You don't?" Laura said.

"No."

Charlotte put her napkin next to her plate. "You like fish tacos."

Trina made a face at Charlotte and carried her plate to the sink. Laura watched as she stood there, her back to the room, shoulder blades like little fins. She wheeled around and said, "I think it's rude that he hasn't called you."

"Maybe his phone died," Laura said.

"Then he should borrow one," Trina said. "Duh."

Charlotte cleared her plate, and both girls went to do homework. Laura scraped their uneaten enchiladas into the garbage. Matt didn't like it that she let them complain about her cooking, but what was she supposed to do, say they had to like everything? He was a stricter parent than she in just about every way. His kids had firm bedtimes, and so now hers did, too, fairness being the number one rule in every self-help book about stepfamilies and blending. "Blending?" Trina had said. "What are we, ingredients?" But it was an apt enough metaphor. And a tough enough task. Two adults, five children, and twenty-one relationships. A few days before the wedding—ten months ago now, they were coming up on their first anniversary—he had said out of the blue that of Laura's two he thought the marriage and all it entailed would be harder on Charlotte. She'd adored him for that. Not because he was right—though she believed he was—but because he had thought about it. He was such a funny combination: orderly, precise, even a little controlling about certain things . . . but also remarkably intuitive.

By nine-thirty dread had invaded her body. She went upstairs and waited while Charlotte brushed her teeth, then she turned off the light and sat on the edge of Charlotte's bed.

"Mom?"

"Hmmm?"

"Do you think he went out for barbecue?"

Charlotte was referring to a conversation they'd all had a week or so ago—Matt, Laura, and all five kids—when Matt said he'd been craving hickory-smoked ribs, pulled pork sandwiches, mashed yams.

Laura kissed Charlotte's forehead and pulled the blanket to her chin. "Maybe so."

In the master bedroom, heart pounding, she called his partners at Sierra Mountain and Gravel, but they were both so concerned that she ended up trying to reassure them. Next she tried the company secretary, who said he hadn't mentioned anything out of the ordinary. His cousin Frank—his closest friend—didn't answer.

She went into the bathroom and looked in the mirror. There were bits of dried spit at the corners of her mouth, and her pulse was wild. She turned on the shower and tried to cry, but she was too terrified.

Early on, she'd told him in passing that it was scary dating him. Puzzled, he asked why, and she said: "Because I like you." She had by then lost Adam, lost their family life, and she lost the girls every few days to the inexorable tides of joint custody. Matt was toned and fit, but he was well over fifty: behind the thick ropes of his triceps, over his sculpted pecs, his skin was soft and starting to droop. He took cholesterol-lowering drugs and would probably have knee surgery in the next few years. Now, standing in the bathroom, she imagined that tender body of his, that body she loved: bleeding by the side of the road somewhere. She wanted to fling herself on it, shield it from harm.

Downstairs, she found Trina on the family room couch, binders and books open all around her. She'd gotten her hair cut very short just before the wedding, but it was growing out, and she'd pulled it into stubby pigtails.

Laura stood there for a moment and then went to the kitchen for her purse. When she came back, Trina was on her feet, hands planted on her slender hips. "Have you called Kevin?"

Kevin was Matt's son, his oldest. Laura shook her head. "I don't want to worry them."

"Yeah, but what if Matt called them?"

"I'm going to drive around a little. Obviously if he calls or comes home, call my cell."

The night was freezing, the moon little more than a sliver in the blue-black sky. There were clouds in the east, in the direction of the mountains. She climbed into her car and started the engine, shivering a little as she waited for it to warm up. Sometimes, after work, he went running at the regional park, but never without telling her beforehand. Still, that's where she went first, eyes scanning the parking area before she turned around and headed toward town, with a detour past the company on the off chance he was still there. The parking lot was empty, though, the office dark. Out back, great mounds of rock lay in the moonlight like giant, slumbering animals.

She made her way to 49 and headed south, slowing as she passed the parking lots of shopping centers that were just closing for the night. She crossed the Interstate and drove around Old Town and downtown, then headed for the high school, where on spring nights he sometimes took Kevin to do sprints on the football field. At last she drove to his ex-wife's house, aware she'd been saving it for last but still surprised by the relief she felt when she saw the two cars parked outside, Kevin's and his mother's, and no others. She hadn't really thought he'd be there, had she?

She turned around and headed home. Something was terribly, horribly wrong. Was he lying in a ditch somewhere? Trapped in such terrible wreckage that the Jaws of Life couldn't get him out? She was so panicked that when she finally turned off the main road, she braked and rolled down the window and gulped at the cold air. Then she imagined arriving home and pulling up behind a police car, and she flew the last two miles, the picture insistent: the black-and-white parked in Matt's parking place, its blue light swirling, the front door of the house open as Trina faced the officers.

It wasn't until she reached the turnoff for the driveway that she got ahold of herself. Why a police car if she was going to make things up? Why not Matt's car? She drove the quarter-mile of the driveway at a reasonable twenty-five miles per hour, convinced in some small part of her mind that her behavior during these seconds would determine what she would find, that only slow, moderate driving would give her Matt. At the very end of the driveway there was a sharp turn to the right, and she sucked in her breath, then sighed hard when she saw the empty parking area. She felt dizzy and rested her forehead in her hand before going into the house.

Trina was in the kitchen, holding a jar of peanut butter and a spoon. She looked up as Laura came in, and her face fell. "It's worse now!" she said. "Why is it worse now?"

Laura was too tired to reassure her. "Because before, even though we told ourselves he wasn't just hanging out somewhere nearby, we secretly believed he was. Hoped he was. And now it seems he wasn't, and we have no idea what's going on."

"Well, I watched the news," Trina cried, "and it's supposed to snow." She tossed the spoon into the sink and left the room.

Laura retrieved the spoon and put it in the dishwasher. If his car had broken down somewhere and it started to snow . . . She pictured him walking in a blizzard, snow pummeling his head and shoulders. He was resourceful, though: he had a collapsible shovel in the cargo area of his car, a package of flares, a down sleeping bag. Snow he could handle. Snow was such a familiar adversary that when Kevin turned sixteen and got his mom's old Camry, Matt outfitted that trunk, too, even though Kevin wasn't allowed to drive into the mountains alone yet. "He's a kid," Matt said. "Who loves skiing fresh powder. You do everything you can to keep them safe, and then you do a little more."

Her husband took a powder. Wasn't that an expression? He took a powder, took off, disappeared.

Laura picked up the phone and called the hospital. She called the highway patrol and waited while they typed Matt's name into their database. She called the sheriff and was told they could send someone out to take a report, but she might want to give it a little more time.

She went upstairs and lay on the bed. If he were at all sentient, he would have called her. And so clearly he wasn't . . . or he couldn't. Maybe it wasn't a car accident. Maybe he'd been robbed and tied up somewhere. Robbed and shot. Someone coming up behind him at the ATM, pressing a gun into the center of his back. She ran into the bathroom, ready to vomit, but the feeling passed. This time she didn't look in the mirror.

Finally, near two, she changed into pajamas and took a sleeping pill. But what if he called, and she was out so deeply she didn't hear the phone? She went downstairs, found both of the household's cordless phones in case one wasn't working, and brought them to bed with her, sliding Matt's pillow out of the way and laying them, along with her cell phone, in its place.

The first time she ever saw him was in a 7-Eleven, late on a weekday night. This was about a year after her separation. There was a guy in her way, a big guy wearing a tan windbreaker and pre-faded blue jeans that somehow accentuated his height. He was 6'4", 6'5"—exceptionally tall, with a thick chest and close-trimmed snow white hair. He was standing right where she needed to be, and she couldn't move or say excuse me—she just stood there. Why this paralysis? Love at first sight, he joked when they finally compared notes, but it was fear, not love—or fear-plus-its-opposite, fear plus an incongruous feeling of calm. His height, his posture, his *competence:* he was in command, he was going to terrorize her or save her, it didn't matter what she did. This was an embarrassing reaction, piddly and womanish, and she didn't tell him about it until they'd been sleeping together for months and there were ways in which she was in command of him.

Coffee filters—they were both buying coffee filters. "Not only did I let myself run out," he said a little later, the two of them finished paying and standing in the dark parking lot, each holding a flimsy plastic bag—"Not only did I let myself run out, I let it happen twice." He explained that in order never to wake up in the morning and discover he had no coffee filters, he habitually maintained two boxes at a time, a main one and a backup one. "My rule for myself is, when I move the backup filters into the main filter position, I'm supposed to buy a new box to take over the backup function. What am I going to do now, add a backup for the backup?" He grinned, and she was charmed. She liked how crowded his teeth were. His hair was so short she could see the skin above his ears.

She hadn't been on a date since the separation. Just a week or two earlier, Trina had surprised her as she was clicking through Match.com. "Mom," Trina cried, all priggish preteen though she was already in seventh grade. "Gross."

Of course it was for coffee that they first got together. At Dwell Time, a café he suggested, a tiny, dark-walled place with the bitter-rich smell of freshly ground beans. "I admit it," he said, pulling out her chair for her, "I'm a coffee geek." He told her about a trip he'd taken, the first summer after his separation—a coffee safari in Kenya. Wildebeest by day, espresso by night. The tour group went to three small-harvest farms, and now he was a convert to single-source coffee and a fair trade buyer whenever possible. Laura couldn't get her mind around a man who looked like a marine but would fit in perfectly in Berkeley.

She'd met Adam in Berkeley—at Berkeley, where they were both students—and she told Matt about this as the sun moved higher in the café window. It was 1985, Reagan had just been reelected, and she and Adam spent their first few evenings together talking about what a bubble the Bay Area was. They fell in love and got married and stayed on, happy in the bubble, until Laura finished her PhD in education and was encouraged to apply for a newly created position with the Auburn Union School District. "Why not?" Adam had said. "Let's give the real world a try." Now the poor guy was stuck in the boonies at least until Charlotte was grown, all because his ex-wife had gotten a good job offer once upon a time.

"Wait a sec," Matt said in response to this, and she remembered, too late, that he was a Sierra Foothills native, born in Grass Valley and an Auburn resident since high school. The "boonies" comment wasn't why he stopped her, though. He said, "It sounds like you feel guilty," and she sat back in her chair and studied him more closely: this man who looked like a marine and understood feelings.

They talked on, and the friendly feeling at the battered café table turned into curiosity, excitement. They were from similar families (both with the distant father, the passive/hysterical mother). They'd had similar marriages (instead of tenderness, resentment; instead of passion, apathy; it was better to be alone, they agreed, than to live like that). And as far as their kids went— nothing was more important. Dating, they said, eyes averted, would always come second.

This was a Saturday in late spring; out the window of the café, forsythia was in flashy yellow bloom, and flocks of birds flew north again. His shirtsleeves were rolled to just below his elbows, and his forearms were covered with white or maybe blond hair. She longed to put her hand on his arm, to feel the fine, silky fur over the sinewy muscle.

In the morning it was thirty-five degrees out. The sky was the color of concrete. She left a note for him on the front door, just in case, then took the girls to school and drove to the police station. Her heart rate, her skin, her stomach—everything was off. She was sick.

A uniformed young man asked her a series of questions and then handed her a form to fill out.

"So now what happens?" she said when she was finished.

"We'll enter your information into the national database."

"And?"

He hesitated, putting the form on the counter and smoothing it out. "We can't really go looking for an adult, ma'am." He blushed and brought his finger to his mouth, holding it sideways over his upper lip for a long moment. He looked her in the eye. "Was everything OK at home?"

"He didn't run away," she said. "He's either hurt or in trouble. Or dead."

"In trouble."

"I don't know! I was hoping the police might help me figure it out!"

She went to work and somehow made it through the morning. The parents she saw were themselves so worried—Laura did educational testing, evaluating kids with possible learning issues—that she kept a grip on herself, which meant feeling stricken but keeping the bloody highway movie at bay, though she could feel it there, waiting.

At lunchtime she had half an hour free. She called the highway patrol again and then every hospital within a hundred miles. With her twelve-thirty already in the waiting room, she tried his ex-wife's cell phone, leaving a message requesting a call back "at your earliest convenience." Such an awkward phrase. It made her think of a line from Dickinson: "After great pain, a formal feeling comes." Also during. She'd been vague enough that it might be late afternoon before Sandi called back, but that would just have to be OK. Laura was one of the people who might call Sandi if a child of hers were hurt, and she didn't want Sandi to worry about that for a single minute.

Two more hours, and she was finished for the day. She locked up and started across the parking lot. Something brushed her head, and a snowflake hit the bridge of her nose. She looked up, and the sky had gone yellow. In a moment the flakes fell fast.

All five kids were due tonight. Matt was supposed to pick up both his girls from school, and if Sandi didn't call soon, Laura was going to have to plan something fast. She drove to the high school, where kids were just coming out and discovering the snow: twirling with their arms outspread, sticking out their tongues to catch a flake or two. She found Kevin's car in the parking lot and pulled in next to it.

A sharp knocking startled her a little later; she'd drifted off. Kevin stood beside the car, a tiny furrow in his forehead. Embarrassed, she tried to roll down the window, but the button wouldn't work. She started the car and tried again.

"What are you doing here?" he said.

"Kevin." It had gotten colder; she felt it on her face. Her windshield was dusted with snow. She opened the door and stepped out next to him. "Kevin," she said again. "Did you talk to your dad last night?"

Alarm on his face. "Why?"

"He never came home. I don't know where he is."

Kevin's face filled with color. His mouth twisted into a lopsided grimace and his eyes went glassy.

"Don't worry," she said. "I'm sure there's some explanation, I'm sure he's OK."

Kevin turned and pounded the roof of his car, and she reached for his arm, opening her sleeve to the falling snow. He shook her away.

"Kevin, it's OK. I've called tons of hospitals, I don't think he's hurt."

"Of course he's not hurt," Kevin said, turning back. His dark hair hung straight and stringy beside his face, and his forehead was an unnatural white.

"What do you mean?"

"He left."

"Left . . ."

"You," Kevin said. "Us. Didn't he even warn you? That's what he does."

. . .

He had a history, it turned out. Matt. Of leaving, going AWOL—
he'd done it three times during his marriage to Sandi. He took off
without a word, was gone for several days, and then came back as
abruptly as he'd disappeared. Laura heard about it from Kevin and
then again, later in the afternoon, from Sandi herself. Sandi was
terse, descriptive. Her voice a careful monotone.

She had plans for the evening, and Laura insisted she'd take
the kids as scheduled. She figured they could distract each other,
the two sets of kids, but when she told her girls she still didn't
know where Matt was, they asked if they could stay at their dad's.
She pulled some dinner together for herself and Matt's kids, and it
wasn't until they'd finally dispersed for homework that she could
collapse on the family room couch to try to figure out how this
could have happened.

Because he wouldn't do this. *He wouldn't do it!* Every morning,
he counted out vitamins and calcium and glucosamine chon-
droitin for her joints and left them in a little dish by her coffee.
Was that someone who would run away? In bed, he liked her to
put her palm on his bare chest and just hold it there, flat and still.
Was that someone who would run away?

She was enraged—at Matt but also at herself, for being so
wrong about him. She'd been in too much of a hurry to bother
finding out who he really was—or in too much of a lie, to herself,
about how you could step out of one broken vehicle and into
another and expect it to run smoothly.

"The worst thing about me," she said to him one rainy afternoon, maybe eight months after they met, "is that I don't say
when something's bothering me until it's really bothering me,
and then I cry. It's not pretty." He said, "I kind of do that, too—
but with me it's more, I give people the silent treatment." He
didn't say: I walk out on people. He didn't say: I scare people to
death.

She had been scared to death. Now she was mortified.

She thought there ought to be a hint, something from the last few days to suggest, at least in retrospect, that he was unhappy—but she couldn't come up with a thing. They'd had the weekend to themselves, both sets of kids gone. They made love Sunday morning with the bedroom door wide open. She remembered looking at him afterward: the white stubble on his jaw, his wrinkly earlobes, the creases in his neck. He looked his age, and she liked that.

He'd never given her the silent treatment, never given her any indication that he was anything but content. He was quiet sometimes in the evening, but she thought he was tired. Or, very occasionally, angry about the war. In fact, the only times she'd heard him raise his voice had to do with the war. A couple of weeks ago there was a thing on TV about the army's policy of forbidding the media from filming the flag-covered coffins of the dead coming home from Iraq, and he spoke out with great heat, with fire. It was a *travesty,* he said, a *disgrace,* and then he didn't say anything for quite a while.

But it wasn't the silent treatment. And mostly they talked a lot. Way more than she and Adam had. How could he have left? What had she done? "You're not bothering me," he'd said on the phone yesterday afternoon, but obviously she was. In how many different ways?

She tried calling his cousin Frank again, and this time he answered. "Oh God, no," he said once she'd told him. "He didn't. He didn't."

"You knew? That he did this? You should have told me."

"I told *him* to tell you. He said it wasn't going to happen with you." Frank was silent for a moment and then said, "He loves you, Laura. A lot. He's happier with you than he's ever been in his life."

She didn't know how to respond. Frank was right—Matt told her this all the time. And yet . . .

"*What* happens?" she said. "What *happens*?" And Frank told her what he knew about how it was for Matt, how this feeling of restlessness built until he felt he had to leave. He had to leave, he had to leave, he *had to get out of there.* The first time, he drove north, putting miles and more miles between himself and home, and it was exhilarating at first: the freedom, the wind, the road, the radio—the components of bliss. But after several hours he began to feel bad. He drove for three days, feeling worse and worse but unable to turn around or even stop and call.

"And when he got back?" Laura said. "Sandi didn't make him promise he wouldn't do it again?"

"Of course she did. So the second time was worse."

"Worse how? Worse for whom?"

"Well, I meant Matt. He felt awful."

"Poor fellow." She stood up and began walking. She paced to the foot of the staircase and back to the couch. "And the third time?"

"The third time he didn't seem to care much. He called me from a motel and told me about a hawk he saw flying over the desert."

"He called *you*? Has he called you this time?"

"Hell, no—he'd be way too ashamed to call. Listen, Laura, try to put it in perspective. I mean, it's lousy, I know that. But he's a good guy. Everyone has something."

She laughed, bitterly to her own ears. After they said good-bye she sat down again and stared into the empty fireplace. Matt's fireplace, just as it was Matt's house. She'd brought her dining room chairs, some rugs, the girls' beds and some odds and ends, but it was still his house, and she was a guest. A figure in a drama. A woman in a Hitchcock movie: walking blithely in the direction of some terrible woe while the audience watches and thinks: No! Stop! Frank was the audience. Sandi was—Sandi and Matt's kids. *They* should have told her. Had any of them been tempted? Suddenly a terrible idea occurred to her: maybe he'd married her so he'd never have the chance to leave his kids—to leave *only* his kids—so there'd always be a woman he'd be leaving first and foremost, and the injury to the kids would be inadvertent, secondary.

This was creeping paranoia, almost pleasurable. You could lie down in it and never get up. He had married her because he loved her. She was sure of that.

And: *He said it wasn't going to happen with you.* He had thought it would be different with her, that he'd be different. This almost made her feel sorry for him, but it was also arrogant. He could be a little arrogant, though in good times she thought of it as confident. Of a golf game he had scheduled: "I know I'll win. I'm better than all three of those guys." Of their division of household tasks: "I'll vacuum—you probably aren't as thorough as I am." Even emotionally he was a little arrogant. He said it wouldn't be a problem, the fact that Laura had a hard time saying when she was upset. "I'll sense it," he said, "or you'll find a way to tell me. You'll be honest with me. You'll feel safe with me."

What ecstasy it had been, hearing him say those things. It didn't seem like arrogance, it seemed like a dream come true. And he was right: she was more open, closer with him than she'd ever been with Adam. When she and Adam finally went for counseling, the therapist listened to them for twenty minutes and then said, "Do you want to be married? Because you're not married, you're coworkers."

He had to leave. He had to leave, he had to leave, he *had to get out of there.* What did that feel like? Extreme irritation with everyone around him? Or something physical, his skin crawling, his legs heavy with need?

She heard Kevin turning a page in the kitchen, and she went and stood in the doorway. "That first time," she said. "Do you remember how he was before he left?"

Kevin looked up. After a moment he shook his head.

"How about after he came home?"

He shook his head again. He'd been six the first time, a little boy; now he was sixteen. He had an exquisite body, the muscles swelling over the bones. She had read a book about evolutionary psychology that suggested losing a child was most painful when the child was an adolescent or in his early twenties. At peak repro-duction time, in other words. The grief was greatest because this was the moment when the genes should carry forward.

And the loss of a spouse? She was nearing menopause, way past reproduction; her genes had done all the carrying forward they were going to do. Did that account for the emptiness she felt tonight?

Because it was over. She was going to have to leave him. She would never go through this again.

Kevin got up and went to the fridge. He held it open and stood there with his back to her, one arm slung along the top of the door. He came back to the table with the leftover enchiladas from last night.

"You don't want those," she said.

"They look OK." He sawed off a bite and chewed. "I was waiting outside for him," he said, "but when he pulled into the driveway I ran back into the house."

Laura was confused. "Wait, the first time?"

"I just remembered."

"What did his face look like?"

"I ran into the house."

There were footsteps, and in came Carly, the older of the two girls. She was only fourteen, but she was as tall as Laura, with long, twiggy legs and knees that were angular and beautiful. She had her mother's light hair and slightly jutting chin. She was the only one of the five kids who had expressed any resistance about the marriage. She'd written Matt a letter, saying she didn't "expect or want"—those were her words—Matt to break up with Laura; she just thought he should wait a few more years.

She was holding a cell phone, and Laura's heart raced. "Is that him?"

Carly shook her head. "Lizzie got a text. An old one, from yesterday. You know how sometimes you'll get a message, and it'll be like two days late? Like it was in cell phone jail and just got out?" She held out the phone, and Laura took it.

The message said: "Cant make game show em yr stuf xo dad." Sent yesterday at 3:52. Laura had spoken to him from her car at 3:35.

Her cell phone rang in the family room, and she hurried to answer, but it was just the girls, calling from their dad's.

"Trina?" she said, because Trina was the one who always called. "Sweetie, let me call you in a few minutes."

But it was Adam—calling to tell her that Trina needed her math book. The idea of driving to his house and back, fifteen minutes in each direction . . . It was the straw that broke the camel's back, she imagined saying to someone.

Matt, of course.

The book was her responsibility: it was a Tuesday, Trina should've been with her. She was about to say she'd drive it over when Adam said he'd come get it, and her eyes stung, she was so grateful.

She was still holding Lizzie's phone, and she headed upstairs to return it. "Knock, knock," she said outside the closed door of the room Lizzie and Carly shared. "How are you doing in there, Liz?"

No response. She bent down to set the phone on the floor and was just straightening up again when a tiny voice said, "You can come in if you want."

Lizzie was lying on her bed. She was on her stomach, chin propped on her fists, eyes red. At her side lay Bodie, her stuffed giraffe. Bodie was among the things that went back and forth between households; it was a bad evening when Bodie was forgotten.

"Hey, there," Laura said.

Lizzie didn't look at her.

"I brought your phone back. I'm glad you got the text."

"My game was yesterday."

Laura racked her brain. What could she say to help?

"My mom said this would happen," Lizzie added.

Laura looked away. On the bulletin board there was a photo from the wedding, of her and Matt and all five kids; it had been pinned to the board in such a way that the thumbtack went through her face. Once, when the house was empty, she moved the tack to the top edge of the picture, but the next time she looked it had been moved back. In the photo, Lizzie was standing directly in front of Matt, his wrists crossing under her chin, holding her close. On the morning of the wedding, she had made a point of telling Laura that her mom was spending the weekend at a spa. "She's having the biggest splurge of her life," she said. "She's going to spend a thousand dollars." Carly, the objector, had been gruesomely polite. Kevin had given Laura a long hug. Because he was the oldest? A boy? "Because he's Kevin," Matt said. Ever since then Laura had waited in vain for a special bond to develop between her and Matt's son.

She turned back to Lizzie: ten years old, butterfly barrette in her hair. She said, "Your dad loves you a lot."

Lizzie pulled Bodie close and turned her face to the wall.

"Come down if you feel like it," Laura said. "I'd love your company. We could make cookies."

She closed the door behind her and went back downstairs. In the family room she poured herself some wine. How was she supposed to help these children? Maybe she should have let Sandi cancel her plans. "I'm sorry I didn't call you right back," Sandi had said. "It's worst the first time, when you think he's dead."

The first time would be the only time. Laura had sold the cottage where she and the girls lived after the split; now they'd have to move again. Trina would probably figure out this period of life in a therapist's office, but Laura feared Charlotte would bury it and be one of those people who never felt at home anywhere.

You weren't supposed to apologize to your children—that was the conventional wisdom for divorced parents. She couldn't remember why.

A car pulled up in front of the house. She hurried to the door, but it was just Adam, come for the math book. She stood on the porch watching as he turned off the lights and climbed out. Snow still fell, and it was sticking, a layer of white covering the driveway.

He came most of the way up the steps and stopped. He wore a watch cap over his shaggy hair, and his eyes appeared more deep-set than ever, retreating into their sockets.

"Oh, I forgot the book," she said. "Come in and I'll get it. You can warm up for a few minutes."

"Just have to get cold again," he said with a shrug.

She left him on the steps. This was Adam through and through: the resigned martyr. "Hey, I come by it honestly," he used to say. "It's one of the great Jewish positions." Laura had mentioned this to Matt as a way of illustrating Adam's style of humor, but Matt had focused on the content. He said it was no wonder Laura felt guilty—who wouldn't if they lived with a martyr?

And living with a liar, she wanted to ask him now. How does that make people feel?

She had a math book to find. Back up the stairs she went. It looked as if a tornado had hit exactly half of Charlotte and Trina's room. On Trina's side the floor was covered with clothing: inside-out T-shirts, twisted panties, and three pairs of jeans that looked as if someone had just stepped out of them, legs accordioned, waists standing open like giant cans.

The book wasn't immediately visible, and Laura kicked through the debris and then felt down the bed in case Trina'd been doing homework there.

But no, last night Trina had done her homework in the family room; Laura remembered talking to her just before she headed out to look for Matt. She went back down, but the book wasn't on the coffee table, or under it, either. She headed for the kitchen, where Trina had been having a snack when she got home from her search.

Kevin was back at the table studying, and Carly had the paper open to the comics. Laura looked at them, tried to glean their states of mind. It was hard to tell what the older two were feeling: that's what she'd tell Matt. Lizzie was pretty upset.

No. She had to stop.

She said, "Have you guys seen Trina's math book?"

Simultaneously they looked up and shook their heads.

She lifted stacks of newspaper, magazines, her Mexican cookbook, still open to the enchilada recipe. She left the room and went back outside to Adam.

"Look, you should come in. It's taking me a minute to find it."

He looked away from her, tilting his face to the sky.

"I'm sorry. I should've had it waiting for you."

"Did you call her?"

"I will."

"I'll be in the car."

Charlotte answered the phone, and Laura didn't want to rush her, not with life so strange tonight, so she listened to a scene-by-scene summary of a TV show Charlotte had watched before asking for Trina.

"I don't know," Trina said indifferently. "My room. Did you look there?"

Laura snapped the phone closed, ending the call, and then opened it again and called back. "Sorry," she said. "That was my phone, I think. Anyway, listen, yes—I looked in your room and it's not there."

"Well, then I don't know," Trina said.

"No ideas?" Laura said. "Should I just send Dad home?"

"I *need* it."

"Well, then give me a little help here, honey. Where did you last have it?"

There was a silence, and then Trina sobbed, "I had a *terrible day* in case you're interested."

Laura looked at the fireplace. She imagined herself pierced from head to toe, roasting on a spit over a huge, hungry fire. She flopped onto the couch but got up again because she'd sat on something hard. "Never mind," she cried. "I found it, it was on the couch!" It was under a blanket Trina had brought down from her bed. "Let me take it out to Dad. You'll have it in fifteen minutes."

"We were supposed to be with you tonight," Trina said, still sobbing.

"I know, sweetie," Laura said. "I know."

It was only twenty yards, but she put on her coat and gloves before she went outside. She took her time, careful not to slip on the icy steps. The clouds had mostly lifted, and there was a crevice of dark sky straight overhead that would widen by morning, letting the real cold in.

Adam saw her coming and rolled down his window. He took the book and set it on the passenger seat. "What about tomorrow night?" he said; Trina and Charlotte were supposed to be with him. "You can have them if you want."

"I have no idea about tomorrow night. I'm supposed to do things, but I don't know what I'm supposed to do."

"What do you mean?"

"Well, Matt's kids. I've got all three of them in there, and I don't know—" She put her hands over her eyes. "God," she said, and she squatted suddenly, or fell—she wasn't sure what happened. She was still on her feet, but her knees were completely bent. She steadied herself against Adam's car. Her own car was a few feet behind her, and she stayed like that, closeted by metal, her breath visible in the freezing air.

"Let me help you," Adam said. He started to open his door, but it pushed her off balance and he stopped. "Do you want to get in for a second? Just to catch your breath?"

"I don't know if I can stand up." Saying this annoyed her, and she stood, then immediately lowered her face into her hands, she was so dizzy.

"Get in for a sec," he said. "They can wait."

She circled the car and got in. He drove the same Subaru he'd had during their marriage. She remembered deciding to walk home after a counseling session they'd just come from, and how he drove along beside her for a few seconds, crept along beside her, casting looks at her through the open window. Ask me to get in, she thought, ask and I'll get in, but he just looked.

She said, "So I actually have some news, kind of. Information."

When she finished talking, he sat in silence, staring straight ahead. She'd given him the bare bones but for some reason had included the name of each place where Matt finally turned around during his previous disappearances, and as she thought of these again—Vancouver, Arkansas, and Baja—a silly question came to her: Did he bring home souvenirs? She laughed and clapped a hand to her mouth.

"What?" Adam said.

"Nothing. The good news is you shouldn't have to drive out here anymore. Once I find a place."

"You're not going to leave him?"

"Are you kidding? I'm not living with this. I would never go through this again."

"But you won't have to," Adam said. "You'll know."

"I need to go inside, the kids are waiting."

She got out, crossed in front of the car, and started toward the house.

"Laura," he called.

She stopped and looked back.

"The good news is he's alive."

His eyes were on hers, determined but watchful, and she stood there, frozen, until at last he started the car and backed away.

In the house, the smell of popcorn drifted out of the kitchen, and she heard Lizzie's voice along with the other two. Should she join them? Or let them have the time together without her? She wondered what would happen, how it would be to see them once she'd moved out. How would it be for Trina and Charlotte to see them? That would happen all the time: at school, at the movies, down at the Confluence. Worst would be the Confluence, where the two sets of kids had been introduced; it was the spot where the north and middle forks of the American River joined to form one body, and Matt had made a little speech about how it was the perfect place for their first get-together. Laura remembered the friendly, awkward picnic beside the rushing water, and the tense game night a few weeks later, and the surprisingly easy ski weekend some time after that: the early assemblies of their fledgling nation-state. Trina's contempt for Kevin, veiling a crush; Lizzie's insomnia the first few nights she slept under the same roof as Laura. Laura recalled Matt coming home from returning the kids to Sandi after one of those sleepless nights: she was groggy, sitting on the front steps when he drove up. His blue eyes were bloodshot, his face was drawn. This isn't going to work, she was afraid he would say. But he eased himself down next to her and shrugged. "What shall we do," he said, "go back to bed or go for a swim?" It was summer, hot and bright; they could be at Lake Clementine in twenty minutes, moving side by side through the cool, clear water. But she was so tired. She leaned back and stretched. The rest of the day was wide open, and so was the evening, and so was the next day. There was something to be said for the lulls in parenting, each emptying of the house a new season, bringing weather you remembered or perhaps had never known before, it could feel like such a lovely revelation. "Both," she said.

On that first date, at the café Dwell Time, the midday crowds thinned, and soon Laura and Matt were the only people in the place. They had drunk coffee, two cups each, and eaten lunch, and now it was clearly time to go.

"Dwell Time," she said, not wanting to break the spell yet. "Funny name."

"It's the amount of time the water's in contact with the coffee grounds. With some coffeemakers you can adjust it. I have one—there's a switch."

"And you use it?" she said. "More dwell time for certain kinds of coffee?"

He smiled. "Told you I was a geek."

"I wouldn't use that word for you."

His eyes were on her. She wondered if he'd ask what word she would use. That would be the flirtatious thing to do. Don't, she thought. Flirting would be sexy, but she didn't want that. She didn't want only that.

"Well . . ." she said.

He grinned, revealing for the first time a nickel-colored crown toward the back of his mouth. "I couldn't agree more."

They slid their chairs back, looked at each other, stood. He held open the café door and she walked out, into such yellow sunnyness, such warmth that she gasped.

He said, "Are you OK?"

"No, it's just so nice out. It's beautiful. The perfect spring day."

"Would you like to go up to the park? Take a walk? I mean, I know we should go our separate ways now and I should call you tomorrow and ask you to dinner next week, but what do you think? We could drive separately."

"Can we drive together?"

They were at her car, and so it was into her car that they went. She was impressed: he was ten years older than she, almost from another generation—a generation of men who were not comfortable being driven by women.

He slid the seat back to make room for his long legs. "You know what else dwell time is?"

She'd started the car but turned to face him, hand on the gearshift.

"It's how long soldiers have between deployments. By contract they're supposed to have a certain amount of downtime before they can be shipped off again, but not this war. This war they just keep getting screwed."

Laura smiled.

"What?"

"At the 7-Eleven I didn't peg you as a liberal."

"Am I one?"

"Fair trade, antiwar."

"Better get my hair cut."

At the park they strolled past spring flowers, past a play area crawling with small children. She saw young families, couples so new to parenthood that they didn't have any idea of the dangers ahead, the way having kids could split you apart. That had happened with her and Adam. That and other things.

She looked at this man at her side—this Matt. We met in a 7-Eleven, they would say; or the whole thing would dissolve into something that had barely happened, and she might wonder, ten years from now: Wasn't there a man once, in a parking lot, shortly after the divorce? She'd have an image—a man who looked like a marine, a convenience store parking lot—but she might not know if they were actually linked, or if a trick of the brain, a pair of crossed wires, had brought them together by accident.

Matt's kids were in the kitchen and she was upstairs, lying on the bed, still in her coat and gloves. The room was close, warm air rushing up from the vents. She covered her mouth and breathed in, her gloved hand like something inanimate against her skin.

Dwell time. How long would the next one be, the next period at home before he went off to war again?

But no. It seemed home was war. He left for downtime, to rest before returning to battle. Was that how he felt? About marriage? Is that what got into him?

He had to leave, he had to leave, he *had to get out of there*. That wasn't the full story, was it? He had to get out of there, *and* he had to tell no one. You were part of it—your feelings were part of it. Your terror, your confusion.

If she stayed, she wouldn't be afraid next time. Not that she would stay, but if she did: she wouldn't be afraid, she'd be mad. If he were ever late, she'd be angry, automatically. Looking at her watch, adrenaline starting up. A nightmare.

A week was all she'd need to find a new place. She and the girls would start again. They had become a good threesome over the years since the divorce—and she didn't have much time left with them. Maybe she'd even go back to her group, the eight or nine divorced women who met weekly to talk about their new lives, their children, the future. Would you marry a man with diabetes? they asked each other. How about emphysema? No, most of them said. I am through taking care of people. One woman, though—a shy bank teller with tidy dyed blond hair—told Laura privately one evening that she had met someone, a man with a

pacemaker and clammy hands and a habit of cleaning his fingernails in front of her, and she was thinking of marrying him. Just
to have a man, Laura thought, and, as if she had read Laura's mind,
the woman said: It's not to have a man, it's to have a person.

A pacemaker, clammy hands. A habit of running away.
Everyone has something.

Laura sat up and took off her gloves. The curtains were still
drawn in front of the balcony door, and she went over and slid
them to the side. The balcony overlooked the backyard, a half-
acre of groomed lawn that ran all the way to the fence separating
the yard from the hill behind it. She opened the door to see, but
the whole of her view was steeped in darkness.

What if she could be blasé, indifferent? Take away from him
the part of it that wasn't his anyway: her reaction. It was fine, she
could tell him. Feel free, whenever you want. Would that spoil it
for him? Enough to keep him from doing it again?

It would take a great effort to pull it off; she'd have to find
just the right tone. And it would work only if he never found out
how she really felt: the vivid dread, the excavated heart.

She crossed the bedroom and turned off the overhead light.
Behind her, a swath of snowy air blew in through the open door.
She returned to the balcony and stepped outside again. Soon she
could see better, the snowy lawn, the faint trace of fence dividing
it from the snowy hillside. She leaned on the rail.

Matt? she could say if he called right now. Honey, is that
you? Oh, don't worry, never mind that—I have to tell you something. Listen, it snowed, and I'm standing on the balcony, and
you can't imagine how beautiful it is. It's all over the grass, and the
trees are dusted with it, the branches are frosted. And you know
how snow lightens everything? It's almost like daytime out here.
The longer I stand here the lighter it gets. We're so lucky, she
would say to Matt. We're so lucky we live here.

Her Firstborn

. . . . .

Dean goes to the window and stares at the dark parking lot, half looking for Lise though she won't arrive for another ten minutes. It's after six and the lot is all but empty, just white lines glowing with new paint. He wonders what she's doing right now. Finishing a snack? Or already locking up and heading for the car? Or, no: gathering their bed pillows and *then* heading for the car. Tonight is their first childbirth class, and the flyer said to bring pillows. He imagines them piled on her backseat—flowered, lumpy, faintly scented with the deep smells of bodies asleep—and he shudders. It seems wrong somehow, a broken rule of nature: no personal bedding outside the home, please.

She pulls in right on time, her headlights sweeping the wooden fence, and he shuts down his computer and heads out to the reception area, calling goodbye to Gregor as he approaches the elevator.

"Dean, Dean, hold on." Gregor appears in the doorway of his office with a stack of CDs in hand, an amused look on his face. "I just want to give you a little encouragement." *Incurgement* is how it sounds to Dean: Gregor's from West Virginia, which shows up in about a fifth of what he says.

"Thanks," Dean says. "It's nice to know you care."

"I do—in a kindly, avuncular way."

Dean laughs: Gregor is thirty-eight to his forty-one, blond and robust to his dark and stringy. Gregor is about as avuncular as Dennis the Menace.

"Come on," Gregor says, motioning Dean closer. "You want to be prepared, don't you? It's like anatomy class. When Jan and I went the woman had big illustrations and a pointer. She said, 'This is the uterus, these are the fallopian tubes.' "

"That was in Morgantown," Dean says. "This is Eugene, remember? There's practically a *street* named Uterus here."

Gregor laughs, but he's looking Dean over all the same. "Everything OK?" he asks in a carefully blended mixture of concern and nonchalance.

Dean nods.

"Sure?"

"I'm *fine*," Dean says. "Lise's waiting, I've got to go."

He pounds the Down button, then doesn't want to wait for the elevator. The fire stairs are at the other end of the hall, and he takes off at a gentle jog.

"I want a full report tomorrow," Gregor calls. "In exchange for bearing the lion's share of our mutual burden here."

Dean flips the bird over his shoulder, but he's grateful: he and Gregor run a small company that publishes software guides, and this is their busy season, galleys to look over, a tight production schedule to stick to. Gregor'll be here until ten or eleven tonight, easy. "You can't have a baby in the *fall*," he said when Dean gave him the news. He was kidding, but only just.

Outside, Lise's car is idling at the curb. Dean slides in next to her and says, "Sorry, Gregor had to ride me a little."

"Wimmin been birthin' babies a long time, Dean."

"No, it was about how Mickey Mouse the class'll be." He pulls her close for a kiss, then takes her hand from the steering wheel and kisses it, too, on the little valley between her first two knuckles. When she returns her hand to the wheel he notices a tiny oval sticker with the word "Kegel" printed on it, right at twelve o'clock. "Where'd you get that?"

"At my appointment today," she says with a smile. "I got a whole sheet of them—I'm supposed to put them all over the house as reminders."

A Kegel is a toning exercise for pregnant women: it's like stopping your urine midflow, according to one of Lise's books. For a while, Dean found himself trying it nearly every time he peed, just to see how it felt.

"I put one over the kitchen sink," she says, "and one on my bedside table, but I figured that'd be enough."

"Moderation in all things."

"Right."

He reaches for her belly and strokes it. "How was the appointment?"

"Fine, except I've gained *five pounds*. I've got to pace myself."

"Like a marathoner?"

"I've got the carbo-loading part down anyway."

They exchange a smile: Dean's the runner in the family, although he's tapered way down since their marriage. Used to be he wouldn't miss a morning with his group, but these last two years have taught him to question pretty much everything he thought he knew about himself, like that *running* was the only path to well-being. Most mornings now he sleeps in, Lise breathing quietly beside him.

"Everything else OK?" he asks her.

"Yeah, the head's down, I'll have my internal next time probably."

"That it?"

She doesn't reply, and when an odd, faraway expression comes over her face he's suddenly washed with tension, certain he knows what's on her mind. But then she says, "And twenty, and that's a hundred today, and that's *all* I'm doing, damn it," and he lets out a big breath. Kegels. That's what she was doing, just Kegels, not thinking back after all.

The class meets in a church basement, in a room with plastic chairs set up in a circle and the air of having seen a lot of twelve-step programs in its day. Dean and Lise carry their pillows in and take seats opposite the only other couple there yet, the woman tiny and auburn-haired, dwarfed by her belly. Lise's small, too, but her belly is more volleyball-size to this woman's Great Pumpkin.

The woman leans forward eagerly. "How far along are you?"

"Thirty-three weeks," Lise says. "How about you?"

"The same. Looks like forty, though, huh?"

"No, you look fine."

"I look enormous."

Lise shrugs but doesn't disagree. She has a knack for getting along with strangers—not so much cultivating them as keeping her distance in the most amiable possible way. Dean's just the opposite, comes off as an asshole even when he's thinking there might be a friendship in the offing.

"Do you know what you're having?" the woman says.

"We decided not to find out." Lise looks at Dean and gives his leg a pat. At the beginning, thinking it would be easier that way—easier for her—he told her that he wanted to know, but she absolutely didn't and he's grateful now. He likes to think of the baby living its secret life in there, waiting to surprise them.

"How about you?" Lise says.

The woman smiles. "A girl. I was so nervous finding out,

because I really wanted it to be a girl." She shrugs. "I have a friend who's pregnant with her second and she's not finding out, either. Do you have older kids?"

Dean feels his pulse quicken and turns with concern to Lise, but she just shakes her head placidly.

"I guess you wouldn't be here," the woman says absently, and this time Lise doesn't react. They're here for him, of course.

Gradually the room fills, and soon every seat is taken. Dean's certain he and Lise are the oldest, which shouldn't matter but somehow does. The teacher is a tall, blowsy woman with a patch of red high on each cheek. She has an easel and a stack of illustrations but, Gregor will be sorry to hear, no pointer. When the clock over the door says seven, she picks up a piece of chalk and writes three letters on a portable blackboard: "i-n-g."

"I'm Susan," she says. "Welcome to everybody, especially the moms. This class is going to hopefully get you ready for childbirth, and since that's a pretty intimate thing, I'd like us to get to know each other a little. Let's go around the room and say our names and also something you like to do." She points at the letters on the blackboard. "I wrote 'i-n-g' because I want you to tell us something you like *do*-ing." She turns to the woman at her left. "Let's start with you."

The woman blushes. "I'm Patricia, and I guess I like gardening." She looks at her husband, and he nods.

"Yeah, I'm Jim, and I like skiing."

"I'm Stephanie, and I like folk dancing."

"I'm Gary, and I like playing soccer."

Two more people and it'll be Lise's turn. Dean leans close to her. "Can I say that I like be-ing alone?"

She smiles and then takes his hand and places it on her belly, just in time for him to feel the baby move. "I'm Lise," she says a moment later. "It's pronounced Lisa, but it's spelled L-i-s-e." This is something she generally tells people within minutes of meeting them; it was one of the first things Dean ever heard her say. "I like reminding myself I won't be pregnant forever."

The whole class laughs, and Dean says, "Yeah, I'm Dean, and I like the fact that that's true."

The next person starts to talk, and it's only then that Dean realizes he didn't use an i-n-g word. I like fail-ing to follow simple instructions.

Finally it's the last couple's turn. The woman says she likes making jam, and then her husband, a big guy with a florid face and a Hawaiian shirt, says, "She's like this, so you know one thing *I* like doing!"

The class titters, and Lise digs her elbow into Dean's side. Dean looks at the guy to see if he's kidding, but the guy just seems puffed up and proud. I like fucking? *This* is what Dean will tell Gregor about tomorrow.

In a moment Susan starts talking about fear and pain. Fear causes tension. Tension causes pain.

"Actually," Lise says under her breath, "*contractions* cause pain."

Susan takes up the chalk and turns to the blackboard. "OK," she says, "let's go over what happens during labor."

Halfway through the class she gives them a break. While the women line up for the bathroom, Dean climbs the stairs and goes outside to get some air. It's an early October night, still and cool, the rains a few weeks away although the air feels moist already, expectant.

After a few minutes Lise comes out to join him. For work she wears her hair pulled back, but it's down now, and the dampness has curled the shorter bits near her face. She looks pretty in the vaguely European way she looked pretty when they met, dark tendrils and dark eyes and a small, dark-red mouth. French or Italian, he thought then, and when they started talking it was all he could do not to compliment her on her excellent English.

He reaches out and fingers a lock of her hair. "Don't they give us milk and crackers?"

"Juice and crackers. Little paper cups of apple juice and three Ritz crackers each."

Back inside, the basement room seems overheated. All of the women are flushed. They've got something like two extra quarts of blood in their bodies, a slightly unnerving figure to Dean. Think of the pressure on their veins. How could you be the same afterward, shrunk back to your usual volume?

"Let's wind up," Susan says a little later, "by going around the room again and this time telling about any experience you've had with childbirth—if you've ever been with a woman during labor, or if you've actually attended a birth. And tell us your name again."

Stricken, Dean turns to Lise, but she just smiles and keeps within herself, inside the chamber where she keeps all of that.

One woman tells about having been with a friend for the first part of her labor, another says she watched her sister give birth. None of the men has anything to say.

Lise and Dean have switched seats, so Dean has to go first this time. "I'm still Dean," he says. "I have no prior experience with childbirth."

Then it's Lise's turn, and Dean feels that the whole class has been waiting for this moment, expecting it somehow. "I'm Lise," she says. "I went through childbirth myself, eight years ago." She turns to Dean and gives him a look that's almost—*apologetic,* he finds himself thinking. She holds her eyes on his, but just as he's finally mustering a dumb smile she turns away.

"I had a little boy," she says to the class. "I was married to someone else then. The baby died when he was five months old."

Dean's lips are dry, and he licks them. He doesn't know how she can stand this—he can't himself stand the fact that she has to. He looks around the room: the women are staring at her, the men at their own hands. Susan clears her throat. "How did he die?" she asks in a gentle voice that makes Dean think of murder.

"He died in his sleep," Lise says, "crib death," and then there are no more questions, no more answers, just the sound of the clock ticking and the feel of a group of people waiting for something to be over. Dean stares into the center of the room and waits, too, moment giving way to moment until finally, mercifully, the woman next to Lise takes her turn.

In bed at home later, Dean tries to look at proofs while Lise arranges the pillows she needs for sleep. He's used to this, but he half watches anyway, thinking the pillows look different tonight, distorted somehow after their time in the bright lights of the church basement. Next week, Susan promised, they'll use them.

Lise puffs a little with the effort of getting comfortable. She's on her side with one pillow between her legs, another under her belly, and a third smaller one that she's tucking between her breasts. "Can I get you anything?" he says, and she gives him a rueful look.

"A surrogate? I guess it's a little late for that."

"How about a backrub?" He gets off the bed and goes around behind her, easing himself onto the mattress. He lays his hands onto the soft flannel of her nightgown and begins kneading, pressing into her muscles with the heels of his hands. There's more flesh than before, and it seems loose somehow, sliding across her back as if not quite a part of her but rather an extra layer of clothing.

"Right there," she says, and he presses harder. "It wasn't so bad, was it?"

"The class?" he says. "It was OK. Susan's a bit caring."

She laughs, but he feels tense. In her dresser, in the top drawer, there's a picture of the dead baby, and as he stares at the drawer front he can almost see it: the blond wood frame, the baby with his little topknot curl and his toothless grin, his drooly lower lip catching the reflection of the flash.

"I thought what you said . . ." he says. "I thought you were amazing."

"About Jasper?"

The name gives him a tiny shock, as always. "Yeah."

"It was fine."

They are both silent, and for a while Dean just moves his hands across her back, kneading and pushing, pushing and kneading, until from her breathing he knows that she's asleep. The light's still on, but whereas before this pregnancy she was the finickiest sleeper he ever slept with, requiring perfect darkness and silence, she now falls asleep effortlessly, at will—even against her will, over books, carefully selected DVDs, sometimes even Dean's conversation.

He turns off the light, but rather than climb in next to her he goes to the window and looks outside. A misty night, starless, the rooflines of his neighborhood jagged against the lightish sky. What happened to her is just too horrible. It's unspeakable—*literally* unspeakable, in a way: when he first heard, it became for a while both all he could think of about her and also something they couldn't really talk about—*didn't* really talk about, because what was there to say? Horrible horrible horrible horrible horrible. In some true, essential way that was all that could be said.

By feel he finds shorts and his running shoes, then makes his way to the front door. It ca-thuds shut behind him and he locks it, then slips his running key into his Velcro pocket. He does stretches on the front lawn, just a quick set to take the edge off, then he sets out, first an easy trot but soon he's running all out, heaving hard, racing toward the University. His first run in how long—a week? Ten days? The dark feels like a material thing he has to penetrate. He passes the development office where Lise does graphic design, the science complex, Oregon Hall. On Agate he turns and presses even harder to get past the track—track town, he's a runner in a town of runners, out here again but alone this time, legs burning, lungs burning, sweat sliding off him in streams.

That weekend, Dean and Lise are in a Thai restaurant on Willamette when Gregor and his wife, Jan, come in. Dean hunkers in his chair, but of course Gregor spots him right away. "Dean and Lise!" he booms from across the crowded restaurant, his arm moving over his head like a windshield wiper at top speed. "Great! What say we join forces?"

Dean groans. After five years of working with Gregor, Dean thinks of him as a family member, but the kind with whom you don't want to be seen in public.

"It's OK," Lise says.

The hostess leads them over, Gregor beaming, Jan just behind him with a shy look on her face, her brown hair in a new, shorter style that makes her look—there's no other word for it— matronly. Dean knows her pretty well, from his bachelor days, when once or twice a month she'd phone the office late in the afternoon to tell Gregor to bring him home for dinner, but she and Lise aren't well acquainted. The four of them have been out together only once before, back when Dean and Lise weren't married yet. Jan was pregnant then, now that Dean thinks about it. Pregnant with two kids at home. She kept getting up from the table to call the babysitter.

She sits next to Dean, leaving Gregor the chair beside Lise. He sits down and pulls forward, then gives Lise a broad smile. "I haven't seen you in must be ten or fifteen pounds," he says. "Are you eating everything in sight? You're just huge."

Lise smiles good-naturedly, but Jan gasps. *"Gregor."* She catches Dean's eye and shakes her head apologetically. "Ignore him," she says to Lise. "How are you? You look great."

"Thanks."

"Are you ready?"

Lise shakes her head. She tucks a strand of hair behind her ear and says, "All we've got is a bassinet, plus some boxes of old clothes."

Dean swallows and stares at his placemat, the tips of his ears getting hot and, no doubt, red. The old clothes are the dead baby's, and he's afraid of what will happen next. Early in his relationship with Lise, he told Gregor about what had happened to her, and though he immediately felt he'd betrayed her and swore Gregor to secrecy, he can't imagine Gregor didn't tell Jan. He's afraid to look up, afraid to see the sympathetic, probing look he's sure Jan's giving Lise.

But: "Go shopping," Jan says, and now Dean does look up, to find Jan smiling innocently. "Seriously. Borrowed stuff's nice to have, but you need to get your own stuff, too. I didn't with our first, and I felt so guilty, putting him in these ratty little stretch suits. With the others I bought new stuff, and it really made a difference, really made me feel I was welcoming them right."

"Thanks," Lise says. "I'll keep that in mind."

Gregor gives Dean a defiant look, and Dean shrugs. OK, so he doubted Gregor. OK, so he was wrong.

"Do you have a stroller?" Jan says.

Lise shakes her head.

"That's where to spend some money. The expensive ones really do last a lot longer. There's probably nothing you'll use more."

"OK," Lise says. "We'll look into that." Under the table, she presses her stockinged foot against Dean's ankle, and he brings his other leg forward and holds her foot between his calves until their food comes.

At childbirth class the following week, Susan has them all lying on the floor, heads on their bed pillows, tensing and then relaxing each muscle group in their bodies. Tense your toes. And now relax them. Tense your ankle. And now relax it. Dean's nursing a cold and lying down should feel good, but the ceiling lights bore into his eyes and he can't stop coughing.

After the break Susan shows a short movie. It features a couple straight out of the seventies—man with sideburns and a tight, striped sweater; pregnant woman with Farrah Fawcett hair and eyebrows plucked to oblivion. The film opens with them in their motel-style living room in early labor: Dean knows this because the first thing the woman does is lean back in her chair and start breathing very deliberately, as if she were following difficult instructions. Soon the couple is in their car heading for the hospital, and she's breathing harder; next they're in a hospital corridor, walking and then stopping and then walking; and finally she's on the delivery table with a doctor nearby, his gloved hands ready. Dean turns away at the moment when the crown of the baby's head first bulges out, but he forces himself to watch as it bulges again, and then the whole head appears and it's all there, born, covered with white stuff, its arms and legs curled close to its body. Near Dean one of the women in the class sobs, and through the dark he sees Lise reach into her purse for a Kleenex and pass it to her.

Leaving the class later, the woman touches Lise's arm. "Thanks for the rescue."

"Oh, anytime," Lise says. "I keep one of those little boxes of tissues in my purse."

The woman smiles and waves, but she gives Lise a curious

backward glance as she joins her husband at the door, and Dean knows she's wondering about Lise's emotional state. He understands: he used to assume Lise thought about her baby dying all the time. She's said it's not like that, but every morning she opens her top drawer and looks at his picture while she's fishing for underpants, and Dean has to fight the urge to tell her to stop. *Don't,* he wants to say. *That'll just make it worse.* Like pressing a bruise.

Out in the parking lot, Lise hands him her purse to hold while she pulls her sweater over her head. Actually it's his sweater, a baggy old shetland he's had since college, burgundy and a bit moth-eaten, and he smiles a little, remembering a line from one of her pregnancy guides.

She tilts her head to the side. "What?"

"I was thinking of that book: 'Your husband's closet is a great place to find maternity clothes, but be sure to ask first!' "

She grins. "Like they know you better than I do. It should be called *What to Expect from an Annoying Author.* That's the same book that told me to ask myself before taking a bite of a cookie whether it was the best possible thing I could be eating for my baby. When I want a cookie I want it *because* it's a cookie, not just because it's something to eat."

"Do you want a cookie? We could go to that café."

She shakes her head. "I want a quart of mocha chip ice cream, but I think I'll just have an apple at home instead."

They make their way across the rutted parking lot, skirting puddles, walking slowly. "She reminded me of me," she says once they're in the car.

Dean looks at her.

"That woman."

His throat tightens. Was Lise crying during the movie? He was next to her the whole time, wouldn't he have noticed? Shouldn't he have?

"I mean the other time," she says. "We saw a movie every week, and every single time I cried right when the baby was born." She slides her car key into the ignition, then gives him a thoughtful look. "I don't know why I didn't tonight. I kind of thought I would, although I didn't put the tissues in my purse for that very eventuality." She smiles. "She sure thought so, though—did you see how she looked at me? Like she wondered why I needed a *box,* but it's this little thing, look." She fishes in her purse and pulls out a box of tissues about the size of a wallet. "So I blow my nose a lot."

"People have an incurable interest in what's not their business," Dean says. "They want to *know.*"

Lise nods and then starts the engine, pulling onto the wet street with the car tires swishing. Dean looks out the window at the porches going by—the big, wide porches of communal living, fraying easy chairs in front of plate glass windows, bicycles chained to railings. The kind of place he lived when he was new in Eugene. He had a bedroom on the third floor, half a shelf in the refrigerator. Fourteen years ago. What he remembers is the dankness of the bathroom, how his towel never really dried from one shower to the next.

At a traffic light he turns and looks at Lise's profile, her high forehead and long, narrow nose. He thinks of the woman at class tonight, her wanting to know. What he knows isn't much: that it happened during an afternoon nap, only the second time Lise went out without him; that her husband was the one at home, the one to go in after the nap had gone on much too long. Dean still remembers the night when he heard all of this, at a little Mexican restaurant out near the airport, with red-checked oilcloths covering the tables and mariachi music coming from a radio in the kitchen. She spoke evenly as she told him about the blur after the funeral, the half-year of living back to back with her husband, the two of them moving through their house like ghosts until finally she left, taking nothing but her own clothes and the baby's. Not because she hated her husband, she said, and certainly not because she blamed him: It was just that they couldn't go on. She couldn't go on.

She's lost track of him. She doesn't even know if he's still living on the West Coast. There are moments, though, like now—sitting in the dark car beside her, knowing he could ask more about it all but not wanting to press, not wanting to press on the bruise—when Dean gets a sudden intimation of the man, of a guy his own age with a permanent pain wedged in his side like a runner's stitch, and a cold fear slides through his veins.

Very early Saturday morning, Dean is woken to complete alertness by a pack of runners passing by outside, their feet slapping the road, the muted, heaving sound of their breathing checked once or twice by a low voice. Beside him Lise's deeply asleep, her dark hair a tangle, the faint, sweet scent of her hand lotion just there under the fresh-laundry smell of the sheets. He feels as wide awake as ten a.m., but he doesn't want to get up, doesn't want to go running any more than he wants to be alone in the kitchen with the gray dawn lightening outside while he makes coffee and pages through the *Register-Guard*. Up against the headboard he finds a small pillow, a stray, and he rolls over and holds it against his ear. A few months ago, a friend of Lise's from the Bay Area told him it was the early mornings rather than the interrupted nights that were hardest, but he thinks that if the baby were born already, were down the hall crying right now, he wouldn't mind at all getting up. She was passing through Eugene, Lise's friend, on her way to a family reunion in Portland, her husband and three kids in tow. She was an old friend, a neighbor from Lise's old life, and her presence had an odd effect on Lise, made the color in her cheeks a bit brighter, the pitch of her voice a bit higher. Toward the end of the visit, the friend's oldest child lifted his baby brother from the floor and flew him through the air like an airplane, and Lise said, to no one in particular, "Jasper loved that."

When Dean wakes again it's midmorning, he can tell by the light, by how empty the bed feels next to him, as if Lise's been up for a while. Her nightgown is on a hook on the back of the bedroom door, and he wanders out and finds her dressed in her denim maternity overalls, standing in what will be the nursery, a small corner room with white walls and a square, jade green rug.

"What a sleeper," she says when she sees him.

"I do my best."

"Was there anything you wanted to do today? I was thinking we could go buy a rocking chair, maybe a few other things."

An hour later, they borrow a neighbor's pickup truck and drive downtown, where they buy a rocking chair, a changing table, four hooded towels, a four-hundred-dollar stroller, a package of cloth diapers, a footstool for nursing, five flannel blankets, a car seat, a stack of pastel washcloths, a Snugli, a mobile with multicolored zoo animals hanging from it, a lambskin, and the tiniest fingernail clippers Dean has ever seen. Driving home with the big things in boxes in the truck bed behind them and shopping bags strewn at their feet, Dean is exhilarated.

After lunch he mows the front lawn, and then, because it's something he's been meaning to do for weeks, he gathers up and takes to the supermarket several dozen empty beer bottles, which yield him for his trouble a few wrinkled dollar bills and a handful of change. Back at home he's not surprised to find Lise in the baby's room again, standing amid the morning's loot. He fetches his toolbox and assembles the changing table while she comes and goes, carrying stacks of things to and from the garage: in the distance he hears the washing machine churn and drain, and the thrum of the dryer.

As he's tightening the last screw on the footstool, she goes into the closet and reappears with a cardboard box.

"Careful, I'll do that," he says, but she's already set it on the floor and crossed to his toolbox for a box cutter.

She slices open the edges of the box first, then pulls up the still-joined flaps and cuts them carefully, so the blade won't go through what's underneath. With a feeling of discomfort, he watches as she opens the box, and then there they are, the dead baby's clothes.

She removes a handful of little white caps and sets them aside. Next is a stack of tiny white undershirts, with shoulders that somehow remind him of the way the fly looks on Jockey underwear. Halfway across the room, he doesn't know what to do or say. He feels grossly out of place, and beyond that boorish, and beyond that paralyzed.

"Pretty basic stuff," she says, but then her expression brightens, and she eagerly withdraws a little one-piece yellow coverall with the head of a giraffe on the front. "Look at this," she says, looking up at him. "I'd forgotten about this one. We always called this the giraffe suit."

"I can see why," he says with an idiotic smile.

She looks at him carefully. "What do you think about using some of this stuff?"

There's no reason not to, unless it would make her feel worse. "Sure," he says. "Whatever you want."

She brushes absently at a spot on her overalls, then sets the giraffe suit down and rubs her lower back with both hands. "I do want us to get some new stuff," she says, "but I feel like—I don't know—I'd like to use some of these things, too. I mean, I saved them as Jasper outgrew them, for when he had a little brother or sister. Would it bother you?"

"Not at all."

The doorbell rings, and he hesitates a moment, then makes his way to the front door. Outside, his neighbor's eight-year-old daughter is standing there with a small paper bag. "Dad said you left this in the truck this morning," she says, and Dean takes the bag and thanks her, then watches as she leaps off the porch and runs home. She goes to school just a block away: when he leaves for work each morning he sees her mother watching from the sidewalk until she's reached the schoolyard.

In the bag are the nail clippers. Dean closes the front door and returns to the nursery, not entirely surprised to find it empty. He comes back out and hesitates outside his and Lise's bedroom.

She's standing at her dresser, the top drawer open. She has the picture of the baby in one hand, something small and red-and-white striped in the other. Her head is bent, her dark hair brushing her shoulders, and Dean feels sure she's crying. He crosses the room and puts a hand on her back, and she turns. She isn't crying, but she has an air of crying about her: of just having cried or of being about to. "Sweetie," he says, and she looks up at him with her bottom lip clamped between her teeth.

"Do you know why he was smiling in this picture?"

Dean shakes his head.

"Because Mark had just pulled these from his feet and started tickling his toes." She opens her hand, and the red-and-white thing unfolds into a tiny pair of socks. "He loved having his toes tickled, he'd make this little noise, like 'Arrr.' I remember it so clearly."

Dean doesn't know what to say. His throat is lumpy and he has to try a couple of times before he can swallow. At last he remembers the bag. "Look," he says. "We left this in the pickup."

She hesitates a moment, then turns and puts the picture away, pushing the drawer closed and pausing for a moment before turning back. She sets the socks on the dresser and looks inside the bag. "Oh, the clippers," she says. "Good. We'll definitely need those."

.   .   .

Gregor calls late Sunday night, after Lise's asleep. It's a habit Dean and he have gotten into, to catch up on things before the start of a new week. Tonight they talk for a while, but Dean's distracted, and soon Gregor's voice trails off.

"What?" Dean says.

"Go on to bed, son. Get some sleep while you can."

"That's like telling someone to eat five dinners today because he's going to have to fast for the next week. There's only so much sleeping you can do. Go on, I was listening."

"Nah, you weren't. Everything OK? Got the bag packed for the hospital?"

"Yes, Gregor," Dean says wearily, although in fact Lise packed it just this afternoon. The books said to take all kinds of crazy stuff—lollipops and tennis balls, as if you were preparing to sit in the audience of *Let's Make a Deal*—but she just put in the basics.

"Don't forget your swim trunks," Gregor says.

"What?"

"For the jacuzzi. Jan always made me get in with her so she could lean against me instead of the porcelain."

"You're loving this," Dean says. "Go torment someone else, call a catalog and pick on the operator."

"Come on," Gregor says. "I just want you to be prepared."

"I am. Jesus."

Gregor doesn't respond.

"What? I can't possibly be prepared, is that it? My life is going to change completely, I'll never have a free moment again. I know that, OK?"

Gregor laughs.

"OK, I even know that I don't really know it."

"That's what I want to hear," Gregor says. Then he adds, casually, "How's Lise? Is she—"

"She's fine."

Gregor is silent, and Dean thinks of yesterday, all the excited shopping and then the box of clothes. "She got out his stuff," he says, but then he stops himself. What is he doing? He doesn't want to tell Gregor this. His heart pounds, and he adds, almost against his will, "His clothes."

Gregor exhales. "Jeez." He hesitates and then says, "Is she— I mean, are you guys—" He's silent for a moment. "It must be scary," he says at last, "to think it could happen again. Is she really worried?"

"You'd think so," Dean says, "but she's not." He fingers the buttons on the phone, strokes their faint concavities. Back when they first talked about getting married and having children, she told him that she saw what had happened as a one-time thing, plain bad luck—it bothered her when people expected her to fear a repeat. She said that wasn't how the world was—how she wanted to think of it, anyway.

As for him, he doesn't fear crib death, he fears . . . what? Something.

He fears being afraid.

After saying goodbye to Gregor, he goes into the kitchen. It's nearly midnight but he's far too wired for sleep. He gulps a glass of orange juice, then crosses the room and opens the back door.

The backyard is small, little more than a deck and a tiny patch of grass, but it's nicely enclosed, and last spring Lise hung Italian tiles on the fence and planted lavender and rosemary in terra cotta pots. Dean sits on a wooden bench they chose together shortly after they were married, and he leans back. The night is cool, and he feels the wind stir goose bumps from his bare arms. Overhead the half-moon looks transparent. The faint scent of lavender reminds him of a trip to Provence he and Lise took two summers ago, and he finds himself remembering an evening there, in a village near Arles. Walking after coffee in a tiny café, they happened upon a kind of amateur's night at the local bullfight, and they sat and watched from rickety bleachers while boys barely old enough to shave teased and provoked bulls, then leapt to safety over the low wall of the ring. Near Dean and Lise, a small family called and cajoled to one of the boys, and when his turn in the ring was over he came and sat with them, had his head rubbed by his father and then reached to take onto his lap a little girl dressed in pink ruffles. Dean watched them openly, and when the boy looked up and met his gaze he gave Dean a look of such sweet contentment that Dean felt a rush of love not just for him but for all of them, the proud father and the fat mother, the little, overdressed girl: love and pure longing. If it did happen again, if his and Lise's baby died, too, would they survive? Would their marriage? The thing is, there's no telling. From where he sits, less than a month away from fatherhood, he sees that what they've done together acknowledges the possibility of its own undoing: that what there is to gain is exactly equal to what there is to lose.

Labor starts in the kitchen three days before Lise's due date, with a gathering of color in her face, a low moan as she bends over the counter, her weight on her forearms. In a moment she looks up and smiles, and Dean sets down the pan he's been drying and says the exact thing he hoped he wouldn't say at this moment, a line out of a bad movie: "Is it time?"

It isn't, quite. But close to midnight, after hours with his watch in his hand, timing contractions, Dean helps her to the car and they head for the hospital, Dean trying to avoid potholes while she puffs in the seat next to him, her hands on her belly.

"Jesus," she says, "I better be fucking five centimeters dilated when we get there or I'm never going to make it."

He reaches for her hand, but a moment later she moans and shakes him away. She's already told him that he's not to talk to her, touch her, or in any way get in her face while she's in hard labor. Ice chips. That was all her first husband was allowed to do, feed her ice chips.

Up ahead the hospital looms into view, and he imagines plowing right through the double front doors—the car would just about fit. The walk from the parking area takes forever, Dean standing by while Lise staggers along, bent like an old woman. Inside, a clerk takes her name and phones for a wheelchair. The orderly pushing it doesn't seem surprised when Lise refuses it, nor when, several minutes and only twenty yards later, she changes her mind.

Upstairs, minutes stretch endlessly while hours collapse upon themselves. There's a period of walking in the halls, another of standing nearby while she rests her forearms on a bar and moans. Drugs are discussed, rejected, demanded. Then for a strange interlude Dean sits in a chair next to the bed and nearly dozes, only to be startled to alertness by a bright light aimed at his wife's crotch. All the blowing and panting, the ice chips, the dial on the fetal monitor springing up and down—it's all as he was told it would be and at the same time utterly shocking. Then suddenly Lise cries, "Oh my God, I can't do this, I can't do this," and the room stills to her.

"That's the wrong attitude," the midwife says. "You have to think you can do it."

"I can do this, I can do this," Lise cries; and then she does.

Lise in the rocking chair with Danny curled in her lap. Danny asleep in the very center of Dean and Lise's huge bed. Lise on her side on the couch with Danny next to her, his mouth around her nipple. Danny staring at Dean while Dean stares at Danny. Every moment feels consequential, essential to preserve somehow and yet also infinitely repeatable. Dean watches Lise watching Danny, and his eyes brim and overflow. Lise watches Dean watching her, and tears stream down her cheeks.

Dean has never been so tired in all his life. Two-fourteen in the morning, 3:45, 5:03: walking, walking. His shoulders have never felt so sore, his upper arms. Danny wants to be held. He's five days old, seven, and Dean still hasn't set foot in the office. Gregor and Jan arrive one afternoon while Lise is asleep, and answering the door with Danny in his arms, Dean hardly hears their greetings and exclamations, his only thought that at last he can go to the bathroom. They've brought gifts for Danny—a navy blue sleepsuit, a copy of *Goodnight Moon,* and three different lullaby tapes, but the thing that touches Dean is a huge dish of lasagne, good for at least four dinners. He hugs them both.

The day of Danny's two-week checkup arrives and Dean is ready with a list of questions for the doctor. The blister on Danny's upper lip, the sucking blister—could it pop and what would happen if it did? The spitting up—is it normal for there to be so much of it? The cradle cap, the hiccuping, the way one of his toes sort of curls under the one next to it . . .

In the living room, getting ready to go, Dean buckles a sleeping Danny into his car seat, drapes a blanket over the handle because it's misting a little outside, and turns to Lise just as she's zipping the diaper bag.

"I'll go start the car and get the heater going."

"Good idea." There are rings around her eyes, a small smear of what looks like mustard near the cuff of her white oxford shirt, which is actually his: since Danny's birth she's been living in his shirts—for their looseness, for how easy they are to unbutton for nursing. She follows his glance to the smear. "Oops," she says.

"Tough times call for tough people."

"Still, I think I'll change. There's no one at a pediatrician's office who won't know what that is."

She heads for the bedroom, and Dean takes the blanket off the car seat to look at Danny. He's still asleep, one round cheek resting on his shoulder: his drunken-old-man look. "You nailed Mommy," Dean says. "What a thing to do."

The doctor's office is crowded, full of small children swarming all over a colorful plastic play structure or tapping insistently on the glass of a large aquarium. Dean sets Danny's car seat in a relatively quiet corner, and he and Lise sink onto the bench next to him, each of them sighing a little as they sit down.

Lise picks up a magazine, and Dean rests idly for a moment, then stretches across her to look at Danny. He touches Danny's forehead, his cheek, his impossibly tiny fist. Danny's fingers scare Dean, how fragile they are: little matchsticks in flimsy padding.

A nurse comes into the waiting room and says, "Daniel?," and Lise's on her feet waiting well before Dean gets it. He lifts the car seat and follows her and the nurse back to a small examining room, where the nurse asks questions about feeding and sleep and then tells them to undress Danny. She leaves and reappears when they've got him down to his diaper, which she untapes, then she carries him to the scale, whisks the diaper out from under him, and slides the scale's weights around until she's arrived at his.

The pediatrician comes in a little later. He asks Dean, who's been holding Danny, to set him on the examining table, and then he listens to Danny's chest, rotates Danny's legs, presses his giant fingers into Danny's abdomen. Dean stands just to the side, so alert he realizes he's waiting for Danny to learn to roll over and to roll to the edge of the table: if he does this, Dean will be ready to catch him. Danny's awake now and quiet, and when the doctor finishes his examination and loops his stethoscope around his neck, he and Dean and Lise gather and stare at Danny, watch as his ocean-deep eyes move from one of them to the next.

"Can I hold him?" the doctor asks Lise, and while Dean's wondering what's odd about this, Lise nods, and the doctor lifts Danny and cradles him against his chest. "He's a nice little bundle," the doctor says, and all at once Dean understands that what he's feeling is the awe of ownership, amazement that permission is his and Lise's to give or refuse. Just two weeks and he's an expert on Danny, on his Dannyness, each day placing into an infinitely expandable container every new thing he knows to be true about his baby. He thinks of what he knows about the dead baby—about *Jasper*—and it's next to nothing: he liked to be flown through the air like an airplane, he loved to have his father tickle his toes. Dean's had it all wrong: it isn't that Lise had a baby who died, but rather that she had a baby, who died. He looks at her, creases around her eyes as she smiles at Danny, and he feels a little space open up in his mind, for all she can tell him about her first-born.

The doctor turns to Dean now, holding Danny out like an offering. "Dad?" he says. "Do you want him back now?"

Things Said or Done

· · · · · ·

B y the way," my father says, "I'm probably dying."

Except for sleep, we've been together nonstop for the last thirty hours, ever since we met at the Hartford airport yesterday morning, but he has chosen this moment to unburden himself: this moment, when we're carrying folding chairs through a windowless corridor in a neighborhood community center in Berkeley, California. Well, I'm carrying folding chairs, my elbows sticking out as the bottoms of the chair backs dig into my curled fingers, while he is empty-handed, strolling back toward the storage room.

"Sure, ignore me," he calls when I don't respond.

"You're probably dying," I call back.

Up ahead, the once homely rec room is growing more festive by the minute. Three young women with bare feet wind garlands of flowers up the frame of a makeshift gazebo, and five neat rows of chairs are arranged on the linoleum floor, with a center aisle for the bridal procession.

"My piss smells like raw meat," he calls. "Plus I'm always tired. I'm thinking kidney disease."

"Sounds right," I call back.

I enter the room and set the chairs down for a moment. In the dry California air, my hair, which is curly enough, frizzes with static, and I find a clip in my pocket and pin a section away from my face. Beyond the grimy clerestory windows puffs of cloud float across the sky. It's a crisp September day, auspicious for a wedding. The groom is my middle-aged brother, the bride a very pretty twenty-three-year-old girl who was until recently an intern in his lab at the University of California. Her name is Cressida, but on the plane yesterday my father began referring to her as "Clytemnestra," and because I made the mistake of objecting, he won't give it up.

Cressida's mother directs me to start row number six with my chairs. Like her daughter, she is tall and long-limbed, and she's as calm and unfussy a mother of the bride as I've ever seen. According to my brother she is fifty, a year younger than I, but somehow I feel as if I am by far the less mature of the two of us, probably because in this context she is all mother, whereas I don't have children—unless you count my father.

I head back to the storage room, expecting to find him, but he seems to have vanished. Cressida's younger brother, a high school senior with sleepy eyes, has discovered a cart with wheels, and I help him load a dozen chairs onto it and dispatch him down the corridor, glad for a moment of solitude. We've been working since nine o'clock, an early call after a rehearsal dinner that lasted till well after midnight. Like the wedding, the rehearsal dinner was arranged and catered by Cressida's family, though they allowed my father and me to make a gift of the wine. It took place in their backyard, where a giant paella was served at picnic tables crowded with jars of daisies. There were about forty of us, family and close friends, and toward the end of the night Cressida's mother made a point of telling me how sorry she was that my mother wasn't arriving until today, which was nice but didn't conceal—in fact, communicated—her bafflement that a retired librarian who lives alone could be too busy to spend a full weekend at her son's wedding. It isn't busyness, though, it's history: decades of it, beginning with my mother's decision to leave my father when I was sixteen. She had, for twenty years, tried to hold him together, but there were just too many pieces of him for that, and now she keeps a steady and inviolable distance.

"Ha," he says, appearing in the doorway with his hands on the hips of his baggy khakis—pants so old a wife would not allow them and a daughter shouldn't, but I can't do everything. "There you are. That woman, the mother, is about to tell us to take a meditation break!"

"That woman."

"Meditation and/or stretching. That's what it said on her list."

I frown to show I can't believe he looked at her list, though of course I can believe it.

"Sasha," he says, "she left it lying on the piano. I'm supposed to walk right by that?"

"As a matter of fact you are. Where were you just now?"

"Went to see a man about a hearse."

This is an old family joke—it means he was in the bathroom. He claims it started as a misunderstanding of mine, that as an appealingly morbid little girl I heard "hearse" when someone on a TV show said he needed to see a man about a horse. I don't remember this, but if it happened I'm sure I only pretended to mishear, that the apparent "mistake" was a calculated move to please him. Beginning when I was very young, he conferred specialness on me and then required that I earn it, and I was only too happy to comply, dividing my efforts between precocity (memorizing at age seven the prologue to *The Canterbury Tales,* for

example) and fussiness (insisting on two thick foam rubber pillows for sleep every night; refusing ever to wear green). We lived
in tacit agreement that I could be anything but ordinary. Like
him, I was to breathe only the rarefied air of the never-quite-
satisfied, and the more difficult I was, the more entranced he
became. Which is not, it turns out, the best preparation for life.
Or marriage, as my ex-husband would certainly attest.

"Anyway," my father says, leaning against the storage room
door and peering with apparent fascination at the back of his forefinger, "it can't be good."

"Your finger."

"My health! Something's wrong. My piss smells like chocolate."

"I thought it was raw meat," I say, but then Cressida's brother
returns with the empty cart, and my father gives up both the
promise of a minor skin injury and the opportunity to be
offended by me, both so he can lay a trap for the boy. Feigning
nonchalance, he asks what's next on the schedule.

"Schedule?" the boy says.

"What do we do after the chairs are in place?"

"It's fine," I interject. "We're happy to do whatever."

"Yeah, but there must be a schedule," my father says. "A *list*."

"I don't know," the boy says. "My dad just got here with the
programs, I can ask him."

"The programs!" My father glances at me: this is getting better and better. "What is this, a concert?"

"Well, they're not really programs. More sort of souvenirs?
With photos and poems and stuff?" The boy shrugs. "They're
nice."

At the word "poems," I turn my back on my father and begin
loading chairs on the cart. Long ago, in another lifetime, he was a
professor of English, and he still has proprietary views on what
should be called poetry and what should be called—well, not
poetry. I hope if I don't look at him he'll keep his mouth shut.

"Oh, um," the boy says, face reddening, "now that I think about it—my mom's going to try to get everyone to do partner massages."

I shoot a murderous look at my father and say, quickly as I can, "She wants to make sure we don't work too hard. That's thoughtful."

The boy glances over his shoulder and leans forward. "Do you mind not telling Peter? I told Cress I wouldn't let my parents do anything dumb, and—you know."

"Sure," I say. "No problem."

He pushes the cart away, and now I have to look at my father again: he is grinning triumphantly, showing off his crooked yellow teeth. "What did I tell you?" he says. "Partner massages! Only in California!"

"That's what you told me."

And told me and told me. We're staying at a bed-and-breakfast that offers—unexpectedly, I admit—an afternoon class in self-massage, and after my father made the obligatory joke about how we used to call that masturbation, he declared that in no bed-and-breakfast anywhere else in the country would there be anything offered in the afternoon but sherry or tea. Then we discovered there was a clothing-optional hot tub in the backyard, and it was as if he'd won the lottery. The thing is, we lived in California once ourselves, and his scorn can't erase the fact that he thought of it as paradise when it was his.

My father is not an easy person in the best of circumstances, but he's especially cantankerous when he has to see my mother. It's been thirty-five years since she left him, but I remember it vividly: his heartsick weeping, his enervation, his despair. He was supposedly job hunting at that point, having been "let go" by the Connecticut boarding school where he'd gone when higher education didn't work out, but after the initial shock of her departure he abandoned his search and hung around in his pajamas all day, waiting for me to get home from school. "Come talk to me," he'd plead as soon as I entered the house, and he'd lead me to the study, where he'd been sleeping since she left, on the hard foam pallet of a Danish modern sofa. While I perched on a sliver of windowsill, he'd sit behind the desk and ask if I thought she'd ever come back, or even, incredibly, why she'd left, as if he'd been away for the bulk of their marriage and needed me to tell him what had happened. (He wasn't away. Years later, in that cultural moment when the words "present" and "absent" cast off their classroom meanings and entered the crowded realm of the psychological metaphor, I joked to friends that if only my father had been *more* absent, things might have worked out between him and my mother.)

As we continue arranging chairs, I keep an eye on him, half for damage control and half to monitor his mood. The bride and groom were banned from the proceedings, and at noon the rest of us—assorted relatives and friends, my brother's troop of graduate students—are offered a break and a snack and are instructed that this setup help is the only gift we are allowed to give the couple. "A little late telling us," my father says, but under his breath, and I'm grateful he didn't say it louder. I'm even more grateful that no massages were suggested, partner or otherwise.

I'm recruited to help with flowers, and I join a group stuffing blossoms into every size, shape, and color of vase imaginable. My mother will like the unfussy, inclusive mandate of this wedding, the leggy perennials, the homey appetizers I saw in the community center fridge. Her flight is due to land at three-forty, which is cutting it close even for her. Surprisingly, she will be staying at the same bed-and-breakfast as my father and I, a mark of resignation, or maybe indifference.

I'm putting a bunch of white roses into a glass jug when my father comes over and says he's not well and needs to rest.

"So sit down," I say.

He looks at the ceiling, as if there might be someone up there to recognize my boorish insensitivity. "I have to *lie* down. Right now."

"*Right* now?"

"I'm telling you, I'm not well."

He looks fine, but I know better than to argue. I make our apologies to Cressida's parents and lead the way to the car. Other people throw parties; my father throws emergencies. It's been like this forever. When I was a kid I thought the difference between my father and other parents was that my father was more fun. It took me years to see it clearly. My father was a rabble-rouser. He was fun like a cyclone.

Peter found the B&B, which is on a quiet street in a residential neighborhood and looks very much like an ordinary Berkeley house: painted a bold burnt orange, its front yard landscaped with birch trees and a slate pathway. Inside, the owners' private area is to the right; the breakfast room is straight ahead, already set for tomorrow with a basket of tea bags on the communal table and more of the stiff beige napkins we used this morning (made of bamboo, we were told); and to the left are the guest quarters, down a hallway that is still hung with photographs of the teenagers who once occupied these rooms.

The whole drive from the community center my father complained and sighed, insisting he really didn't know what was wrong, only that something was, but by the time we reach his room he's feeling "a little bit better," and I leave him. There are two more rooms, a very small one next to my father's and a larger one at the end of the hallway, and the proprietor insisted I take the larger one since I'm staying three nights and "the other lady" is staying only one. This means that tonight my parents will go to bed with only a thin wall between them, closer than they've slept in decades.

I'm more tired than I realized, and when I add up the transcontinental flight yesterday, the incredibly late night given that we were on eastern time, and the work of schlepping chairs all morning, I think it's no wonder he wanted to lie down—I do, too. I close the blinds and take off my shoes and stretch out on the bed. There's a separate guesthouse in the backyard, occupied this weekend by a couple from Melbourne, and I hear their voices and the occasional splash as they soak in the hot tub.

I'm just drifting off when my cell phone buzzes with a text. *Viens,* my father has written, as if the French will somehow mask the imperiousness.

I find him not lying down or even sitting but pacing between bed and window. "What's wrong?"

"This Clytemnestra. Do you suppose she thinks we're rich?"

"Uch, Daniel," I say. "I was lying down."

"You're so blasé. My son is getting married."

"And?"

"And I don't want him to get hurt again."

This is an allusion to Peter's romantic history, with its long fallow periods and terrible ecstasies, though it is of course an allusion to my father's, as well. Last night, staring across the picnic table at Peter, I caught a glimpse of the boy he was at thirteen, when his family fell apart, and I thought it made sense, how late he was marrying: he'd waited till he was older than our father was at the time his marriage ended. What this means, though, is that he's old enough to be Cressida's father, and I worry about the strains of gratitude in his voice when he talks about her.

"Also," my father says, "it makes me feel old."

"This is a *happy* thing," I tell him. "You should feel young—most people are a lot younger when their children marry. You were only fifty-whatever when I got married."

"And look how that turned out."

"You know, you can think stuff like that and choose not to say it."

"I was heartbroken about your marriage."

"As opposed to my divorce."

"That's not fair," he cries, but he's smiling now, a coy, aren't-I-a-naughty-boy smile. The truth is he has never been a fan of anyone I've dated.

Now he says, "You didn't take me seriously this morning about my health," a classic kvetcher's bait and switch. I don't respond and he says, "Are you saying you did?"

"I'm not saying anything."

"I noticed!"

"What does the doctor think?"

"I haven't been," he says. "She'll order a scan, I'll be like one of those suitcases at the airport."

I say she might ask a question or two first, but he ignores me, looking off into the distance and caressing his chin. He says, "Have you ever thought about this? They have CAT scans and PET scans, but CAT scans aren't a kind of PET scan—there's a taxonomy problem. CAT scans should be a kind of PET scan, and there should be other PET scans, too—DOG scans, which would be, you know, Diagnostic Oldfart Geriatricography. And RAB-BIT scans, Retired Alterkoker Bladder . . ."

I let myself drift as he continues. I think of this sort of thing as The Daddy Show, and long ago, when I was a little girl, I enjoyed it. In fact, there was a time when he staged a literal show every night before I went to bed, and it was the highlight of my day. Once I was under the covers but still sitting propped against my pillows, he put on finger puppets—a felt Daddy-O-MacDaddy on his left forefinger, a felt Sasha-the-Pasha on his right—and the two of them bopped through literature and history as narrated by my father, joining in the Norman Conquest, acting out parts of *Twelfth Night,* never an idle evening until I was ten or eleven and began making excuses about being tired or having homework. After that, he retired the puppets, but to this day he has not stopped performing.

"Did you see that *New Yorker* cartoon," he is saying, "with the rabbits in the living room, sitting with their legs crossed holding martini glasses? I thought of a *much* better caption than the one they had. It should have said—"

"If you think you're sick," I say, "you need to go to the doctor."

"But I'm scared."

He looks scared, and I give him what I hope will seem like a sympathetic smile. I *am* sympathetic—somewhat, and more for the hypochondria than for whatever ails him—but the algebra of our relationship means it's hard for me to offer compassion when that's so clearly what he wants.

"Seriously," he says. "It's time I told you this. I'm scared, but it's not death I'm scared of, it's dying. It's pain. Will you promise me no pain? I'm not asking you to do me in, just a very fast morphine drip."

"Dan, you're way ahead of yourself."

He looks down his giant, beaky nose at me. "Excuse me for having the bad manners to tell my daughter how I feel." He glares, and I can't decide what to say next. If I were he, I'd try to bump him out of it with a family joke—his joke, which is itself a reaction to his mother, the legendary Moomie Horowitz (as if there could be two Moomies, but that is what we called her), who was one of the great complainers of all time. If dissatisfaction was a virtue in our family, endless talking about it was to take unforgivable advantage of one's good fortune, and whenever my brother or I whined or moaned about something, my father would tell us: Beware the family curse. Beware the Horowitz horror!

We face each other, I perched on the bed, he on the chair. He is, in fact, getting on: his bright blue eyes are hazed by cataract clouds, and his hair, once as red and curly as mine, is beige and cut so short that it clings to his scalp in tiny disheveled patches, looking like nothing so much as a helmet of brown rice. He will fall ill someday, whether he's ill now or not, and someday he will be gone. I have imagined the time after, with its cavern of sadness, and I know that even his most irritating foibles will acquire, in recollection, a kind of charm, and that grief will have its way with me time and again.

I say, "I'm sorry you're scared."

He shrugs, and I go to the window and watch the Australians in the hot tub, their bodies so submerged I can't tell whether they've taken the clothing option or not. They are talking and smiling, and at one point the husband puts his hand flat on top of the wife's head, an oddly tender gesture. They look to be in their sixties; at breakfast this morning they said they'd both just retired and were taking their first ever trip away from Australia.

A mile from here, my brother is alone in his apartment—doing what, I don't know. How do you spend your wedding day if you are one of the sweetest and most solitary people on the planet? He is a man so overwhelmed by his own heart that he arranged a sabbatical the last time he fell in love, an entire year away, effectively guaranteeing that his beloved would meet someone else during his absence and move on. It's extraordinary to me that he is getting married.

"Maybe if you went to the doctor with me," my father says, and I turn and tell him I'd be happy to—which I'd have said five hours ago if he'd only asked. I suggest we both lie down for a while, and when he agrees I return to my room.

The next thing I know, I'm waking in a strange bed to the sounds of my mother on the other side of the wall. I hear the zip of her suitcase, the slide and clatter of plastic hangers moving along a bar. If my father is awake, he can hear this, too. I last saw her about eighteen months ago, when I drove from Western Massachusetts, where I live, to Old Lyme, Connecticut, where she'd just finished remodeling her cottage. On that particular trip I didn't stop in Hartford to see my father—I visit at least once a month, often more—but even so I felt what I always feel, that in the most literal of ways, as in all others, he is between us.

I wash my face before I go knock on her door. We chat for a few minutes, exchanging travel stories, marveling at the weather. She tells me I look great, and I tell her she looks great, which she does, in her proudly unkempt way: her nearly white hair hangs past her shoulders, thick and flyaway; and she's unapologetically frumpy in a mid-calf calico skirt and running shoes. She gave up vanity the way other people give up sugar, and her arms and hips and stomach are as soft and plump as bread dough.

"Fat, anyway," she says cheerfully. "I hope I won't embarrass Peter."

"He can't wait to see you," I say, which is surely true, though not something he said to me.

"Where's Dan?"

I point at the wall dividing her room from my father's. "He's a little under the weather," I say in a low voice.

Her face betrays nothing, neither concern nor skepticism; for thirty-five years she has been the very embodiment of the correct way to behave with your children after a divorce. In my twenties, I tried to get her to open up: "It's been ten years," I said. "I'm an adult, we can talk." This was just after my divorce, and I guess I wanted to dish with her, but she wouldn't budge.

"What's Cressida like?" she says now, backing up and sitting on the bed. She puts her hands together and holds them between her knees, a gesture I've known forever.

I fill my mother in about Cressida and her family and then move on to last night's party, leaning a little harder than I should on how welcoming everyone was and how much fun we all had. "They're big hikers," I say. "After the thing tomorrow they're going to take us on a hike." This, too, is unkind: I happen to know that my mother is on an early flight—booked, she claims, before she knew there would be a brunch.

She smiles, ignoring or maybe not even noticing what I've really said. She tells me that last time she was here she and Peter spent a glorious afternoon at Mount Tam. "It was fantastic," she says. "I still remember the view."

From my father's room comes a loud cough, a cough that could have been produced for one reason only, to remind us of his existence. I don't think he can hear what we're saying, just the sound of it, but I have no doubt he's using every gram of concentration to determine from our pauses and cadences how we are getting along. With him, I generally pretend that my mother and I are closer than in fact we are, whereas with her I pretend that he and I are not as close as we are, or rather that we have one of those healthy parent-child relationships characterized by mutual affection and respect, not mutual suspicion and resentment. I think I've done a better job convincing him than her.

"So," she says, glancing at her watch, "we've got half an hour?"

I look at my watch and say, "Wow, that's right."

And here is more pretending: we are both acutely aware of the time, the strain, the welcome need to part so we can dress.

At 5:35 I leave my room and go to the front hall, where I told both my parents I would meet them. I made sure to say we would all three be meeting—no surprises—but even so I've been careful to arrive first. While I wait, the Australians appear in matching blue sweatshirts, each with the word "VICTORY" in giant letters across the front. "We're going to a baseball game," the husband says, rhyming "game" with "lime." "In our team colors." "Our football team," the wife says, and then together they say, "Soccer, that is." They laugh and she says, "Have a lovely time at your brother's wedding. September's the best time to get married in Australia—it's our spring, you know."

They head off, and I think of my own short-lived marriage, which also began in September, at my fiancé's family's reform temple in suburban New Jersey, since I had neither synagogue nor intact family of my own. We had met in college, broken up after graduation, and then found each other again and mistaken familiarity for love. After we married we had some fun traveling together, but once we tried to settle down I began picking at him over tiny annoyances—because the big annoyance, the fact that he wasn't paying enough attention to me, was too unreasonable for me to recognize at that point, let alone communicate. When I wasn't picking at him I was picking at the rest of mankind, going on and on about some slight, a minor social disappointment, an achievement inadequately rewarded. I was twenty-five, I thought it was just a matter of time before people shaped up and started acting as I wanted. Such is the lot of the narcissist's child, to inherit her parent's umbrage over the world's indifference.

And here is the narcissist, looking dapper in a light brown suit and paisley necktie, and loafers with tassels. "She's a little late," he says, glancing at his watch.

"A minute," I say. "Actually forty-five seconds."

"Well, but she's not here yet."

"You look spiffy."

He adjusts the knot of his necktie, smooths his lapels. "And she's . . ."

"Great," I say.

We stand here for an eon of seconds, until my mother's footsteps sound, then we both turn to look at her. She has pinned up her hair and put on lipstick and a sapphire caftan, and she looks marvelous. I hear my father suck in a mouthful of air. "Joanie," he says. "Always a pleasure."

She kisses the air above his shoulder. "What an occasion, hmmm?"

I always think I can finesse these situations—the last was maybe seven years ago, when I received an award at the college where I teach—but in the event I am clumsy and fall back on false hurry. "Right, let's get going," I say, and I leave the house ahead of them and have the car doors open before either has made it to the sidewalk.

The community center parking lot is only half full, and we find Cressida's father and brother greeting people at the entrance. During the car ride, my father went on and on to me about the book he's reading, offering an elaborate critique of its faux Faulknerian dreaminess and moral vacancy, and my mother, once I've introduced her, says she wants to find Peter and vanishes.

"She's certainly haughty," my father says.

"Don't," I say.

Some people I recognize from the party last night come up to say hello, and we talk to them, and then to the next group, and soon it is time to go inside. In our absence this afternoon, the rec room was even further transformed, and it is stunning now, with gauzy drapes covering the walls and dozens of flower arrangements creating a lovely chaos of color.

The programs are lying on the chairs. They have Peter's and Cressida's names in calligraphy on the front, along with today's date. My father opens his and flips through the pages. "They've got e. e. cummings," he says. "And Rumi."

"Could be worse," I say, knowing he wishes it were.

My mother appears and sits with us, sliding her bag, a large silver brocade satchel that's oddly capacious for a social event, under her chair. She tells us she found Peter standing with some of his graduate students in the courtyard. "He looks beautiful," she says, eliciting an offended sigh from my father, I don't know why.

"Did you get a chance to talk?" I ask, remembering the morning of my wedding, when my mother told me she wanted time alone with me and then said in the gravest voice imaginable that her only regret about leaving my father was the message it sent me and Peter about the impermanence of love. "The thing is," she said, "it's up to you, how long it lasts. You get to choose, the two of you together." These words, despite their wisdom, did not in the end make a difference for me and my ex-husband, but I imagine they might for Peter and Cressida, if at some point a difference needs to be made.

"He was with other people," she says. "I just gave him a hug."

Then Peter appears before us, looking, in fact, quite beautiful, in a greenish gray suit and a soft white shirt with no collar. He is tall and skinny, my brother, with high cheekbones from our mother and our father's narrow shoulders. His hands are at his sides, and, holding his arms steady, he looks at us and swings his fingers up and down in an almost imperceptible wave. He got his hair cut today; his ears are pink and vulnerable. We rise from our seats to watch Cressida and her father come up the aisle, and when I look back at Peter, I see that he is wearing the kind of giant grin that just takes over sometimes, when nothing exists but how happy you are.

For the next several minutes tears leak from my eyes, and I'm grateful for the tissues my mother passes me, a fresh one as soon as she sees that the last is sodden. On my other side, my father simply lets his face get wet, and finally a tear splashes onto his program, briefly magnifying a few letters before they thicken and begin to slide down the page.

The reception is at the back of the room, spilling into the courtyard, and my father and I mill around with wine and then wine plus appetizers passed on trays by a small army of teenage girls. He stays at my elbow, volunteering very little of his own conversation but occasionally annotating mine with opinions and contempt. It's not till he heads off to use the bathroom that I search out my mother, whom I find with Cressida's mother, the two of them clasping hands.

"I didn't know your mother was an artist," Cressida's mother says when she sees me. "She's so talented." To my mother she says, "You've got to show her the one of Cress and Peter."

I understand now why my mother brought such a big bag: she's been sketching. It's true, what Cressida's mother said: she is very talented. When I was young, hardly a guest came over whom she didn't capture in a quick sketch, and she drew us— Peter and my father and me—over and over again. After she left him, my father spent days studying the portraits hanging around the house, as if what she'd seen in each of us might reveal whatever it was he'd missed in her. Then one day he took them all down and put them in a large envelope, and for the next few years, until he had the house painted so he could sell it and move somewhere smaller, there were shadow portraits everywhere, faint gray smudges outlining empty rectangles.

My mother hands her sketchpad to me, opened to one of the newlyweds. Cressida is lovely, but in this drawing my mother has discovered something else, and it's a revelation. Cressida and Peter are standing alone together, in front of one of the panels of gauze, and her fingertips are curled onto the waistband of his pants, a gesture not of sexual play or possession, but of reassurance. With her hair spiraling past her shoulders and her pretty collarbones reflecting the diffuse light, she looks at my brother with what I can describe only as faith.

I flip the pages, see sketches of Cressida's delighted mother and distracted father, of her brother pulling at the collar of his shirt. Then suddenly there I am, together with my father: we're standing in a corner, each of us with a glass of wine held bouquet-style, at low chest level with both hands. He looks sad and dazed, and I look—how can I describe this?—like a not unattractive middle-aged woman with overly curly hair who has just sucked on a wedge of lemon.

"God in heaven," I say.

"What?" my mother replies.

"Who's this charmer?"

Cressida's mother has turned to talk to someone else, and my mother moves to my side for a better look. "You look lovely. Beautiful and serious."

I hand the sketchpad back to her.

"You do," she says, looking down at the sketch, "see, through here," and she runs her finger along the charcoal lines of my forehead and temple, bisected by a short coil of hair.

"Listen," I say, "I should find Dan," and I leave and head for the hallway to the bathrooms, thinking I shouldn't've just walked away but also that she won't mind, may in fact prefer it, because now she can continue sketching. She's like a shy teenager with a guitar: her sketchbook helps her connect with other people while keeping her at a safe, busy distance.

I run into my father as he's leaving the men's room. He sees me and says, "Red meat, if you want to know, and speaking of which: Are they having a real dinner? Because I can't stand around eating things off toothpicks all night. It's a wedding, shouldn't there be a skimpy piece of salmon with my name on it somewhere?" I open my mouth to respond, but he continues: "It's not like they're poor. That house was worth a million if it was worth a penny. What about a cold bread roll? What about salad with candied walnuts and too much balsamic vinaigrette?"

"It's not a sit-down kind of reception," I say.

"Obviously."

Back in the rec room, he stops walking and falls into silence. I stand beside him, aware that he could be on the verge of an unpleasant slide.

"Nice what they did with the room," I say.

He grimaces. "Where's Joanie? Has she left already? I wouldn't put it past her."

"She's around. I was just talking to her."

"And why are there no tables? All those chairs from earlier, what are we supposed to do—go sit in rows?"

"Dan."

"What?"

This could be a mistake, but I say it anyway: "Beware the Horowitz horror."

For a long moment it could go either way, but at last he grins, and I relax a little. He chuckles and says, "That made you laugh, you and Peter. But mostly you. Do you know, I used to think of you as my child and Peter as your mother's? Not that you should tell him that, of course."

"Not to worry."

"I feel bad about it. Do you think he knew?" He gives me a sidelong look. "Never mind, he knew, he knew. Ah, God, regret." He falls silent again, and I think it would be a good idea to move on, into the party, out to the courtyard—somewhere. But just as I'm about to suggest this, he proclaims:

> Things said or done long years ago,
> Or things I did not do or say
> But thought that I might say or do,
> Weigh me down, and not a day
> But something is recalled,
> My conscience or my vanity appalled.

"Yeats?" I say.

"Isn't it marvelous?"

"Such a lovely view of maturity."

"But it's true, not a day goes by. Which is worse, do you suppose?"

"Which what is worse?"

"Appalled conscience or appalled vanity?"

I think for a moment. "Appalled conscience for me. For you it's appalled vanity."

He barks out a laugh. "Well, that appalls my vanity right there."

"And that," I say, "appalls my conscience."

He laughs at that, and I begin to laugh, too, and it takes root: we're giggling like children. We laugh and laugh, and my father flaps his hand in front of his face as if he were trying to put out a fire. Then I have a memory, from the year we spent in California. My father had been denied tenure at Yale and had a temporary appointment in the English Department at Stanford. I was thirteen. One evening shortly after we arrived, the four of us went into San Francisco and happened to stroll past a fancy French restaurant just as a well-dressed couple came out and were about to step into the backseat of a waiting taxi. Before they could get into the car, the door to the restaurant opened again, and a waiter rushed out, calling after them and holding in his upturned palm a tinfoil swan. "Your gâteau," he cried, and the couple took the package and thanked him and got into the taxi. Nothing, a nothing moment, slightly amusing, but for the entire rest of the evening and the weeks or maybe months following, that scene split us into parts: my father and me into sick hilarity, my mother into eye-rolling exasperation, my brother into bored indifference. "Your gâteau" with an empty palm held skyward—that was all it took, one of us saying it to the other, my father to me or I to him, and each time we fell into great convulsions of laughter.

I don't mention it, though. The memory actually slows my laughter, stops it. That year in California. If, as the saying goes, adolescence is not a developmental stage but a diagnosis, then I had a life-threatening case of it. Along with the requisite parental dethroning—OK, *paternal* dethroning; that was the year I could not bear my father—there was lying, promiscuity, drug use. For years afterward it was as if I were recovering from a stomach flu and could eat nothing but dry toast and applesauce: I was obedient, cautious, the least likely teenager on earth to cause her parents a moment of concern.

My father is looking at me, and I take his hand and interweave my fingers with his. We stand in silence. As if my teenage rejection of him weren't enough, he was terminated at Stanford after that one year. And the next two were terrible, the fallen university professor discovering how entirely different and difficult it was to teach high school. It wasn't until after my mother was gone that he finally landed, at a small organization dedicated to promoting the work of Wallace Stevens, Hartford's hometown poet. It barely paid a living wage, but he stayed with it—gradually and in the end gratefully arriving at the point in life when you understand there are no great changes ahead. When he retired, a few years ago, he was given a plaque inscribed with these words from the great poet himself: "After the final no there comes a yes / And on that yes the future world depends."

"You're a good girl," he says to me now, and I tell him, "Shhh, be quiet," but he keeps going. "You've given me so much. So much."

"You've given me a lot, too."

He squeezes my hand. "Don't worry, I won't ask you for a list."

"Dan. What am I going to do with you?"

"Throw me in the oven with some garlic and parsley."

This is another old family joke and I smile, but suddenly I'm tired and want this—the conversation, the reception, the weekend—to be over. He exhausts me, there's no getting around it.

He says, "I still think there isn't enough food at this thing."

"Let's find some more."

I pull my hand free of his and look around to see what's available, but at that moment my mother walks up, and so we stay put. Her lipstick has rubbed away, and she's begun to look weary.

"Having a nice time?" I ask her.

"It's lovely. Cressida's very smart."

My father straightens his back, lifts his chin.

"She knows her own mind," my mother continues, ignoring or unaware that he's peeved. "That's unusual in someone so young."

"Knows it?" my father says crisply. "Or thinks she knows it? And how could you decide which without being the expert yourself?"

My mother lifts one shoulder. She turns slightly, putting herself in quarter profile to us. The room is warm, and she plucks her caftan away from her chest several times.

"We've been talking," he tells her, "about regret."

She waits.

"And which is worse, guilt or humiliation. Which is it for you?"

"Sorry, Dan," she says, "I'm not biting," and she heads off without a pause, without even a glance back at us.

I don't look at him, but I can feel him bristling. I'm in awe of her rules of nonengagement. She's so detached and consistent. And yet not entirely avoidant, not as avoidant as I expected. Is this new, or does my memory misrecord her, so that each time she surprises me a little? She stayed at the B&B. Rode with us in the car. Sat with us for the ceremony. She returns and returns, as true and indifferent as the moon.

"What chicken shit," he says.

The teenage girls who were passing trays earlier have disappeared, but one of them left a platter of aram sandwich spirals on a table, and I say, "Look, let's grab some of those."

"I was just making conversation," he grumbles.

"You were baiting her. It was obnoxious."

He presses his lips together and looks away as I load several sandwiches onto a small plate. "You know I'm right," I say. "Now come on," and I hold out the food.

He frowns and picks up a piece. "What is it?"

"Just eat it," I say, and he takes a bite, and the whole thing promptly unrolls, releasing a few strips of turkey, a sodden length of lettuce, and a blob of tomato, all of which land on his suit jacket.

"For Christ's sake," he exclaims, brushing at the mess and creating several trails of mayo on his lapel. "Damn it. Look at me."

I set the plate on the table and grab a napkin. As I dab, I attempt to make consoling noises, which just escalate his anger, and he cries, "Fuck!" loud enough so that the people closest to us fall silent. "Fuck," he yells again, *"fuck,"* and now it's the whole room, silent until the silence itself becomes the objectionable sound and people begin to talk again.

My father stalks away, and I shield my face with my hand, mortified. Why didn't I head him off before he tried to provoke her? Or better yet, why didn't I walk away when she did? I feel someone touch my shoulder and look up to find Peter at my side, frowning, his cheeks ghosted with the kiss marks of well-wishers.

He says, "God, I'm sorry."

"*You're* sorry."

"We didn't want you to get stuck with him tonight."

"*Ma nishtanah halailah hazeh mikol haleilot?*" I ask, the first of the four questions posed on Passover—"Why is this night different from all other nights?"—and he bursts out laughing.

"Wait," I say, "she's not Jewish, is she? Cressida?"

"You can't believe I remember it?"

"It's been a few decades."

"I've been to the odd seder over the years," he tells me, and then we say, simultaneously, "*Very* odd," as if Dan were operating us like a puppeteer from wherever his pique took him.

"We're so glad you're here," he says, and I think I'm not losing a brother, *he's* losing a personal pronoun. This is a sour little thought, but I can't help myself.

"We're glad to be here," I say. "You know that."

My father sits on a folding chair directly in front of the gazebo where the ceremony took place, the set of his shoulders telling a story of boundless indignation. My mother stands against the wall, alone with her sketchpad, her pencil moving quickly over its surface. For a while I mill around, and then I join her and see that she's drawing not people but flowers. "Aren't the lantana pretty?" she says, but after another stroke or two she closes the sketchpad.

"Don't let me stop you."

"No, I'd rather talk." She smiles at me. "I want you to know that I have regrets."

"It's OK."

"No, I want to say this. I have regrets, but only one about leaving your father."

"I know," I say. "You regret the message it sent me and Peter about the impermanence of love."

She looks puzzled.

"No?"

"No."

"That's what you told me on my wedding day. What's your one regret?"

"How interesting," she says. "I suppose that was what I felt, for a long time." She reaches up and touches her earlobe, a nervous habit I remember from long ago.

"And now?"

She takes a deep breath. "Now I regret that you ended up in a caretaker role. I regret," she says, looking deeply into my eyes, "that because of my choice to leave him, that role was available for you to take."

I'm surprised by this—shocked, actually; I never knew she felt this way and can't believe she is saying so—but while all kinds of responses crowd my mind, the one I speak sounds hollow and is, in certain ways, beside the point. I say, "He isn't that bad. He's lived a good life."

And she says, "What about you?"

My entire body warms under the heat of her regard. What *about* me, and why ask now? For years we've been so careful, my mother and I, around the great disappointment that is my circumscribed life, always in concert in our efforts to keep the identity of the draftsman—or, rather, the draftsmen—out of sight. Shall I tell her about the tiny pleasure of tending my herb garden, about the excessive thanks I get from the colleagues to whom I make small gifts of dried thyme? Shall I tell her about the relief I feel now that the "introductions" I am sometimes offered to unattached men have devolved from awkward dinner parties to quick e-mails? Shall I tell her about the unexpected delight of a good TV show, especially a drama that unfolds over many episodes and encourages the blocking out of an entire evening each week for three or even six months? Or shall I tell her that my father's piss smells like raw meat?

The look on her face is classic Joanie, an unlikely mix of impassive and caring. I shrug, deciding to stay quiet—if you could call such inertia a decision—and she raises her eyebrows ever so slightly.

Just then there's a chiming sound from the far side of the room, and I turn to see Peter and Cressida in front of a table bearing a magnificent four-tiered wedding cake. Cressida has a knife in one hand and a wineglass in the other. "Hello," she calls out, and then, louder, *"Hello,"* her voice a good-size bellow that for some reason pleases me deeply. I step closer to them.

"First," she says, "we want to thank you all for being here. And second, as far as this thing on the table behind us goes, did you really think I was going to let my mother bake oatmeal cookies?"

Everyone laughs and applauds, and then there are toasts, and speeches, and finally the cake is wheeled away to be sliced and served. When I finally look back over my shoulder, my mother is gone. My father is still seated, but he is no longer the only one; chairs have been pulled this way and that, into small and large circles, into pairs. His shoulders are curved now, his head is down.

A passing girl offers me a piece of wedding cake. I lift the plate to my face and breathe in the sugary sweetness, then spot my mother near the back of the room. I approach her, extending the plate on my palm when I get close and lifting it high.

She smiles a slightly puzzled smile. "That's something. What is that? I've forgotten."

My father would be cackling by now. I lower the plate but keep it extended. "Wedding cake. We can share it."

She raises her palm, mimicking the way I held the plate. "No, it's something from Stanford. That year."

" 'Your gâteau.' "

"That's right, 'Your gâteau.' That was so silly." She smiles again, but after a moment a sober look comes over her face and she says, "You know, I came close to leaving him that year—I thought about it constantly. I think I would have if it hadn't been for that boy, that friend of yours, remember? From around the corner?"

I shake my head.

"You don't remember?"

I'm thinking: Then? Then you thought of leaving? That

early? This is the kind of information that derails entire histories—the family equivalent of moving the start date of the Vietnam War back a decade, say, thereby throwing off your memory of everything that happened before and since. "Remember who?" I say.

"That boy. Your friend."

"A boy would've been a friend of Peter's."

"No, he was yours. And his mother had left his father, and I felt so sorry for him, such a forlorn, lost child. All I could think was, I can't do that to my kids. It took me three years to figure out that if I wasn't doing it *to* you, then I could do it."

I nod. This is more than she's said to me on the subject in thirty-five years, and I don't really want to hear about it, not now. I don't feel like listening; earlier, I didn't feel like talking. Is this what I do with my parents? Want what I can't have and then once I can have it, stop wanting it?

She reopens her sketchpad. "I should get them as they're saying goodbye," she says, and I look over and see Peter and Cressida at the door, hugging their guests.

Across the room is my father, looking at me. It's long past time for me to begin the process of restoring him to himself. I start toward him, and once he sees I'm finally coming he looks away, like a timid girl at a school dance, afraid to jinx the approach of a suitor.

Acknowledgments

Many thanks to Geri Thoma and Julia Kenny at the Markson Thoma Literary Agency, and to everyone at Knopf and Vintage, especially Jordan Pavlin and Leslie Levine. I wrote these stories over the course of many years and solicited readings, interpretations, and words of advice from more wise people than I can name and thank here. I am especially grateful to Sylvia Brownrigg, Ann Cummins, Nancy Johnson, Lisa Michaels, Cornelia Nixon, Ron Nyren, Angela Pneuman, Sarah Stone, and Vendela Vida, who read many drafts and helped me see how these pages could form a book.

THE DIVE FROM CLAUSEN'S PIER

How much do we owe the people we love? Is it a sign of strength or weakness to walk away from someone in need? These questions lie at the heart of Ann Packer's intimate and emotionally thrilling novel. At the age of twenty-three, Carrie Bell has spent her entire life in Wisconsin, with the same best friend and the same dependable, easygoing high school sweetheart. Now to her dismay she has begun to find this life suffocating and is considering leaving it—and her fiancé, Mike—behind. But when Mike is paralyzed in a diving accident, leaving seems unforgivable—and yet more necessary than ever. *The Dive from Clausen's Pier* animates this dilemma—and Carrie's startling response to it—with the narrative assurance, exacting realism, and moral complexity we expect from the very best fiction.

Fiction/Literature

MENDOCINO
And Other Stories

With humor, wisdom, and tenderness, Ann Packer offers stories about women and men—wives and husbands, sisters and brothers, daughters, sons, mothers, fathers, friends, and lovers—who discover that life's greatest surprises may be found in that which is most familiar. In the title story, on the anniversary of their father's suicide a young woman discovers that her brother may have found a "reason for living" in the love of a good woman. In "Nerves," a young man realizes that the wife he is separated from no longer loves him but that it is his own life he misses, not her. The narrator of "My Mother's Yellow Dress" is a gay man remembering his deceased mother and their vital and troubling intimacy. In "Babies"—which was included in the prestigious O. Henry anthology series—a single woman in her mid-thirties finds that everyone, including her best friend at work, is pregnant, and that their joy can only be observed, not shared. In these and six other stories, Ann Packer exhibits an unerring eye for the small ways in which people reveal themselves and for the moments in which lives may be transformed.

Fiction/Short Stories

SONGS WITHOUT WORDS

Liz and Sarabeth were girlhood neighbors in the suburbs of
northern California, brought as close as sisters by the suicide of Sarabeth's mother. In the decades that followed, their
relationship remained a source of continuity and strength.
But when Liz's adolescent daughter enters dangerous waters,
the women's friendship takes a devastating turn, forcing Liz
and Sarabeth to question their most deeply held beliefs about
their connection.

Fiction/Literature

VINTAGE CONTEMPORARIES
Available wherever books are sold.
www.randomhouse.com